CONRAD EDISON
AND
THE LIVING CURSE

OVERWORLD ARCANUM
BOOK ONE

JOHN CORWIN

ISBN- 978-1-942453-05-5

Printed in the U.S.A.

To my wonderful support group:
Alana Rock
Karen Stansbury

My amazing editors:
Annetta Ribken
Jennifer Wingard

My awesome cover artist:
Regina Wamba

Thanks so much for all your help and input!

Books by John Corwin:

The Overworld Chronicles:
Sweet Blood of Mine
Dark Light of Mine
Fallen Angel of Mine
Dread Nemesis of Mine
Twisted Sister of Mine
Dearest Mother of Mine
Infernal Father of Mine
Sinister Seraphim of Mine
Wicked War of Mine
Dire Destiny of Ours
Aetherial Annihilation
Baleful Betrayal

Overworld Underground:
Possessed By You
Demonicus

Overworld Arcanum:
Conrad Edison and the Living Curse
Conrad Edison and the Anchored World

Stand Alone Novels:
No Darker Fate
The Next Thing I Knew
Outsourced
Seventh

For the latest on new releases, free ebooks, and more, join John Corwin's Newsletter at www.johncorwin.net!

CURSED FOR LIFE

Conrad Edison is cursed.

His foster parents die in horrible ways around his birthday, and he ends up back at the orphanage where he and the other children are treated like indentured servants. Forced to work the farm and other menial chores, Conrad holds no hope for a better life.

When a man with the ability to mind-control animals inexplicably tries to kill Conrad, the harrowing scrape with death gives him a new perspective on life. He discovers the man had a flying carpet and a talking phone and that the orphanage is only the front for an insidious slave ring.

Determined to elude his cursed fate, Conrad decides to escape the orphanage once and for all. The phone leads him to a magical place called Queens Gate and for the first time in his life, he dares to hope for a better life.

But unless he can free himself from the curse, the terrible secret it guards could destroy everything.

Chapter 1

I wondered if this would be the day my parents died.

Their fate loomed, a black cloud on the horizon. I had no love for these people, but death was too awful even for them.

I couldn't remember my real parents, and there seemed little difference between this set of adults ordering me about and the others before them. The only thing they all had in common was they'd either died or suffered another terrible fate on or around my birthday. It was nearly that time of year again, so I reckoned if anything was going to happen, it would be soon.

"We need some bloody eggs, Edward!" Mrs. Cullen glared at her husband. Her small brown eyes narrowed to slits. "That's far more important than you running down to the pub for a pint with the boys."

"I'll get your bloody eggs on the way back." Mr. Cullen, as usual, wasn't swayed by his wife's argument.

I sat in the back seat of the car and watched the two bicker back and forth about when to get the eggs and what other necessities were more important than Mr. Cullen's desire to drink himself into a stupor as he did whenever possible. It was more entertaining than counting the cows we passed in the countryside on our way into town, and more pleasurable than wondering what fate awaited these two. It was also the only thing keeping my mind off the nauseating motion sickness I got when riding in cars.

"I refuse to let you spend all our money on yourself." Mrs. Cullen crossed her arms. "I won't allow it!"

Mr. Cullen growled. "Then come with me, you bleeding twit."

His wife's face darkened. "I'll show you who's a twit." She reared back and punched him in the side of the face.

1

The car swerved, leaving the country lane and scraping against a stone pasture wall. Mr. Cullen, cursed, jerked the wheel, and brought it back onto the road. His chubby face crimson, he swung a backhand at his wife and popped her in the forehead.

Screeching, Mrs. Cullen clawed at her husband's face. The car swerved back and forth. I gripped the door handle. The oatmeal I'd had for breakfast rose in my throat as the motion sickness worsened.

"Please," was all I managed to say before the urge to throw up nearly overwhelmed me. I pressed the button to roll down the rear window but it wouldn't respond.

"I said stop it!" Mr. Cullen shoved his wife hard. Her head cracked against the window.

She began to wail.

My ears hurt, but the motion of the car steadied. Shuddering, I took deep breaths to calm my stomach and kept my eyes on the road ahead. Something black flashed through the air. It smacked into the windscreen. Blood spattered, thick and gray. I knew it was supposed to look bright red, but I rarely saw anything in color, except for brief flashes.

Mr. Cullen shouted in surprise. He turned on the wipers and cleared the dark liquid. A large crow lay on the hood. It cawed loudly. Its wings fluttered. Then the creature went still.

"Did you see that?" Mr. Cullen said to his wife.

She was still too engrossed in her loud crying to respond.

A bad omen. Today might be the day the Cullens died. It might happen in this very car.

I didn't like watching my parents die. The Hughes had been hit by a London bus only ten feet behind me, giving me quite a shock when I turned around to see what was taking them so long to cross the road. The Smiths had died skydiving when a jumbo jet, miles off course, ran right into them after they deployed their parachutes. The Andersons, a very quiet couple, had abruptly decided to call in a death threat against the Prime Minister and were promptly jailed. The Turners had vanished while out for a walk one evening, never to return.

The closest I'd come to dying had been with the Lewises. I'd lived there with three other foster children at the time. Mrs. Lewis was screaming at us to come down to the kitchen for dinner. Just as me

2

and the other children reached the kitchen door, a freakish flood of water washed it away in a heartbeat, leaving us to stare at the great hollow where it had once been.

Thinking about what lay in store for these people only made me sicker.

I tapped on the window.

Mr. Cullen's eyes met mine in the rearview mirror. "What do you want?" His voice was angry.

"Window." I didn't dare say more for fear I might throw up.

"What the bloody hell for?"

I made a gagging motion.

He bared his teeth. "Keep it down, you weakling."

Mrs. Cullen abruptly stopped crying. "Is he sick again?"

"What do you think?" Mr. Cullen snorted. "We ended up with the runt of the litter this time."

"Least he don't eat too much," his wife said with a smirk. "And they pay better to watch after this one."

"Now we know why." Mr. Cullen glared at me in the mirror. "He's stupid and weak."

I couldn't disagree. School was very difficult for me. I was awful with math and science and barely able to keep up with language arts. Sports were too much for my body to handle. I bruised easily and bled too much from simple scrapes. Nobody wanted me. Like the Cullens, most of my foster parents did it for the government money.

I normally would look away from Mr. Cullen's angry stare, but unless he wanted me to sick up all over the back seat, he had to stop the car or roll down the window.

"Blast it," he growled and slammed on the brakes.

My head bounced off the back of his seat. I felt a little dribble escape my mouth, but managed to clench it shut. I opened the door, released the seatbelt, and fell onto the grass outside just in time. My breakfast spewed into the ditch. After a few seconds, of heaving, I felt empty. A bell jingled. I looked up and saw a sheep watching me as it chewed a mouthful of light gray grass.

I tried to remember what green looked like. I'd glimpsed it once while out with Cora. Her name brought with it a flash of memories. In my mind, I saw the rosy cheeks, the orange hair she frequently dyed different colors, and her brilliant green eyes. *That's how I remember colors.*

We stop outside the grocery store. "You're a wonderful boy, Conrad." Cora kisses my cheek.

For the first time, I glimpse her true colors. For the first time, I feel safe.

"Do you remember what to do?" she asks.

I nod.

"Sometimes, good people have to do bad things." She takes my hand and we go inside the store to steal our dinner.

"Baaa," the sheep said, jerking me from the solace of my memories.

Ovis Aries, quadruped, ruminant mammal.

I jerked back. *Who said that?*

Mr. Cullen got out of the car and glared at me. "Are you finished?" He looked into the rear door and cursed. "You tossed up on the back of the seat!"

Before I could cower, he slapped me on the back of the head. I nearly fell forward into my own sick.

I threw my arms over my head. "I'm sorry!"

"I'd hit you again but then you'd just bleed all over the car." He gripped the back of my shirt and jerked me off the ground. "Get in before I leave your scrawny body in the ditch."

I climbed inside and looked down, praying he'd get back into the driver seat.

He grabbed the back of my head and shoved my face into the stream of vomit on the back of the seat. "Clean it off, boy." He rubbed my head back and forth across the fabric. With one final curse, he shoved me hard back into my seat. "Worthless."

I remained absolutely still and kept my eyes down. Mr. Cullen wasn't as abusive as some I'd known in the past. Humiliating me usually satisfied him. I put my hands under my legs so he wouldn't see my fists tightening. My tiny little pitiful fists. I hid my anger behind downcast eyes. Even if I were stronger, I wouldn't fight back. That would only get me sent back to the orphanage. Anything was better than being back there again, even a little abuse.

4

"Why didn't you get that dead bird off the hood?" Mrs. Cullen asked as we pulled back onto the road. "It's getting blood all over the paint."

"Because the stupid boy made me forget." Mr. Cullen slapped his hand against the steering wheel. "I'll make him clean it up when we get to town."

I looked at the bird and wondered if strange words would come into my head again. They didn't. I remembered the words clearly. *Ovis Aries, quadruped, ruminant mammal.* What did they mean? Aries sounded familiar. Mrs. Cullen liked the daily horoscope and I'd heard her mention it before.

"I've never seen a person so useless," she said to her husband. "He's supposed to be nearly twelve, but he looks eight." She turned around and looked at me between the seats. "What did you say happened to your parents?"

I looked down. "I don't know, ma'am."

"Don't know, or won't say?"

"I was a babe when they died."

Mr. Cullen chimed in. "The boy's slow in the head, woman. You're only confusing him."

"Why else do you think they pay extra for his care?" She stared at me for a moment. "Sometimes I wonder if it's worth the extra headache."

"It's worth the few extra pints it buys us." Mr. Cullen snorted. "And it paid for your hair coloring."

"True." Mrs. Cullen ran a hand through her white hair. "Perhaps we could train him to feed himself so we didn't have to take him everywhere."

"Yeah. Maybe he's smart enough for that at least."

I can feed myself. I wasn't smart, but I wasn't mental. The Lewises used to leave me and the others alone for days. We'd survived on bread, jam, and lots of cheese. Sometimes Mrs. Lewis even left food in the fridge when she and her husband left on their monthly holidays. Apparently, the government money was quite good for four children.

The Cullens had been convinced from day one that I was unable to survive on my own. I would rather be left at their house than forced to sit in the car while they drove around and yelled at each other or left me outside while they went into the pub for hours.

"I say we make him get groceries while we go to the pub," Mrs. Cullen said.

"The boy can't tie his own shoe," her husband replied.

She looked back at me. "He's not that daft."

"I don't trust him with money."

"We don't have to give him money. He can put it on our tab." Mrs. Cullen rubbed her husband's arm. "It'll give us more time in the pub."

"True." Mr. Cullen's dark eyes found me in the mirror. "If you mess this up, boy, I'll make sure you don't ever forget it."

I looked away. "I won't."

A few minutes later, we reached Bedford. Mr. Cullen pulled into the parking lot of a supermarket. He got out and opened the rear door. "Clean off the bird."

I walked around to the hood and looked at the dead animal. A little stream of blood dribbled from its beak and one of its legs was twisted and broken. I felt sorry for it.

"Well, don't just stand there, boy!" Mr. Cullen nudged me with his elbow. "We've got places to be."

With trembling fingers, I reached out and picked up the bird by a claw. Just touching something dead made me want to throw up again. I found a rubbish bin and dropped the bird inside.

Mrs. Cullen got out of the car and gave me a sanitary wipe. "I don't want you touching our food with filthy hands." She inspected me. "Be sure to rinse your face. You've got sick on it."

I nodded. "I will."

She handed me a long grocery list in messy handwriting. "You are to purchase exactly what I listed. Don't you dare get a single thing more." She gripped my chin and forced me to look at her. "Do you understand?"

"Yes."

Mr. Cullen stepped next to her. "We'll be back in an hour or two." He pointed to a nearby bench. "Wait for us there." He pulled back his sleeve and checked a large gaudy watch. Light reflected off the fake diamonds on the band. "Let's go."

Mrs. Cullen touched the watch. "I love how it makes you glitter."

6

He chuckled. "I reckon most ladies do."

The pair climbed into the car. It puttered away, leaving a trail of dark smoke behind and vanishing around a curve.

I looked at the list. *Beer, pork, ice cream, frozen chips, frozen pizza, soda.* I couldn't read the next two items. Mrs. Cullen had listed several kinds of pastries and other snacks. She had forgotten to write down eggs. I wondered if I would be in worse trouble if I bought them or didn't buy them. I knew I would be in trouble either way.

There weren't a lot of people in the store. I walked around for several minutes and looked at the shelves. Bags filled with wonderful looking treats lined the aisle. One nice couple I'd lived with had let me have crunchy cheese balls. They upset my stomach, but tasted so good. Corn chips were another snack I'd eaten before.

I found the cookie aisle and walked up and down for several minutes, wishing I could try one of everything. I was tempted to steal something. When I was seven, my fosters at the time, the Taylors, taught me how to nick small items and take them outside to their car while they distracted the store clerks. They even took me to help burgle houses since I was small and could fit through pet doors and small windows.

"Can I help you?" asked a young clerk.

I turned to him. "No thank you, sir." I showed him the paper. "I have a list." *He must think I'm trying to steal something.*

He smiled. "Any cookies on the list?"

"No, sir. Afraid not."

"Well, let me know if I can help you find anything." He walked away.

I looked at the list again and decided to start collecting the items. Since I knew the Cullens wouldn't be back for a long time, I went very slowly and read the ingredients on some of the packages. Most of the food contained a lot of ingredients with very long names I couldn't pronounce. I didn't know if that was good or bad.

The soda drinks were last on the list. I picked up a pack of Mr. Nutter's Orange Delicious and put it in the cart.

Contains Element ZR Thirty. Boil to powder. Applications include rocketry, explosives, sweetener. This random thought surprised me so much I stumbled backwards and knocked over a display of Mr. Nutter's Angel Biscuits. *Where did that thought come from?* What was Element ZR Thirty? I realized another patron was staring at me and pushed myself back to my feet. It took several minutes to reorganize the pastries. I noticed angel biscuits were on the list, so I put two bags into the cart.

No more strange words popped into my mind as I finished shopping. By the time I had everything bagged and ready to go, it was dark outside. The clock in the store showed seven in the evening. My stomach rumbled and hurt. I knew I couldn't stand inside for long without looking suspicious so I rolled the cart outside to the bench and sat down.

A few minutes later, it began to rain. I quickly got up and pushed the cart back under the eaves. The plastic bags protected the groceries from the water, but my shirt and hair were wet. I folded my arms tight and shivered. My stomach made a funny noise to remind me how hungry I was. I did my best to ignore the hollow feeling. I'd survived it many times before. It wasn't any different now.

Still, I wished I'd stolen a cookie or two.

The store closed two hours later. The young clerk who'd spoken to me earlier saw me on the way out.

"Where's your parents, lad?"

"They'll be along soon," I said.

He looked at his watch. "You've been out here for two hours. Do you have a phone?"

I shook my head.

"Do they?"

I shrugged. "I think so."

He shook his head. "Bloody wankers." The clerk held up a finger. "I'll be right back."

"Please don't worry." I forced a smile. "I'm fine."

He didn't say anything else and went into the store. A few moments later, he returned with a plastic bag. "There's leftover chicken and bread from the deli inside." He held it out to me. "I know you must be starving."

My smile turned genuine as I took it. "Thank you, sir."

He looked very troubled. "Your parents aren't right in the head leaving you here like this. Are you certain they're okay?"

I nodded. "They went to the pub."

His face darkened. "To the pub?"

"It's okay, sir, really." I didn't want him finding the Cullens. They would be furious with me if he made them come get me. "They probably got a flat tire. I'm certain they'll be along soon."

The clerk ran a hand through his hair. "I hope so, lad." He nodded toward the bag. "Now, eat up. I'd wait with you, but I have to pick up my wife."

"Thank you, sir." The aroma drifting from within the bag made my stomach rumble with anticipation. "I promise I'll be okay."

"I hope so." He gave me one last look and then got into a small car and drove away.

I opened the bag and looked inside. A plate with two legs of chicken, potatoes, and two slices of bread was inside. I removed the food. There was a small paper bag underneath the plate. I sat down on the walkway and put the plate on my crossed legs. I took out the paper bag and looked inside.

Cookies.

Another smile found me. Some people were so nice. This was the most wonderful gift in the entire world. Cookies were like large edible coins you could use to pay for smiles. Perhaps one day I would make my own cookies. I would find people who looked sad and go up to them and say, "Please, don't be sad. Here, have a cookie. It will make you feel better."

The person would smile and the tears would vanish.

I ate the chicken, the potatoes, and the bread, saving the cookies for last. I had the chocolate chip cookie first. A buttersnap and an angel biscuit remained. I decided to eat the buttersnap next. Through the grocery window, I looked at the clock. It was nearly eleven. I didn't care. I still had two cookies.

It was just after two in the morning when I heard the familiar puttering of the Cullens' car. I finished the last morsel of my buttersnap cookie as the auto screeched to a stop in the parking lot. Mr. Cullen staggered out of the car and walked around to open the boot.

"Get the groceries in the car," he said in a slurred voice.

I pushed the cart to the car and put everything inside.

He shut the trunk.

"Did he get eggs?" Mrs. Cullen shouted out of the window.

Mr. Cullen looked at me. "Well, did you?"

I nodded.

"And the bread?"

"Yes, sir."

He made a noise like a horse snorting. "I'll be right back, dear. Got to relieve myself." Mr. Cullen ambled drunkenly around the corner of the store and up to the bushes. He returned a moment later. "Why aren't you in the car yet, boy?"

I hastily climbed into the back.

"How's my little golden goose doing?" Mrs. Cullen said. Her cheeks were very pink and her breath smelled quite fierce.

I decided not to answer. Sometimes when she acted like this it meant she really wanted to pick on me. Since she was drunk, she might find something else to amuse her.

Mr. Cullen dropped into the driver seat. The car rocked back and forth for a moment. He made a horse snort again and reached into his front pocket. "Where the hell are my cigarettes?" He looked around the seat but didn't find them.

"You probably dropped them in the bushes," Mrs. Cullen said.

He looked over his shoulder at me. "Boy, go look for them."

I climbed out of the car and walked to where I'd seen him vanish a moment ago. As I searched, I noticed my shadow dancing on the ground. It was strange because a moment ago there hadn't been any light on the side of the building. I looked back and saw something bright in the night sky. It grew brighter, closer, and larger. It looked like a fiery meteor.

"What are you standing there for, boy!" Mr. Cullen shouted out of the car window. "Find my cigarettes!"

I nodded, but couldn't turn away from the falling star. Windows shattered and the air rumbled as it streaked low over the town. It seemed as if it would fly right over us, but at the last instant, it veered sharply downward. With a horrendous crunch, it smashed into the car. A blast of hot wind knocked me backward into the shrubs.

Bits of metal and glass flew through the air. A tire bounced past. I felt something under my hand and picked it up. It was Mr. Cullen's pack of cigarettes. I stood and walked toward the parking lot. Of the car there was little left except a few stray bits. Primarily, there was a large black crater in the middle of the parking lot.

"Well, I suppose that just happened," I muttered. Today had been the day. I sat down on the walkway, took out my remaining cookie, and nibbled at it.

Chapter 2

I almost ran away.

Unfortunately, I knew from previous experiences that trying to live on the street would be much worse than living with another foster family. I didn't like the idea of returning to the orphanage, but at least it was safe. Perhaps they'd find me nice people to live with who wouldn't die around my birthday.

Like Cora died.

We walk down the street looking for a new grocery store so we can steal food.

"Stealing isn't right," Cora says. "But when you have nothing, it's sometimes a necessity."

I look up at her and nod. She'd dyed her hair a darker color, but I couldn't tell what it was.

A homeless man begs for coin.

Cora reaches into her small purse and frowns. After a moment, she removes a pound and gives it to the man.

"God bless you, young lady." He tucks away the money.

As we walk away, I say, "I didn't think you had any money."

She smiles. "That was almost the last of it." Cora kneels in front of me. "Always help people if you can, Conrad. Good karma is priceless."

I felt a tear trickle down my face. I balled up on the ground and tried not to cry. Karma had not treated Cora well. She'd died like the rest.

I spent the rest of the night sleeping in a chair at the police station.

"Time to wake up, Conrad."

The familiar voice jerked me awake. I sat up and saw Mr. Goodleigh leaning over me. He smiled pleasantly. I had seen the look enough times to know he was amused. I suspected the misfortunes that found my foster parents entertained him to no end. He was always the one to collect me in the aftermath.

I stood and felt my pocket for the remaining bit of angel biscuit I'd saved for breakfast. It was still there.

"I have finished the paperwork." Mr. Goodleigh motioned toward the exit. "We can go."

I nodded and followed him outside to the old but pristine black car he drove. It looked like a London taxi, but was much larger. I climbed into the back seat and closed the door. Mr. Goodleigh got behind the wheel, started the car, and pulled onto the road.

"Mother will be pleased to see you again," Mr. Goodleigh said. "And just in time for your birthday."

"I will be happy to see her too, Mr. Goodleigh." Due to the bad things that happened to my fosters, I was always at the orphanage for my birthday.

"Tut, tut," he said. "Since your foster parents are dead, Little Angel Orphanage is once again your home. I am no longer Mr. Goodleigh to you."

"Yes, Father."

His gaze met mine in the rear view mirror. I looked down.

"What did I tell you about looking away, Conrad?"

With difficulty, I brought my eyes back up. "To never look away."

"It is a sign of utmost disrespect, son."

"I apologize, Father." I forced myself to look directly at his reflection.

He nodded. "Much better." Mr. Goodleigh began to chant one of his favorite songs as he drove. The words were in a foreign but pleasant-sounding language. I tried to make out the words, but as usual, they slipped away from me no matter how hard I tried to listen.

I fell asleep during the ride as I normally did. It seemed impossible to keep my eyes open for longer than a few minutes after Mr. Goodleigh began singing. A bump in the road just outside the main gates woke me as it had many times before. Tall black iron fences connected to thick gray-stoned walls on either side of the road. The wall surrounded the estate.

Brickle Brixworth, a giant of a man, stood on the other side of the gate. He nodded once at the car and, with a mighty tug, pulled open the heavy iron. Brickle was a groundskeeper, a guard, and even a farmer all rolled into one. I'd seen him tending to the animals, weeding the garden, and repairing the house. Once, he'd fended off a burglar by picking him up, carrying him outside, and hurling him over the front gate.

Mr. Goodleigh nodded at the groundskeeper as we drove past. Brickle nodded back. Once we were through, he closed the gates.

The driveway wound through a wide pasture. Horses and cows grazed in the distance. There were sheep on the farm as well, but they were confined to other fields. The tall gray manor appeared in the midst of tall oaks at the end of the gravel drive. It was not a huge building, but contained thirty-three bedrooms and a large nursery in one wing. Chimneys rose from all sides. The building made an L shape where the residential quarters met with a common room connecting to a large kitchen.

Mr. Goodleigh pulled into the cul-de-sac and parked in front of the door. A pleasant looking woman stood on the front steps. As usual, Mrs. Goodleigh styled her hair in a tight bun and wore a dark dress. Mr. Goodleigh exited the car, walked around it, and kissed his wife on the cheek. The pair looked at me expectantly.

Taking a deep breath, I opened the car door and climbed out. "Hello, Mother." I dropped to one knee in front of her.

"Hello, Conrad." She held out a fair-skinned hand.

I took it and kissed each knuckle. "I ask permission to return to hearth, home, and kin, Mother and Father."

"With open arms, we welcome you," they said in unison.

I stood. "Thank you."

Mrs. Goodleigh inspected me. "You look no worse for the wear. I suppose that will be less work for the doctor tomorrow."

"As you say, Mother." I was surprised that tomorrow was my birthday. It hardly seemed a year since the last one. The weather didn't seem warm enough for it to be June again already.

"Twelve years old," Mr. Goodleigh said. He shook his head. "Perhaps this time will be the charm."

"Perhaps." Mrs. Goodleigh didn't look convinced. She turned and stepped inside the manor.

I followed them into the empty common room. At this time of afternoon, the other children would probably be doing chores on the farm. I knew not even this day would pass before I was expected to do a share of work. Whether that meant cleaning bathrooms or polishing the wooden floors, I didn't know.

"Your bedroom is ready," Mrs. Goodleigh said to me. "You will find your work clothes in the chest of drawers. Put them on and go to the farm. There is a patch of weeds that needs tending."

I nodded. "Yes, Mother." I walked up the wide wooden staircase to the second floor and followed the hallway to the sixth door on the left. A bare metal bed frame sat in the middle of the small room. I unfolded the worn, striped mattress and struggled to put it on the bed. When it toppled onto the frame, the metal feet shifted a fraction, leaving a tiny scar in the wood.

My stomach tightened in apprehension. Mother would not be happy. I straightened the mattress, looked for the sheets, and found them neatly folded in the closet. I placed them on the bed.

"What are you doing?" Mother said from the door.

Startled, I spun to face her. "Preparing the bed, Mother."

"Is it bed time?"

I almost looked at the floor, but forced my eyes to stay on hers. She despised looking away even more than Mr. Goodleigh. "No, Mother."

Her eyes caught on something and hardened. "You damaged the floor."

"An accident, Mother."

She stepped into the room and approached me until her nose was only inches away. "An accident," she hissed. "What did I tell you to do?"

"Change into work clothes and go to the farm."

"What did you do?"

"I prepared the bed."

Her lips pressed tight. When she spoke, her voice was low and cold. "Nearly twelve years of age and you are still as stupid as the day

15

you arrived here. Are you incapable of learning, or do you simply not care?"

I didn't respond because I knew from experience she didn't want me to answer.

"I believe you are guilty of incompetence and apathy." She turned and walked back to the door. Without turning to face me, she said, "Put on your work clothes and go to the farm. You will be punished tonight." With that, Mrs. Goodleigh left.

I shivered. The room felt cold from her anger. I tried not to think about what form of punishment awaited me. The Goodleighs were very inventive. Sometimes the punishment was psychological. Other times it was painfully physical. They seemed to know what worked best on each child in their care.

After quickly putting on my clothes, I walked as fast as I dared—Mrs. Goodleigh didn't allow running in the house—and left by the back door. I felt cold prickles on the back of my neck and looked over my shoulder at the house. I saw the Goodleighs watching me from a second floor window. Averting my eyes back to the dirt road, I forced myself not to shake.

I always end up back here.

The dirt road led between several wooden buildings. Stands of oaks bordered the area. Between the trees, I saw open pastures where the livestock grazed and wondered how pretty it would look in full color.

The chicken coop stood to my left. Hens pecked in the dirt while a bantam rooster colored with several shades of gray kept a watchful eye. He had long spurs on the backs of his legs and liked nothing better than to fly at anyone who dared come too close to his abode. Gathering eggs required a quick hand and agile reflexes. I had neither, and usually resorted to swinging a metal bucket to keep the vicious cock at bay.

Pigs snorted and rooted in the mud in their pen on the right. They were huge creatures, some of them with long curving tusks like wild boars. Thankfully, their feeding trough was easy enough to reach by standing on the fence. From there, I could pour the slop along the length.

Brickle enjoyed telling new residents a story about a boy who enjoyed snorting and throwing things at the pigs. He would climb atop the fence and antagonize them into a frenzy. One day, he'd fallen in and the pigs had eaten him, bones and all. I didn't know if it was true, but had little doubt the pigs could tear me limb from limb if I did fall into their pen.

The sheep and goat pen, now empty, stood next to the pigpen. I saw William and Stephan mucking it out. Their wheelbarrow held a large pile of dung.

William looked up and saw me. He nudged Stephan. "Hey look, Killer Conrad is back!"

"How did you kill your fosters this time?" Stephan asked. He jabbed his pitchfork into the ground. "Did you stab them?"

William made a whooshing noise. "I'll bet he set them on fire."

Brickle exited the brown barn behind the two boys. "No talking during chores." For someone so large, his high voice always surprised me.

The two boys immediately got back to work, shoveling dung as if their lives depended on it.

I approached Brickle. When I drew near, I stopped and waited.

He looked me up and down. "Still puny." He poked me in the shoulder, nearly knocking me over. "Still weak."

I recovered my balance but said nothing. My fists wanted to clench and my jaw wanted to tighten, but to do so only invited more pushing. Brickle saw such body language as a challenge to his superiority. He enjoyed putting me in my place. I kept my eyes straight ahead and waited.

"The chicken coop." Brickle pointed to the building. "Clean it."

"Yes, sir." I turned and went to the red barn across the dirt road from the brown barn. Though I couldn't see the colors, it was what everyone called them. From inside I took a pitchfork, a small shovel, and a metal bucket. I hoped to slip past the rooster and into the coop so he wouldn't chase me. I could probably close the door, but the fumes inside would quickly overwhelm me without fresh air.

I stepped back outside the red barn and turned toward the chicken coop. The sound of a stomping hoof pulled my attention back in the opposite direction. At the end of the dirt road near the compost pile, I saw the old bull staring me down. *What is it doing here?* It was either supposed to be in the pasture with the cows, or locked inside its own pen.

Thankfully, the bull had never been aggressive, except for the time William had mistaken it for a cow and tried to milk it. The bull had not taken kindly to the attention.

I wondered if I should notify Brickle. A strange light seemed to dance in the bull's eyes. The animal bellowed loudly and, without further warning, charged me. I froze with shock. Why was it coming for me? What was wrong with him? Dimwitted as I was, even I knew to run from the path of this raging beast. I dropped the tools and pushed against the door to the red barn but it wouldn't budge. I rammed my shoulder against it, but the door didn't move an inch and only made my shoulder ache.

The bull sped past the other outbuildings. I turned toward the sheep pen and ran. I climbed over the fence and ran through the mud toward the opposite side. William and Stephan were gone, perhaps into the brown barn. I went to the barn door and tried to open it, but like the red barn, it was also sealed tight.

I wondered if someone was playing a prank on me, or if this might be my punishment. The Goodleighs had used the farm animals many a time to punish me and the others. I heard a loud cracking of wood and turned as the bull crashed through the fence. I cried out with fright as the beast veered toward me.

Bos Taurus. Temperamental.

"What?" I shouted. The strange thoughts couldn't have distracted me at a worse time. I jumped to the side an instant before the bull gored me. The beast rammed into the side of the brown barn hard enough to make the building shudder. Its thick, curving horns plunged through the wood.

I heard a loud pounding from inside the door of the brown barn and Brickle shouting something. There wasn't time for me to hear what it was, for the bull was already working its horns free.

The manor was too far away. The barns were locked. As a last resort, I might be able to run into the oak trees and dodge around them until the bull tired or help arrived. I turned toward the trees and saw dozens of bovine eyes looking back at me. The cows stood behind the wooden fence. They pushed forward as one. The fence cracked and fell over. The line of cows moved forward in lockstep. With an angry moo, the bull jerked its horns from the barn.

I ran straight across the pen. There was only one force mighty enough to take on the cows. I simply had to hope they didn't eat me before the bull reached me. I climbed the fence and leapt into the pigpen.

A large sow squealed and ran from me, a group of piglets trotting in her wake. A large mound of mud shuddered and rose to reveal a monstrous boar. It snorted and pawed the ground. With a loud squeal, it raced toward me on stubby legs. The bull crashed through the fence behind me. When I turned, I saw its eyes flash bright. I had never seen such a thing. I might have stood and stared, but common sense prevailed.

I ran for the boar. Footing was treacherous in the thick mud. My breath came in ragged gasps, my legs wobbled with fright. I felt certain I would die. *Why should I care if I die? Nobody else in the world cares.* The thought nearly made me pause. Perhaps this was the fate designed for me, crushed between a boar and a bull in a muddy pen. The others would remember me if only for the entertaining story.

Weak as I was in mind and body, my survival instinct proved strong. As the two beasts thundered my way, instinct took control of my legs and leapt me out of the way. The bull and the boar crashed hard into each other with an awful bellowing squeal. Something hit me hard on the back of the head. My face burrowed into the muck and I slid forward several feet.

Strange symbols flashed behind my closed eyelids. I remembered seeing some of them during a math lesson. Others looked completely alien. I might have wondered longer at this strange sight, but my mouth and nose were buried in the mud and I suddenly realized I couldn't breathe. I jerked my face up and spat while scraping the mud from my face. My hands were so muddy it took a little while.

I felt warm liquid mingling with the cool mud. When I finally cleared my eyes, I saw thick crimson blood pooling where I knelt. I turned. The bull and boar lay in a huge heap. Blood poured from the bull's mouth. The boar lay on its side, its mouth hanging open, tongue lolling in the mud.

Red blood? I can see color?

The sow squealed and rooted at the boar. Her piglets danced around her feet, each one trying to reach one of her many nipples. Her skin looked quite pink beneath the coarse hairs on her hide. The oak trees looked bright and full of green leaves. It was as if someone had taken a gray landscape and painted the world.

The herd of cows meandered aimlessly within the pigpen while some of the other swine dashed for freedom through the broken fence.

Suidae suinae sus. Swine. Most notable for bacon.

The strange words I'd been hearing in my head suddenly made sense. They were scientific classifications for animals.

Yes, it's a pig. They are very tasty.

We hadn't learned these classifications in school, so how did I know them? I closed my eyes and saw strings of mathematical symbols flowing like a river of nonsense. The schoolwork at the orphanage was rudimentary, nothing so advanced as this.

I heard the mud sucking at someone's feet. Before I could turn to see who it was, I was lifted by my scruff and jerked into the air. Brickle held me in front of him, face red with anger. It was so interesting seeing the color in his face, I nearly forgot I was in trouble.

The Goodleighs stood on the dirt road outside the pigpen. I could tell by the looks on their faces that the blame for this debacle rested squarely on my shoulders.

My first day back was not going well at all.

But at least I can see in color.

Chapter 3

I shivered violently as cold water slammed against me from the high-pressure fire hose. Brickle smiled malevolently as he cut off the water for a moment.

"Still not clean."

Mrs. Goodleigh shook her head. "No, he is not."

Brickle pushed the lever on the nozzle. The world vanished behind a liquid barrier as water hit me in the face.

I stood as still as I could and endured the punishment. I knew if I screamed, cried, or begged, it would do no good whatsoever. In fact, it might prolong the punishment. I tried to close my eyes and put myself in limbo, a quiet disconnected place where I'd often found refuge from the real world. The cold water made it nearly impossible. One positive I observed was that my body had nearly acclimated to the water and it no longer felt as chilling. It was also possible that my skin was simply numb.

To test the theory, I pinched the sensitive skin beneath my wrist between two fingernails. It hurt. *Therefore, I have acclimated.*

It occurred to me that I couldn't remember reasoning out anything like this before. I usually just accepted cause and effect, but didn't try to connect the dots. Had I suddenly grown smarter?

I imagined a simple math addition problem and achieved the answer immediately. I then calculated the square root of the answer by a random number to the fourth power. Again, the answer came easily. A smile stretched my lips. *I am smart!* This was unbelievable. I wondered what had caused this change in me and immediately felt the urge to conduct experiments.

The water cut off.

21

"He's smiling," Brickle said, lips peeled back. "I can make him not smile."

Mr. and Mrs. Goodleigh looked at me with narrowed eyes.

I almost told them about my amazing improvement, but a little voice in the back of my head warned me not to. *Let them think you're stupid.*

"Why are you smiling?" Mr. Goodleigh asked.

"I am happy," I said.

"Happy?" Mrs. Goodleigh's eyes flashed. "This is punishment. You killed the bull and our prized boar."

"The bull chased me." I looked toward the muddy, bloody pigpen. "Why do you think I'm responsible for its death?"

The Goodleighs looked at each other. I realized they were probably puzzled at my defiance. I rarely defended myself.

"You should not have provoked the bull," Mrs. Goodleigh said. "You made it angry so it chased you into the pen."

I wasn't sure what to do. I could defend myself, but the new smarter voice in my head told me that they had already decided I was at fault. A causal timeline developed in my head. They suspected I'd freed the bull from its pen, teased it until it chased me, and then run all the way back here to the pig pen. It should only take a rational person a matter of a few thoughts to see how preposterous their theory was.

They are not being rational. They do not care to be rational. Something bad happened. They wish to assign blame.

In other words, hard evidence would not sway them. A paradox.

This new way of thinking was very unsettling. There were so many variables to account for. Unfortunately, the Goodleighs were two absolutes I could count on. Memories of other punishments I'd suffered came to mind. Most were for minor infractions. There were several instances where I had not been the guilty party and yet had been punished. My new thought processes made clear that the Goodleighs had not even attempted to connect the dots of logic that might have exonerated me.

I suddenly wondered if being ignorant might be better. When I was too stupid to understand why I was being punished, I hadn't felt the void of hopelessness forming in my stomach right now.

22

Seeing no other recourse, I spoke. "I'm sorry, Mother and Father."

The alarmed looks the Goodleighs had cast at me melted back to normalcy. I was now acting within normal parameters.

"More water?" Brickle asked.

Mrs. Goodleigh shook her head. "No, he is clean enough. Now he must butcher the poor animals."

Brickle rubbed his hands together. "We're going to have fun."

The bull and boar were quite old. Their meat would be tough and stringy. Then again, Oadby, the cook, rarely served the orphans meat. Nearly everything was mushed into unidentifiable casseroles. On second thought, we might actually eat more meat than I realized—it was simply impossible to distinguish it from the other ingredients.

I followed Brickle back to the dead animals. He sent me to fetch a heavy-duty wagon. When I returned with it, he hefted the bull onto it with little difficulty. I knew the man was strong, but my newly heightened senses informed me he was stronger than most men.

When Brickle and I finished the butchery, it was already past suppertime. Blood covered me from head to foot, so the brute made me stand while he sprayed me with the water hose again. Brickle had somehow remained mostly clean during the gruesome process. Proving he was a jack-of-all-trades, the man had carved both beasts into neat steaks using a set of stainless knives he'd pulled from his locker. He'd effortlessly hacked through bone and tendon and then made me package the meat in wax paper.

After I was thoroughly doused, Brickle smiled. "Go inside."

I complied without a word. I removed my boots at the back doorstep and put them next to the other work boots. I squeezed excess moisture from my shirt and pants so I wouldn't drip. That would simply add to the list of infractions I already had to answer for. I hoped my penance for the bull and boar was done, but Mrs. Goodleigh probably had something in store to punish me for damaging the floor in my room.

After changing into clean clothes and putting my dirty ones in the hamper at the end of the hallway, I went downstairs to the empty dining hall. The clock showed it was an hour past suppertime.

"You're late," Mrs. Goodleigh said from behind me.

I turned and bit back an acerbic retort. Instead, I adopted the guise of my old self. "I'm sorry."

"Those who are late to meals must go without eating." She pressed her palms together and pointed her hands at me as if sublime wisdom could be transmitted directly to my mind.

"I understand." I walked toward the hallway.

"I did not excuse you, Conrad."

I stopped at her cold tone, turned, and faced her.

Mrs. Goodleigh stared at me for a moment. "You have obviously forgotten your manners while away and become wild and unruly. First, you disobeyed me when I told you to get into work clothes by instead preparing your bed and damaging the floor. Next, you ignored your task, choosing instead to tease the bull. I can assure you that you will repair every bit of damage you caused." A small smirk curved her lips. "Every time you return to us, you must relearn something. This time it appears you have forgotten everything."

My mind swarmed with cold contempt. There were so many things I wanted to say to this woman, but I didn't dare. I was no longer stupid. I didn't know how my intelligence compared to other people. I might simply be average, which was definitely above what I'd been before. Even if I were a genius, I was still a weakling. I would be hard pressed to physically overcome Mrs. Goodleigh or anyone but the weakest among us.

"I'm sorry, Mother." The words caught in my throat, but I forced them out.

"Apologies are not enough." She released a long sigh. "After your visit with the doctor tomorrow, Father and I will discuss how to handle your reeducation."

I nodded.

Mrs. Goodleigh held my gaze for a long moment. "Now you may go to your room, Conrad."

"Thank you, Mother." I left and went upstairs. Once there, I closed the door and put the sheets on my bed. I changed into pajamas and laid in bed, listening to my stomach rumble and complain. It was an uncomfortable but familiar feeling. The Cullens had given me cereal, oatmeal, or bread pudding for nearly every meal they remembered to feed me. Oftentimes they'd taken me to the pub with them, though I'd waited in the car until the wee hours of the morning.

Cora had been the only one to feed me well. Whatever food we stole, she shared with me.

"Why are you nice to me?" I ask Cora.

She kneels in front of me, eyes troubled. "Have people been mean to you Conrad?"

I don't want to answer the question but nod. "Sometimes."

"Always treat people with respect until they show you they deserve otherwise." She kisses my forehead. "Would you like a cookie?"

"Where's the government paycheck?" Cora's husband, Bill, staggers into the kitchen. His face is red, and his eyelids droop.

"It hasn't come yet, sweetheart." Cora motions me to go to my room.

"You spent all the money!" He slams an empty brown bottle onto the counter.

I know what Bill is like when he acts this way, and quickly leave the kitchen before the yelling and hitting begins.

I jerked awake, stomach growling.

I wish I had a cookie.

I remembered the remains of the angel biscuit from yesterday. I had been stupid, but at least my feeble mind had known how to survive. I ate the last half of the pastry. Instead of partially satisfying me, it only made me hungrier.

Oadby kept the kitchen stocked with food for the adults. The garbage he cooked for the orphans was barely fit for consumption. I'd seen the bountiful harvest in the pantry while helping Brickle install new shelves. My stomach rumbled.

Find food!

I'd suffered near-starvation many times before. I would endure this maltreatment no more.

I cracked open the door and peered up and down the hallway. The other children were behind their own closed doors. Aside from the occasional creaking of wood as the house settled, I heard nothing else. I closed my eyes and imagined the layout of the manor. The stairs were a hundred footsteps to the right and twenty-four steps to the common room on the first floor.

Taking a right from there and walking another hundred and thirty steps would take me to the dining hall. The kitchen was behind the serving counter. This time of night, the door would be locked. Oadby and the Goodleighs each possessed a key. I tried using my new powers of reason to solve the dilemma of finding the key. Unfortunately, I lacked the data necessary to reach a conclusion.

When I closed my eyes, I marveled at how easy it was to imagine the dimensions of the manor. Despite my inability to reason before the incident this afternoon, my brain had retained all the details like a sponge. For example, I'd noted a faulty lock on a window in the back of the kitchen while cleaning them. The window offered a way to bypass the minimal security. Using that route added other variables I'd have to account for. Tracking mud inside would be the primary issue. Opening the window silently would be another—that particular window had squeaked when I'd once opened it at Oadby's request. A third, but no less important variable, were Brickle's hounds. Each night they patrolled the area around the manor.

The initial idea to sate my appetite by stealing food was more complicated than I'd realized. In other words, I would need longer than the space of a night to prepare for a culinary infiltration. I felt a smile crease my face. This was fun. I enjoyed thinking about things even if I couldn't solve the problem right away.

I rubbed the bump on the back of my head where something had hit me during the collision of the boar and bull. I hoped whatever had rewired my brain was permanent. I never wanted to return to the gray specter of a person I'd been before. I closed the door, turned out the light, and eased into bed.

My mind raced through scenarios for overcoming the challenges to reaching Oadby's hidden fridge. It helped me keep my mind off tomorrow—my least favorite day of the year.

My birthday.

Chapter 4

I started my morning chores at five AM. Mrs. Goodleigh had reassigned the chores from several other children and given them to me, no doubt a punishment for yesterday.

Gathering eggs was first on the list. Dread built in my stomach as I thought of fighting off the rooster. I might be smarter, but I was no more physically adept than the day before. I saw the brightly feathered bird strutting around in front of the coop as I drew closer and stopped to enjoy how pretty it looked, despite its savagery. Scenarios ran through my mind. Other children, myself included, had hit the rooster with rocks or buckets to keep him away.

That approach hadn't worked. If anything, it had made him meaner.

Roosters were essentially the fowl equivalent of a boar and a bull. They wanted to be dominant. How could I make myself dominant over the rooster? The only person the rooster never attacked was Brickle. I'd only seen the rooster fly at him once. Even then, Brickle hadn't backed off. He'd shielded himself and then picked up the rooster immediately after.

In fact, that was how Brickle handled any bullies, by subduing them. I'd rarely had any issues with the bigger or stronger boys bullying me, but that was because Brickle didn't allow anyone to be a bully except himself. He didn't hit anyone, but he would hold them down or humiliate them somehow.

Approach the rooster with confidence.

As I closed in on the coop, the rooster began to cluck in a warning tone. It faced me and strutted toward me. I saw the sharp spurs jutting from the backs of its legs. It had hit me with them on more than one occasion and the experience had not been pleasant.

Do not fear the chicken.

I had to be like Brickle and not show cowardice. I paced straight toward the rooster without hesitation. The rooster fluttered its wings. It stopped and crowed. In a moment, it would fling itself toward my leg and strike. It ran at me. Wings flapping, it leapt. I jumped to the side. The rooster missed me and landed to my right. Before it could recover, I grabbed it, hands firmly around its wings. As an added precaution, I tucked it beneath an arm and held its legs with the same hand.

The rooster went absolutely still. It glared at me from one eye. It clucked, but thankfully, it didn't try to peck me. Using my free hand, I did something else I'd witnessed Brickle do, and ruffled the rooster's feathers.

"Who's the boss now?" I said. "I am. Don't attack me again."

I set down the rooster and walked toward the chicken coop. It crowed. I turned and faced it. The rooster came at me. Once again, I dodged, scooped the bird into my hands, and ruffled its feathers. I held it out in front of the hens as they clucked in concerned tones and watched the spectacle. I set down the rooster in the middle of the hens and once again went for the chicken coop.

The rooster clucked, but it didn't crow. Still bracing for a sneak attack, I entered the coop, gathered the eggs, and exited. The rooster kept a wary eye on me as I walked back toward the house, but it didn't attack.

A surge of pride lifted my heart. It was so liberating to be able to reason through a problem and solve it. The rooster might forget this lesson by tomorrow, but I didn't care. Over time, it would learn to respect me like it did Brickle.

After depositing the eggs inside the kitchen, I walked to the cow barn at the far end of the dirt road and milked the black-spotted Holstein cows. Feeding the orphaned lambs came next, followed by serving the pigs slop. Brickle must have installed the temporary fence around the pen. Later today, I would have to assist him building a proper one.

I finished my chores by six, went inside, and cleaned up for breakfast. Oadby served pasty, tasteless porridge for the morning meal. I took my usual seat at the back corner of the room. William and Stephan smirked at me as I walked past. The girls sitting at the table began to whisper among themselves, their eyes darting to me as if I were a criminal. I overheard some of the conversation.

"He killed the bull!"

"I can't believe he survived."

"Such a puny boy…"

As usual, I ignored their comments and continued on. I took my seat and tasted a spoonful of the white goop. Thankfully, it had very little flavor, though the texture was quite disgusting. I looked at the Goodleighs and other staff at the front table enjoying scrambled eggs, bacon, and orange juice.

Anger formed a fiery pit in my belly. The government paid good money to feed and care for the children here. Instead, we were used as free labor to maintain a farm, which provided delicious food for the staff while we ate garbage.

"Are you ill?"

I jerked with surprise and realized Ambria, a girl my age, stood to my right. She smiled. My mind flashed back to several occasions where she'd approached me and asked how I was doing. I usually muttered something, lowered my head back to my food, and ignored her.

How impolite. Cora would not approve.

"I'm well, actually." I mustered a smile. "How are you?"

She blinked in obvious surprise. "I'm splendid." Without asking, she slid into the seat next to me and put her bowl on the table. "I heard you had an adventure yesterday. Alice and I haven't stopped talking about it all morning."

"The bull attacked me." I was going to leave it at that, but the hunger in her eyes alerted me to something that only just now occurred to me. Girls enjoyed drama. I'd observed the phenomenon several times as a dullard. Thankfully, my memory had retained the pertinent data and was able to formulate a solid theory. In order to craft a suitable story, I'd need to embellish.

"Do go on," Ambria said, eyes alight with desire.

It took a moment for me to arrive at a suitable opening. "There I was standing on the dirt road when I heard a snort. I turned and saw the bull, eyes red with fury, its hoof pawing the dirt, head tossing back and forth." I let the hook sink in for a second. "It was then I knew the old bull wanted to kill me."

By the time I finished my story, Ambria was nearly breathless. "Goodness, Conrad!" She touched my shoulder. "I'm so glad you survived. Who knew what that bull was thinking?"

"I don't know, but apparently I'm to blame for the temperamental beast."

"The Goodleighs don't care about the facts," she said with certainty. "They only care about pinning the blame."

"That's the truth." I sighed.

Ambria regarded me for a moment. "What happened to you? You're so much livelier than normal." A grin lit her face. "It's as if you were a rainy day but now the sun's burned away the clouds and the birds are singing."

I couldn't help but laugh. "That's a better explanation than any I could imagine."

We continued to talk as it helped keep our minds off the tasteless food. It seemed a scant number of minutes later that Mrs. Goodleigh rang the bell and dismissed everyone to their chores.

Ambria squeezed my hand. "I very much enjoyed talking with you, Conrad. May we do it again soon?"

I nodded. "I won't be here for lunch, I'm afraid."

Her eyes grew worried. "The doctor?"

"Yes."

"I visited him three months ago. He seemed excited about something."

My forehead tightened. "Excited?"

"Yes. Even the Goodleighs seemed happy." She shrugged. "As usual, they wouldn't tell me why."

"I suppose you're in excellent condition which means they don't have to worry about medical bills." By now, the dining hall was nearly empty. "I'm sure the government wants to be sure we're not burdening the taxpayers with poor health."

Ambria stood and gathered her bowl. "I believe you're right. Good luck, Conrad."

"Thank you." We dropped our bowls into a large sink just outside the kitchen. Two girls were already putting on aprons and rubber gloves so they could wash dishes while others began cleaning the tables and sweeping the floor.

The Goodleighs made sure everyone capable of working had a task. Even the very young girls like little Mary and Beth busied themselves wiping the tables.

I met Mrs. Goodleigh at the front door. She looked me up and down. "Are you ready, Conrad?"

"Yes, Mother." I reverted to my old personality. The less they knew, the better. I followed her outside.

Mr. Goodleigh pulled up in his black sedan. I opened the front door for Mrs. Goodleigh. She slipped inside the car. I closed the door and climbed into the backseat. The car pulled out of the driveway and headed down the long, winding road to the highway.

As usual, Mr. Goodleigh began to sing his strange song. Despite my newfound mental prowess, I could not translate the words. As I listened, I felt myself growing sleepier despite having been wide awake only moments ago. I fought the smothering blanket of exhaustion.

I woke up as we turned into the circular driveway at the doctor's house. Dr. Cumberbatch lived on a sprawling estate that seemed larger even than the orphanage, though he didn't have a farm or cattle I'd ever seen. It made no sense why someone would want so much land if they didn't plan to put it to good use. The faint sound of the ocean greeted me when I got out of the car. *We must be somewhere on the coast.* Since the country was one large island, that coast could be anywhere.

A butler answered the door when Mr. Goodleigh knocked. He led us inside, down a flight of stairs, and into a large wine cellar.

Dr. Cumberbatch reclined on a leather couch, a glass of red wine in his hand next to two massive casks. He stood and nodded. "A pleasure to see you again, Felicity." He kissed Mrs. Goodleigh's hand and extended a hand to Mr. Goodleigh. "That time of the year for Conrad again, eh, Marcus?"

Mr. Goodleigh shook his hand. "Indeed, Rufus." His voice held no enthusiasm.

The doctor stood a head taller than Mr. Goodleigh, with pale skin and washed out blue eyes. His thick, unruly black hair contrasted strikingly with the rest of his nearly colorless features. Unlike other doctors I'd seen, he wore silky gray robes over his thin frame and never used a stethoscope. He didn't even have a nurse or assistant. Before this trip, I'd never thought about the obvious differences.

During my stays with foster parents, it wasn't uncommon for me to come down with an illness every other month. Since health care was paid for by the government, many of my caretakers would drop me off at a doctor's office for an examination. This doctor was the only one we always met at his home. On rare occasions, he would come by the orphanage, but I'd never discovered the reasons for his house calls.

Dr. Cumberbatch motioned me toward a tall stool. "Have a seat, Conrad." He took a gulp of wine and set it on a nearby table. "This won't hurt a bit." He winked. "I promise."

"Blindfold," Mr. Goodleigh said.

The doctor produced a black piece of cloth with an elastic band and placed it over my head, blotting the word from my view. Under no circumstances had another doctor ever done this. I wanted to question the necessity, but it would be out of character for me to ask. Instead, I sniffed a couple of time and feigned a sneeze.

"Achoo!" I jerked forward into my hands and managed to push the cloth up just enough so I could see through the crack if I looked down.

"Bless you," Mrs. Goodleigh said. I heard her high heels click on the stone floor. "Which wine do you recommend, Rufus?"

"Definitely the seventy-three." His clothes rustled, presumably as he motioned toward the bottle in question. "You'll find it delightful."

"Fetch a glass for me, dear," Mr. Goodleigh said.

The doctor spoke to me. "Please place your hands in your lap, Conrad."

I complied.

He began muttering under his breath. I felt a slight tug on my hair. A moment later, the hair on my arms began to stand on end. I looked down through the crack and saw the doctor's hand moving a stick over my lower body. Usually, I felt nothing during these annual checkups. This time, I sensed a distinct emptiness buried deep within my abdomen. It was as if a part of me were filled with a void that needed to be filled. The sensation faded as the doctor moved the stick down my leg.

32

Light sparkled on my arm. I tried in vain to discover the source, but didn't want to move my head too much and risk giving away my limited ability to see. Just as my curiosity swelled to a nearly uncontrollable urge, a small sphere of light floated down my torso, over my arms, and toward my legs. Numbers and symbols danced in the center of the energy. I couldn't make sense of any of them.

I stiffened with alarm.

"Sorry if that tickles, Conrad." Dr. Cumberbatch chuckled. "Not much longer."

"Still nothing," Mr. Goodleigh said with a trace of anger. "Makes no sense."

"Agreed," Mrs. Goodleigh added. "Perhaps we should resort to more extreme measures."

Dr. Cumberbatch stepped to my right side where I could see the lower half of his body through the crack in the blindfold. "I don't know that it would do any good."

"It certainly wouldn't do any harm," Mr. Goodleigh said. He spoke a strange word and suddenly the sounds in the room became muffled. I heard him speaking again but it was as if I were underwater.

Deprived of two of my senses, I began to feel confined, claustrophobic. I wanted desperately to jerk off the blindfold. *Do it!* My hands trembled. The others in the room spoke, but I couldn't understand what they were saying. What was wrong with my ears? I put a finger in my ear and tried to clear it.

An insubstantial presence like the air itself wrapped around my wrist and pulled it to my lap. I felt it loop around my arms and bind them to my legs. I tried to stand but my legs were immobilized.

Fear overwhelmed me. "What's happening?" I shouted. My own words sounded clear, which was something of a relief. Being bound, blind, and deaf, however was still too much to bear.

I saw the glowing orb moving up my legs. It stopped just over my stomach. I saw the doctor's stick moving around the light globe. It turned a sullen red. The empty feeling in my stomach grew until it seemed as if a black hole were forming at my very center and consuming me. Electricity jolted through every nerve. I thrashed and felt the stool begin to topple. A pair of hands gripped my shoulders and steadied me. Another shock hit me so hard my body went rigid and my mouth opened wide in a silent scream of pain.

Prickles ran up my spine and into my scalp. Every single hair felt as though it was being pulled from my head. Blinding pain shattered my thoughts for an instant. My head lolled with wooziness. I couldn't tell if I'd been physically struck or if the doctor had sent electricity directly into my brain. What sort of mad scientist was this man?

I heard loud voices, as if people were arguing. For a moment, there was silence and the pain faded. My body relaxed as endorphins soothed me.

Without warning, agony stabbed into my abdomen. I might have doubled over, but something held me fast. I looked through the crack in the blindfold, fully expecting to see a dagger protruding. Instead, I saw only the light globe. Tears blinded what little vision I had. The pain increased until it was so excruciating, I could barely hold onto consciousness while a loud whining buzz shattered my hearing.

I had never endured such pain. While the annual checkup sometimes felt unpleasant, it had never reached such extremes. Tears poured down my face and I began to sob uncontrollably.

How much longer the pain lasted, I couldn't say. At long last, the piercing agony in my abdomen withdrew. The jolts of electricity ceased. I heard muffled voices again. They seemed to speak for a very long time before my ears popped and suddenly, I could hear once again. The bindings on my body slipped away and the blindfold came off.

I wiped the moisture from my face.

The doctor handed me some tissues. "Sorry, Conrad. You had an illness that required desperate measures."

I wiped my snotty nose and simply stared at him.

"He's too stupid to understand your apologies or explanations, Rufus." Mrs. Goodleigh sounded extremely annoyed.

"Please keep those thoughts to yourself." Mr. Goodleigh raised an eyebrow and gave her a warning look.

"As if he's capable of comprehending what we're talking about," Mrs. Goodleigh said. "I no longer care."

"You should." Mr. Goodleigh nodded at the doctor. "We'll be off then, Rufus."

The doctor nodded back. "My sincere regrets we couldn't arrive at a more promising conclusion, Marcus. I'll study the results and get back to you if I discover anything."

"Please do," Mrs. Goodleigh said in a clipped tone.

My knees buckled when I tried to stand. My head ached, and my stomach gurgled angrily.

Mrs. Goodleigh briskly motioned me to come. "Oh, do come on, Conrad."

"The boy's had bit of a shock," Dr. Cumberbatch said. "Perhaps he needs a moment—as a matter of fact, why don't you leave him here tonight for observation?"

"He's young. He'll recover." Mrs. Goodleigh gripped my bicep and jerked me forward.

Taking deep breaths to keep the nausea in my stomach at bay, I staggered along. Climbing the stairs was a monumental effort, legs protesting with every step. We finally reached the car. I crawled into the back seat.

"Conrad, I know I taught you better manners," Mrs. Goodleigh said.

I opened my bleary eyes and saw her waiting expectantly near the passenger door.

Repressing a groan and wincing at the sharp pains racing through my body, I stood and opened the door for her. Once she was inside, I shut the door and fell once again into the back seat.

"I do wish you'd told me where his last fosters lived," the doctor said as he spoke to Mr. Goodleigh outside the car. "I've always wanted to observe the phenomenon."

"I'm sorry, Rufus, but you know we have to keep that information confidential." Mr. Goodleigh's polite voice held a sharp edge to it. "It always happens near his birthday."

Dr. Cumberbatch looked at me and offered a friendly smile through the car window. "Yes, yes. And what's more special than the day you were born?"

"Supposedly, this birthday," Mrs. Goodleigh said in a very sharp tone. "Let's go, Marcus."

What's so special about this birthday?

Before I could consider it further, my muscles cramped violently and I doubled over. Anger nearly equal to the pain in my bodies ignited deep in my solar plexus. What had the doctor done to me? Why would he trace a stick over my body, and what sort of device was that light sphere? The Goodleighs had ordered him to probe me like a sick animal. His supposed treatment had been torture. If I had this to look forward to year after year, I couldn't simply sit by and do nothing.

Perhaps my next foster family would be better. If not, I would have to run away and pray I found better circumstances. There had to be something better in the world. Someplace safe I could run to and hide.

There just had to be.

Chapter 5

I woke up when we reached the orphanage. After getting out of the car and opening the door for Mrs. Goodleigh, I headed inside.

"Brickle needs your help repairing the fence," Mrs. Goodleigh said.

I felt my hands clench and my cheeks grew hot. I almost spun and shouted at her. It took everything I had to hold it all inside. Trembling with rage, I went inside and upstairs to change into work clothes.

Mrs. Goodleigh's voice echoed up the stairwell behind me. "Bloody waste of time."

As I dressed, I couldn't stop thinking about her words. Why was I a waste of time? I did more than my fair share of work on the farm. I behaved within specified parameters. Overall, I should have rated high compared to the others in the orphanage. Instead, they derided me and subjected my body to cruel treatment. I squeezed shut my eyes and took a deep breath. Angry thoughts swirled through my mind.

Kill them. Make them suffer.

Eyes flicking open, I gasped. Had that been my thought? I touched my forehead as if I could divine the origin of the idea. It brought me no closer to understanding my murderous thoughts. I looked at my hands and wondered if I was capable of murder, or if perhaps my anger had simply driven an extreme idea into the realm of possibility.

I didn't want to think about such awful things.

The patter of rain drew my attention to the window. The sunny afternoon had turned dreary and wet. Most people would abandon working on the fence until better weather prevailed. Brickle would not. If anything, working in adverse conditions only made him happier. He always seemed eager to prove he was a pure, unstoppable alpha male. Nothing would dominate him. Nothing could stop his relentless march.

I made my way downstairs, put on my rubber boots, and went into the steady downpour. Brickle stood next to the brown barn. Water poured down his head and into his thick, bushy beard. A grin creased his face, no doubt because he observed how miserable I was.

Yet another person who revels in misery.

My muscles still ached and my stomach threatened to heave its meager contents. A bundle of posts lay just outside the barn. Instead of the triangular oak posts from the old fence, these were thick and coated in tar. There were also many more than necessary to repair the fence. In fact—I knew before Brickle opened his mouth what he intended. We were to replace the entire fence and not just the damaged section. The swine were absent, relocated somewhere else.

"Is it really necessary to replace the entire thing?" I asked just as he began to speak.

He glared at me as if I'd stolen his thunder. "Ain't going to look right if we just patch it." His high-pitched voice thwarted the attempt to sound menacing.

It suddenly occurred to me why Brickle was so intent on proving his manliness to everyone, including nature itself. He was compensating for his puny voice and perhaps a terrible childhood. I tucked away the observation and spoke. "Well, let's get started. No sense in wasting time."

His eyes flashed, whether with disbelief or anger, I couldn't tell. "Fine, boy. Start digging holes."

I took the post-hole digger to the location of the original fence posts. Gritting my teeth to prepare myself, I jammed the metal blades into the ground. Tears in my eyes accompanied the jolt of pain in my muscles. Every time I stabbed the earth, it seemed to stab me back. I knew there was no point in complaining. The doctor might have done more harm than good to my body, but Brickle would only deride it as weakness.

Looking up, I saw him smirking at me. "This is work a real man can appreciate." I mustered a fierce grin, as if hard work in the pouring rain was reward instead of punishment. "None of that child's play, feeding animals and milking cows." I stabbed the shovel back into the ground and gritted my teeth, forcing the smile to stay on my face. "I'm glad I destroyed this fence."

Brickle's forehead pinched. "The bull destroyed it."

I spread my hands, looked up at the rain and laughed maniacally. "Yeah? Well look who killed the bull and the boar." I jabbed a thumb into my chest. "Me! How many men can brag about something like that?" I narrowed my eyes at him. "Nobody but me."

The hulking man's back straightened. "Yeah, well I killed a bear with my bare hands."

I didn't doubt it for an instant. "To real men!" I shouted as I ripped a clod of earth from the ground and threw it into the meager piled I'd made. "We're the only ones capable of building a fence in harsh weather." I laughed again. "Mother Nature doesn't know who she's messing with!"

Brickle suddenly roared with laughter. "Right you are, mate." He rammed a much larger shovel into the dirt and tore loose a huge clump. Teeth bared like a lion, he threw the dirt into the pile, raised his fist, and howled.

I estimated my competitive posturing had increased his testosterone production by another ten percent. Sure enough, he dug the larger holes quickly and then uprooted the other fence posts, hoisting them overhead like a victorious gladiator. I did my best to keep up, but I was no physical match for this brute. As we worked, I threw in more comments about real men and about how nothing could dominate them.

By the time the rain stopped and dusk absorbed the light from the sky, all the new fence posts were set. Placing the sturdy new slats in their notches would be much easier. Though Brickle had done most of the work, it took every ounce of energy I could summon to keep moving. The rain had masked how much I'd cried from pain during the task. All I wanted now was food and sleep.

Brickle brushed the dirt from his hands as it grew too dark to work. "Unstoppable." He spoke the words in a murmur, as if congratulating himself. His stomach grumbled loudly. "Think I'll have steak tonight."

I'll have gruel or oatmeal as usual.

After cleaning up, I went to the dining hall. Oadby dumped a blob of meat porridge in my bowl. At least I thought the dark specks and chunks in it might be meat. I found my usual seat and took a bite. After chewing on a hunk of meat until my teeth ached, I realized it was probably from the butchered bull. I inspected a cube of brown beef and noticed gristle laced through it.

Ambria came to my table. Her eyes filled with concern. "Conrad, you look awful."

I glanced at the bruises on my arms from picking up the heavy fence posts. "Thank you."

"How was the doctor visit?" She dropped into the seat next to me.

I told her everything.

"You can't be serious." She touched my arm. "That's inhumane, even by the standards of this fine establishment."

I looked at the head table where the Goodleighs drank red wine and feasted on juicy red meat. Brickle took a large haunch of beef and tore into it. The juices ran down his beard. "The only standards here are that the staff members get treated like royalty."

"Without doubt." Ambria frowned. "I wish we could change that."

"We're powerless."

She looked forlornly at her meat porridge. "I'm afraid you're right."

Avoiding the inedible bits of bull in my porridge, I finished it and told Ambria good night. I wished I could break into the kitchen for better food, but I was far too tired to plan an insurrection tonight. I went upstairs and, after changing into pajamas, fell into bed and a deep sleep.

I dreamt of a dark, ominous shadow hovering over me. It took a humanoid shape for an instant before melting back into a dark cloud. The dream held me in a lucid state. I knew I was fast asleep, but couldn't seem to purge the wraith haunting me.

My internal clock woke me at five in the morning. Still tired and sore, I dragged myself out of bed and dressed. When I viewed the downstairs chalkboard with the daily assignments, I noticed the Goodleighs had given me yet another task. I had to check the water tank for the sheep and goats. Staring with disbelief—for it was at least a fifteen-minute walk to the tank—I realized the handwriting looked different. Mrs. Goodleigh wrote in a lovely flowing cursive. Mr. Goodleigh preferred neat print in all capitals. This handwriting approximated Mr. Goodleigh's, but fell short of his immaculate lines.

I wondered if someone else was trying to play a trick on me, but the idea was preposterous. The Goodleighs were adept at discovering such things and would deal swift punishment on the guilty. William had once tried foisting one of his chores on me. The Goodleighs had somehow traced it back to him and doubled his chores for a week.

I decided to play it safe and do the task. If the Goodleighs discovered subterfuge, the person would be punished. If, however, another staff member had actually assigned me this task, I could not ignore it. Rare as it was for anyone else to schedule such things, it had happened. Perhaps Brickle decided I needed something else to do after my boasts the previous day.

Fresh, cool air greeted my lungs this morning. I drew in a deep breath and adopted a brisk walk down the dirt road. As I passed the chicken coop, it suddenly occurred to me that something was missing. I looked inside the building and all around it. There were eggs aplenty in the hen's nests, but the chickens were nowhere to be found.

Perhaps Brickle removed them because he intends me to rebuild this shack.

My time was limited, so I pressed onward toward the end of the road, my mind processing possible reasons for the missing chickens. The sheep pasture lay to the left. The water tank was located a little way past the gate. I reached the end of the road and entered the pasture. A wall of wool blocked further progress. I flinched from my thoughts and looked up.

A stocky ram stood at the head of the sheep formation. Goats, ever prone to strange behavior, stood atop the sheep. One of them made an awful screaming sound. The sheep bleated in response.

To the side of the formation stood a middle-aged man dressed in black robes. He stood perhaps five feet tall with a head of thinning brown hair. His face bore a resemblance to someone I'd seen before, but couldn't place. The man glared at me with what could only be described as pure hate. "Here to clean the tank, Conrad?" Malice formed daggers of his words.

"You put that assignment on the chalkboard?" I asked. *Is he a new staff member I haven't seen?*

"Yes." He held a wooden staff up and motioned it forward. The ram took several steps toward me. The sheep and goats followed right behind.

I backed up a step, my eyes widening with surprise. *The sheep are acting just like the cows did yesterday. The ram is acting like the bull. Does this man have some way of controlling them?* "How are you doing that?"

"Zoomancy." His sparkled like cold hard diamonds. "Then again, you should know that."

I've never heard of such a strange term. I took another step back. "Did you send the bull to kill me?"

He giggled hysterically, though the anger on his face remained. "Oh, yes, you seed of evil." Spittle foamed on his lips. "I know who you are, Conrad Edison. Your parents hid you before they died, but I dug and dug and dug and dug and dug." Giggles burst from his mouth. "I found you!"

"My parents hid me?"

"Don't lie!" He shook with rage. "Those evil monsters killed my family, boy. Now I will snuff the rest of their bloodline."

Clucking sounded from behind me. I spun and saw the chickens forming another wall behind me. I quickly decided the chickens were far less dangerous than the ram. Still, this man knew about my parents. He'd called me by a last name I'd never heard before. The Goodleighs never discussed dead parents with the orphans.

I held up my hands in surrender. "I don't know anything about my parents. What can you tell me about them?"

"After the war, they tried to seize power. They had powerful relics. Killed so many people." He slammed the end of his staff into the ground. "Murdered my family!" Panting in shuddering breaths, he turned his furious gaze on me. For a moment, sanity seemed to find him. "You cannot be allowed to live." With that, he thrust his staff forward.

The ram, the goats, the sheep all rushed me. The clucking behind me reached a fever pitch. Ducking my head, I ran through a forest of feathers and sharp claws. The chickens' clucks turned to screeches of pain. I looked over my shoulder and saw the sheep trampling the birds that hadn't managed to flutter above the stampede.

Every pounding step sent throbbing pain into my legs. Somehow, I managed to keep upright. The wide metal gate hung open at a ninety-degree angle to the fence. I grabbed it as I ran past and swung it shut behind me. The latch clicked into place an instant before the ram's horns rang against it. Unlike the pigpen, the pasture walls were made of stone with sturdy metal gates.

The flock of sheep crashed against the gate but failed to budge it.

I heard the angry man shouting from somewhere behind the fracas.

My body trembled with relief and with anger. Who had killed my parents and why? Why had they supposedly killed this man's family? I knew if I didn't do something to stop him, he would eventually succeed in killing me. I had to apprehend him and let the Goodleighs handle the rest.

I ran inside the red barn and grabbed a shovel. The stone wall bordering the pasture ran behind the red barn. Stones jutting from the wall made it easy enough to climb despite my sore muscles. I crawled over the top and ducked behind a tree. The man stood behind the sheep, yelling at them. He didn't see me as I sneaked closer and closer. The last tree stood twenty feet from the man. I peered around it and made sure he was still preoccupied. Steeling myself, I crossed the open pasture in a steady pace.

One of the goats gave me away at the last instant, its horizontal pupils allowing it tremendous peripheral vision. It turned my way and bleated. The man started to turn. Panicking, I swung the shovel as hard as I could. Steel rang like a bell as it cracked the man in the temple. He went limp and slumped to the ground.

The goats and sheep collapsed. At first, I feared they'd all died, but within seconds, they wobbled on unsteady legs and began eating grass as if nothing had happened. I breathed a sigh of relief.

"You're going to see the Goodleighs," I said to the unconscious man. Kneeling, I searched the man's robes but found nothing except for a crooked stick that looked much like the one Dr. Cumberbatch had waved over me. It had a neatly polished handle and strange symbols inscribed in the wood. The man's staff bore similar inscriptions. Just as my mind had readily identified the scientific classifications of some animals, it tingled as though trying to dredge up the significance of these items.

Instead, a sharp ache formed in my forehead. I pressed my hand against it, but the pain was too deep. When my vision cleared, I realized blood was pouring from an open wound in the man's head.

Check his vitals.

I remembered how doctors put a finger against my neck or wrist to check the pulse and mimicked what I'd seen. I found no pulse in the man's wrist or neck. I put my ear to his mouth and realized with horror he wasn't breathing.

Chapter 6

I killed him!
My stomach heaved so hard, the world went black.

A loud thumping wakes me up. I leave my room and see Cora standing at the top of the stairs, eyes focused on something below. Standing beside her, I follow her gaze. Bill lies at the bottom. His eyes are wide. His left foot twitches.

Cora goes into her bedroom and returns with a brown bottle. She tosses it down the stairs after Bill. Liquid splashes with each bump. It comes to rest next to him, leaving a puddle.

"Sometimes, bad things have to happen." Cora squeezes me in a hug. "It doesn't mean you're evil, does it?"

I squeeze her tight. "You're the best person in the world." This is the truest thing I know.

I staggered to the side and caught myself on a tree.

Almost incapacitated with nausea, I forced myself to think. Even if the man had been up to no good, the Goodleighs would be very upset that I'd murdered him, accident or not. In fact, they would likely do as they had before and blame me no matter the circumstances. They might send me to jail for the rest of my life. The only hope of avoiding such a fate lay with the tool that had killed the man.

I found a spot beneath the trees and dug. I cut the sod into neat squares and carefully put them to the side. Ignoring the awful aches in my body, I burrowed as deep as I could. Because of the trees, roots made the chore difficult. I hacked through the small ones until the hole was about four feet deep. I dragged the man into the hole. He was too tall so I rolled him on his side and bunched up his legs. I

45

filled in the hole quickly and patted it flat. The sod fit over it neatly, disguising the patch of disturbed dirt from its surroundings.

Using the same method as before, I climbed the stone wall, rinsed the dirt from the shovel, and then put it back inside the red barn. Time was slipping quickly past, so I hurriedly gathered the eggs and put them just inside the door. I grabbed the milk buckets and raced to the cow barn. Unfortunately, milking the cows could not be rushed. Taking deep breaths to overcome my panic, I put my mind to the task at hand. I finished my chores perhaps ten minutes late.

After rinsing my muddy boots and cleaning my face and hands, I walked into the dining hall and tried to pretend that all was well. My insides were another matter. My bowels churned and my heart felt as if an invisible fist clenched it tight. Not only had I killed someone, but the attack on me had likely killed several chickens and sheep. So preoccupied had I been with burying the body, I hadn't even thought to check on the animals or clean up the carnage.

Someone will discover them for sure.

"Something serious must be on your mind."

I flinched and found Ambria seated to my right. "Sorry, I'm very tired from yesterday."

"I imagine you are." She scooped a spoonful of watery oatmeal from her bowl and made a face when she put it in her mouth. "Slimy."

Shoveling a mound into my mouth, I winced in agreement. "At least it's a change from porridge."

Ambria touched my arm. "Conrad, your eyes look practically black and blue this morning. You look as though you haven't slept for a week."

"I feel as though it's been a month."

Her eyes softened with worry. "Perhaps you should ask the Goodleighs to let you stay in today. Tell them you're sick."

"You know they won't care." I stuffed more oatmeal in my mouth and forced it down my throat.

"Maybe you can take a nap at lunch."

I nodded. "I'll try."

The smell of blueberry pancakes wafted past my nose. I looked on with envy at the feast on the main table. "How are we supposed to survive on this rubbish?" Without proper protein, my muscles wouldn't heal very quickly. I looked around the room and noted even the sturdier boys were quite thin, though not as scrawny as me.

"I hope this is the year I find real parents." Ambria sighed with longing. "Unfortunately, it seems the only ones who find permanent homes are the ones the Goodleighs actually like."

I remembered those who had gone on to better homes. Most had done so within weeks of their visit to Dr. Cumberbatch. "I'm afraid the Goodleighs don't consider me good enough." I remembered what she'd told me about her visit to the doctor. "They seemed very happy about your last doctor visit. Maybe that means something."

"It's possible. You've had several fosters at least." She frowned. "I've heard stories about what happens to them. Are they true?"

"Is what true?"

"Do all your fosters die?"

I looked down at the nearly empty bowl. "Not all, but most. I can always count on a freak accident." Even when dumb, I'd noticed it always happened close to my birthday. "I might be cursed."

"Cursed?" Ambria giggled but abruptly stopped, a troubled look on her face. "When I think about how many times you've been fostered, it makes me think you might be right."

It was fantasy, of course. There was no such thing as magical curses. Then again, before this morning, I hadn't realized a human could control animals. I wondered if I should tell Ambria, but quashed the idea. She would be horrified to know I'd killed someone. Instead of thinking I was cursed, she'd conclude I was a murderer who'd intricately plotted the deaths of my foster parents and might possibly start dispatching the other children next.

Kill them all, a harsh voice whispered in my head.

I flinched, but Ambria didn't seem to notice.

"I can't get over how much different you are now than when you left with your last fosters." She peered into my eyes as if trying to see through dirty windows. "What changed?"

I shrugged. "I must have hit my head."

A smile stretched her plump lips. "I'm sure that's it."

Despite the pleasant conversation, I couldn't stop thinking about the debacle with the sheep and chickens this morning. I couldn't decide if I should leave breakfast early and try to clean up the mess, or act as if nothing was wrong and go about my day. I decided on the latter. There was no time to bury the dead animals, and certainly no way to disguise that several chickens and sheep were missing.

On the other hand, I was the only one with the early morning chores. If someone noticed the extra chore to check the water tank, they could easily conclude I was to blame. Since neither of the Goodleighs had come and asked me about the additional task, it likely meant they hadn't checked the board yet.

"It's been nice talking," I told Ambria. "I'm going to rest for a few minutes before the work day begins."

She touched my hand. "Take care of yourself, Conrad."

Her touch warmed my heart. Was this what it was like to have someone genuinely care about you? "Thank you."

I put my bowl in the sink and went into the back hallway where the chalkboard hung. After looking both ways to be sure I was alone, I erased the forged handwriting and looked it over to be sure no traces remained.

"What do you think you're doing?" Mrs. Goodleigh said.

I nearly jumped, but somehow managed to retain my composure. "I was looking at the rest of my duties."

She walked up behind me and peered at the board. "Even a dullard such as yourself should be able to see you'll be repairing fences the rest of the day."

"Yes, Mother." I let my shoulders slump and adopted a dull look in my eyes. "I'm sorry I disappoint you."

"Apologies are poor substitutes for inadequacies." Her gaze sharpened into a severe look. "I'm afraid you'll never rise to expectations." With that, she marched toward the main office.

A long breath escaped me. My hands shook. *That was too close.* I had to remain calm and hope things played out in such a way I didn't catch the blame. I looked over the chalkboard and saw that William and Stephan were assigned to walk the perimeter and check the pasture walls. If they followed their usual route, they shouldn't end up near the sheep pasture for a couple of hours. All the other boys were assigned various lawn and grounds maintenance tasks, which took them nowhere near the sheep pasture.

I also realized for the first time there were only four other boys left at the orphanage according to the duty roster—William, Stephan, Toddy, and Sam. Since I'd been living with the Cullens, six of them must have been either adopted or fostered. I couldn't remember how many females there'd been before, but eleven were listed on the chalkboard. As usual, their tasks dealt with cleaning the manor.

I walked onto the back porch and noted with some relief the surviving chickens had returned to the coop. The rooster had apparently survived and was patrolling his reduced flock. Two of the hens limped and hopped about; another fluttered a crooked, possibly broken wing. I returned inside and sat on the mud bench. I didn't want to be the first outside.

A few minutes later, Brickle came along and collected me. We finished the pigpen by lunchtime. As we were putting away the equipment, William and Stephan raced over to us from the direction of the sheep pasture.

"Mr. Brickle, you have to come!" William said. "Something's happened to the sheep and chickens."

The big man narrowed his eyes. "What's happened?"

"A bunch are dead."

Brickle set off at a brisk walk toward the pasture while the rest of us jogged to keep up with his long strides. He stopped abruptly when he reached the pasture gate. "What in the name of the moon happened here?"

Even though I knew what to expect, the sight twisted my lips into a grimace. Spattered blood painted a canvas of soil, grass, and corpses. Crimson streams pooled where hooves had carved a depression in the earth. Feathers and chicken parts littered the area, making it difficult to count how many had actually died. Three sheep, including the ram, lay broken, limbs askew, on the ground.

A beautiful masterpiece of gore.

I shook myself from the troubling thoughts and spoke. "What happened? Was it a wolf?" I didn't actually know what sort of predators existed in the countryside, if any.

Brickle knelt next to the sheep and shook his head. "They did this to themselves." He scanned the ground. "Looks like something spooked them."

"Why were the chickens out here?" William asked. He gave me a suspicious look. "Conrad had the morning duties. I'll bet he chased the chickens out here and scared the sheep."

49

"The chickens wander all over the place." Brickle stood and looked further into the pasture.

"Look there," Stephan said. "A footprint."

I saw the large imprint in the soggy ground where the madman had stood. Thankfully, any footprints I'd made had been obliterated by the stampede.

Brickle walked to the footprint and inspected it. He looked at our feet. "Come over here."

Repressing the urge to run away, I walked over to him and put my boot next to the footprint. Even if my boot were as large as the footprint, the tread wouldn't match. Brickle made each of us put our boots next to the footprint. He seemed satisfied it didn't match any of ours.

He stood and walked a few paces around the area where he discovered a few more traces of the interloper. "Whoever made these footprints scared the sheep. Probably made them stampede right into the fence." Brickle sniffed the air. "Wait 'til I find whoever did this." He turned to me. "Go tell the Goodleighs."

I swallowed a nervous lump. I was not currently in the good graces of the Goodleighs. As the bearer of bad news, I would likely be the one to bear the blame. "Maybe William should tell them since he found the dead sheep."

Brickle narrowed his eyes at me. "Go tell the Goodleighs."

I maintained eye contact with him so it wouldn't appear I was submitting to his will, though in reality that was exactly what I had to do. "You're right. William isn't brave enough to face the Goodleighs."

"I'm not afraid of them," William protested. "Let me go tell them."

Brickle shook his head. "No, you help me look around for more footprints. I want to trace the path."

I hadn't even thought about backtracking the crazy man's origin. Had he left a car parked nearby? If so, it might have his identification and more clues inside. Somehow, I had to reach that car first. I walked purposefully toward the gate and rounded the corner on the road back toward the house. The moment I was out of sight of Brickle and the others, I raced for the manor. Stopping on the back porch to catch my breath, I pulled off my boots and went inside.

The main office was adjacent to the common room with the doorway just inside the main entrance. I knocked on the office door. The latch must not have been fully engaged because it swung open. The Goodleighs were not inside. I remembered it was lunchtime so they were likely in the dining hall. As I turned to go, I noticed a glowing screen on the desk.

It appeared to be a tablet computer. Though I'd seen them plenty of times, I'd never had the pleasure of using one. I walked over to the thin device and examined it. The screen dimmed. I tapped it with a knuckle and it brightened. The Goodleighs must have just left the office seconds ago.

I resisted the desire to toy with the tablet since my fingers were dirty and swiping across the clean screen would leave marks. My eyes focused on the open document on the tablet. Ambria's name caught my eye. I went back to the beginning of the text.

Mr. Hova:

> *We have an ideal female candidate for you. Though Ambria is not physically fit, she can be trained and brought up to standard. Cumberbatch measured her AP at a healthy fourteen, which should lend itself well to your particular line of work.*
>
> *The previous candidates we've sold to you have met or exceeded expectations. As you know, we procure only the finest of specimens. We will be listing this new candidate for auction at the end of this month in the usual location. Please find her pedigree attached.*

Yours,

Felicity Goodleigh

My heart turned to solid ice. *Auction?*

They weren't finding parents for Ambria—they were finding a buyer!

Chapter 7

I simply couldn't believe what I'd read. But upon rereading it, certain words refused to let me believe it was simple misinterpretation. One did not refer to an orphan as a specimen. And how did they procure their specimens in the first place?

This tablet held the answers.

Unfortunately, I had only minutes before Brickle wondered at my long absence, and someone could happen by at any moment and see me in this forbidden zone. It was no wonder the Goodleighs had been so strict about keeping us out of this room.

Using a clean knuckle, I scrolled down and found other open documents. Some of them referred to other children I'd assumed had recently been adopted. Instead, the letters detailed the final sale of each one. Another who'd not met expectations by his thirteenth birthday had been given away as a servant—a bonus prize to a valued buyer.

I looked at the clock and realized I'd been poring over this for nearly five minutes. I quickly scrolled back to the letter about Ambria and left on the screen since it would eventually deactivate on its own. Peering around the corner, I saw the common room was empty. Just as I was about to close the office door, an idea came to me. I ran back to the window and unlatched it then quickly exited the office and pulled the door completely shut behind me.

Time was of the essence, so I briskly made my way to the dining hall and approached the Goodleighs at the front table.

"Mother, Father, there has been a serious incident in the sheep pasture and Brickle asked that I come get you." I made sure to keep a dull, submissive aura about me.

Mrs. Goodleigh stabbed a spear of asparagus on her fork. "What have you done now?"

"Brickle said someone scared the sheep." I maintained eye contact with her.

Mr. Goodleigh sighed and threw down his napkin. "Let's go see what the fuss is."

When we reached the pasture, Brickle was still pacing around the same area, his nostrils flaring as if he hoped to sniff out the culprit. Even his ears seemed to twitch. I occurred to me that he would probably get his hounds to find the scent of the perpetrator.

They'll find the body for sure.

My knees wobbled at the thought.

The Goodleighs pulled Brickle aside and spoke to him, faces deadly serious. I pretended to look on the ground for footprints. I found several fresh dung heaps from the sheep. They were small and black, shaped like berries. Though the odor wasn't too strong, I hoped it might confuse a dog's sense of smell. Kneeling as if to inspect the ground, I gathered what I could in my hands and took the droppings into the trees near the grave. I dropped the feces around the tree and over the grave.

As the Goodleighs continued their conversation, I repeated the dung relocation process several times. William and Stephan stood a little ways from the group of adults, worried looks plain on their faces. Everyone seemed preoccupied. Thinking furiously, I came up with one more idea that might keep the corpse hidden.

Running back to the barn, I grabbed a small shovel, then ran into the other barn for one of the buckets filled with discarded bits from the bull. With the others preoccupied, I dug several small holes and deposited bull guts into them, then tossed the shovel and bucket over the stone wall to hide them.

Several minutes later, the adults broke their huddle. Brickle went to retrieve the hounds.

"Look for footprints," Mrs. Goodleigh commanded. "Walk back and forth across this field and mark everything you see."

"Yes, Mother," we three boys replied, meek as mice.

I walked a distance from the others and surveyed the field. In the mornings, the sheep usually congregated beneath a stand of trees in the middle of the field. The tree stood on a slight rise, which offered them a better view of the pasture. Although I knew of no predators in these lands, the animals' instincts probably guided them to seek safety at night. On rare occasions, someone herded them into a stockyard on the farm, but not during the night. Mrs. Goodleigh complained they were too noisy.

If the sheep had been in the center of the field, it made sense the strange man had gone there first. If so, I might find his footprints and determine the direction they'd originated. Two roads bordered the pasturelands but I wouldn't have time to survey them both. I needed to find his car quickly to see if he'd left his identification inside.

William and Stephan adopted a more deliberate approach and began walking back and forth where the massacre had occurred. I pretended to do the same but wandered in what I hoped looked like an aimless pattern. The Goodleighs, thanks to their low opinion of my intelligence, likely wouldn't suspect anything. I walked into the grove of gnarled oaks in the middle of the pasture and tripped on a bundle sitting at the base of a tree.

My knee slammed painfully into a large root. I bit back a cry. Rubbing my joint to sooth the pain, I looked back at the neatly rolled bundle. It looked like a carpet. I unrolled it and discovered it was just that. Hidden within the folds was a smartphone. I quickly pocketed it.

"Why would he stash a phone in a carpet here?" Though the ground beneath the trees was quite firm, it was mostly bare earth. I found two footprints leading away from the middle of the grove, but none leading into it. I wondered if he'd used the carpet to drag over his tracks, but dismissed the idea. The man hadn't bothered to conceal his tracks anywhere else, so why bother doing it from the road to the grove?

Besides, the grass in the field would hide most tracks unless he happened through a particularly soggy area. I heard baying in the distance and saw Brickle leading his hounds on the search. The carpet seemed rather innocuous, but my improved intellect told me it was something more than a decoration. Why else would the man bring it with him into a sheep pasture? Had he intended to bundle my corpse into it once the sheep trampled me to death? I needed time to solve the mystery, but there was no way I could spirit a rug across the field. If I left it on the ground, the hounds would sniff it out.

Thankfully, the sheep had rubbed against the trees, leaving wool and most importantly, their scent all over the trunks. I looked up and knew what I had to do. One tree offered an easier climb than the others, so I tucked the carpet under one arm and shimmied up to the first branch. From there, I was able to climb two thirds of the way up and nestle the bundled carpet between two branches.

The height also provided a good view of the surrounding area. I peered at the roads paralleling the stone pasture walls but saw no trace of a parked car near either one. Unless the man had driven into a ditch, I should be able to see his vehicle from here. I climbed back down and looked toward the Brickle and the others.

The hounds were sniffing around the trees where I'd buried the man.

Panic frosted in my chest. I walked quickly back toward the others as they observed the hounds.

"Got something!" Brickle shouted.

My heart pounded in my chest, the echo of its beat thudding in my ears. I followed Brickle around the tree just as a big brown hound ripped something bloody from the ground. The other hounds joined the first, two of them dragging a string of guts from the dirt.

"What is the meaning of this?" Mrs. Goodleigh said. Her gaze whipped toward me.

"What's that doing here?" Brickle stared at entrails.

"You told me to get rid of the remains." I kept my voice as steady as possible. "I thought you wanted me to bury them."

"Idiot!" Mrs. Goodleigh blew out a frustrated breath and turned back to Brickle. "There's nothing over here but whatever this fool child buried." She motioned toward the rest of the field. "Take the hounds out there and see what you find."

Brickle sniffed the air as if he could detect the scents better than the hounds. "There's something around here that don't smell right."

"The field," Mr. Goodleigh said. "Go now."

The big man narrowed his eyes and looked as if he wanted to retort. Instead, he growled and turned toward the field.

"The rest of you get the dead sheep to the slaughterhouse." Mrs. Goodleigh turned her piercing eyes on me. "You will assist Brickle with the butchery."

My stomach growled. I still hadn't eaten lunch. I knew for a fact Brickle wouldn't go without eating, though he wouldn't care if I ever received food or not.

"Yes, Mother." I walked toward the closest sheep.

"You're a moron." William clenched a fist. "Wish I could punch you in the face."

I kept my face calm and regarded him. "You could waste time being mad, or we can get these sheep into the slaughter house quickly and still have a chance to eat lunch."

"I'm really hungry," Stephan said.

Surprise lit William's eyes. "Since when did you start talking in complete sentences?"

I reached under the dead ram. "Are we going to hurry or not?"

Stephan reached under the ram's back. "I am."

Grudgingly, William gripped the ram's head. "Fine. Let's do this."

We synchronized our steps and got the ram into the slaughterhouse quickly. Within another ten minutes, we had the other dead sheep inside as well.

William and Stephan turned back toward the pasture. I held up a hand to stop them. "We should run inside and eat first. Otherwise, they'll probably just give us another assignment."

William folded his arms across his chest. "If we don't tell her we're done, we'll probably get punished."

I shook my head. "They weren't paying attention to us. We finished at least fifteen minutes faster than it should have taken us. That gives us time to eat."

Stephan counted on his fingers. "I'm so hungry, I could eat these dead sheep."

"We'll probably end up eating them anyway," I said. "Most likely the ram."

Stephan made a face.

Not wanting to waste another minute, I left the slaughterhouse. The other boys followed close behind. We quickly cleaned off the blood and took off our shoes. We got our food just as Oadby was preparing to put it away.

"One more minute, and no stew," he said in his strange accent. "You get here just in time." He served us each a bowl of something resembling pig slop.

The three of us sat down and wolfed down the thick concoction. I saw Ambria sitting in our usual spot and waved at her. She looked at me with a confused expression then smiled and waved back. I imagined she was wondering why I'd sat next to William and Stephan.

As I waited for William to finish eating, I looked around the dining hall and counted the other children. There were seventeen of us in all, including me. The last was a little boy I hadn't seen before. He looked about four years old, which probably meant he was the youngest of all the children here.

I pressed a hand against the lump in my pocket. I desperately wished to pull out the phone and inspect it, but the others would wonder where I'd gotten it. I thought about taking it up and hiding it in my room, but time was short. We needed to return to the field and tell the Goodleighs we were done.

William finally choked down his last mouthful and we took our bowls to the sink. After donning our shoes, we walked outside and down the road to the pasture.

"How was your last visit to the doctor?" I asked William.

His head flicked my way. "What do you care?"

I gave him a steady look. "I don't."

"It was good. The Goodleighs were happy." He puffed his chest. "Guess that means I'll be getting a permanent family soon."

Not the kind you want. "What about you, Stephan?" The other boy was a year or so younger than us.

"Mrs. Goodleigh said my results looked promising." He grinned. "I hope that means I'll get a family too."

"I heard you were a huge disappointment." William sneered at me. "Guess you'll be living here 'til you die."

Likelier, I'd be given away as a servant if the documents on the Goodleighs' tablet were to be believed. This orphanage was the center of sinister activities. Thankfully, I would probably be doled out to another foster family soon. Once outside these walls, I would escape and take my chances with the real world.

What about Ambria?

I imagined her smiling face and realized it would be unconscionable of me to abandon her to such an awful fate. But how could I, a puny boy, hope to rescue her when Brickle's hounds patrolled the grounds at night? The Goodleighs would quickly hunt us down if we attempted a jailbreak in the middle of the day. What about the other children? Surely even William didn't deserve life as a slave.

I had to recognize my limitations. Escaping from this place alone would be a monumental task. Saving even one person would be the hardest thing I'd ever done and double the chances of being caught. I felt a little pain in my chest when I thought of leaving Ambria behind. I thought of the way she made me feel warm as Cora had. *She is my only friend in the world.*

The added risk of saving her was worth it. With her, I wouldn't be so alone in the outside world.

I looked up and saw we were nearly to the pasture. The Goodleighs and Brickle stood near the middle of the field. The dogs sniffed around the grove of trees. Heart in my throat, I looked toward the trees near the pasture wall where I'd buried the man. Though his makeshift grave was partially hidden by the tree, it looked undisturbed. Burying the bull guts had thrown the hounds off the scent.

We reached the Goodleighs and informed them we'd finished.

Mrs. Goodleigh gave us a disapproving look. "Took you long enough."

I replied with the only thing she wanted to hear. "I'm sorry, Mother."

She sniffed. "Well, don't just stand there. Help Brickle inspect the grounds."

We did as commanded and spent most of the afternoon scouring the field and the nearby roads. When evening came, we'd found no other trace of the man.

Brickle held his baying hounds by thick leather leashes as they lunged at us, their large noses sniffing the air. A scowl covered his face. "I know someone was here."

"Well, they're gone now." Mr. Goodleigh gave his wife a knowing look.

He suspects someone—an outsider. Their nefarious dealings probably attracted competitors. I couldn't imagine the sorts of lowlifes the Goodleighs knew. It was vital I quickly plan and execute my escape before someone else continued what the dead man had failed.

For all I knew, he was the first of many who wanted me dead.

Chapter 8

Brickle decided to butcher the dead sheep the next day, so William, Stephan, and I put the corpses in the slaughterhouse refrigerator then went inside and cleaned ourselves for supper. The minute I got into my room, I shut the door and pulled out the smartphone. It was small, thin, and sleek. A logo with a partially peeled orange decorated the back. I couldn't find a button to activate the screen and flicking my finger across it did nothing.

"Turn on, you stupid phone."

The screen flickered on.

I almost dropped it out of surprise. The phone looked similar to ones I'd seen former foster parents use. This one even had a picture of two older people as the background, each wearing a robe similar to the one the crazy man wore. A young boy stood between them. The boy looked like a younger version of the man who'd attacked me.

An icon in the shape of a winged horse glowed a little brighter than the others. I touched the icon and a list of messages appeared.

The first email was from a Shelly Darwin.

Levi, you told me you'd given up this mad quest of yours. Please don't do anything foolish.

xoxo

Shelly

"Who is Shelly?" I wondered aloud.

"Shelly is Levi Baker's friend," the phone replied in a monotone voice.

I dropped the phone on the bed and leapt up as if it were a snake. "You can speak?"

"This device understands verbal commands."

I dropped back on the bed and picked it up. *This is marvelous!* I posed it another question. "Does Levi have other family?"

"Levi has no living relatives."

"Where does Levi live?"

"He lives in Queens Gate at one twenty-five Concord Avenue."

I'd never heard of this town. "Where is Queens Gate?"

The phone's screen shimmered and abruptly projected a three-dimensional image of a map above it. The map traced a route from Little Angels Orphanage all the way to London. From there, the blue line corkscrewed downward into what appeared to be a large underground cavern.

"Phone, how do I rotate this image?"

"To rotate a holographic image, the user may instruct the phone to do it or simply use his fingers by swiping across the image. To zoom the image, the user may pinch his fingers together and spread them, or move his hands together or apart. An in-depth tutorial is available." The phone went silent.

I tested the instructions and found it easy to manipulate the map. It was so intuitive, I stumbled across a way to view the map from a first-person perspective. Using this method, I discovered the entrance to Queens Gate was beneath an apartment complex just across the road from Hyde Park, and not far from Buckingham Palace itself. A winding ramp went nearly half a mile below ground and ended in a massive cavern.

The view there became even more bizarre. There was a giant black arch looming in the middle of the cave. Less strange was the parking lot, but a stable promptly undid the normalcy right away. *Why is there a stable in the middle of a parking lot?* The route line went to a pair of large wooden doors in the cave wall. Queens Gate was apparently on the other side.

My stomach growled loudly and reminded me I hadn't yet eaten supper. "Phone, deactivate the display."

It went dark.

I tucked the phone back into my pocket and went downstairs to eat. As I choked down a pile of tough ground beef, I began to think about other uses for the advanced bit of technology I'd inherited. I wondered if it could copy the contents of the tablet in the Goodleigh's office. If so, I could gather enough evidence for the police to put the pair in jail for a very long time. I finished my meal and realized someone was conspicuously absent—Ambria. The Goodleighs' chairs at the front table were empty. *They must be talking to Ambria.*

I took my plate to the sink and left the dining hall. Tiptoeing, I made my way to the common room and peeked around the corner. The Goodleighs' office door hung open. I heard muted conversation and moved closer so I could hear.

"...is very good news, wouldn't you say, dear?"

"Yes, Mother," Ambria replied.

"They'll be by to collect you in two days," Mr. Goodleigh said. "We're very proud of you."

"You are a rare jewel," Mrs. Goodleigh added in an effusive voice. "Now, go eat. We'll be along shortly."

I ducked into an alcove between two wooden support columns running up the wall. Ambria walked past, her face lit with excitement. A moment later, the Goodleighs began to speak again.

"He didn't even want to wait for the auction," Mr. Goodleigh said. "I still can't believe he paid quintuple the starting price."

"A fourteen is rare, even among the children we procure." Mrs. Goodleigh sighed with contentment. "This is the largest payday we've seen by far."

"If only Conrad would blossom like Ambria." Disappointment deadened Mr. Goodleigh's excitement. "That boy should have been our retirement."

"There's something more to his condition than simple immaturity," Mrs. Goodleigh said. "Anyone with his genes should have at least an inkling of ability."

"Rufus would have discovered it."

She sighed. "I believe you're right. He makes too large a percentage of our profits to hide anything."

"I feel like celebrating," Mr. Goodleigh said. "Let's have dinner in London after the sale."

"That would be lovely. I'm so tired of these dreadful nuisances." Mrs. Goodleigh groaned. "I suppose we should foist Conrad on another couple in the meantime. I don't enjoy having the murderous little wretch in the same house."

"I've already located a suitable pair, but it will be at least a week before they come in."

There was a click and the sound of their voices muted once again. I looked from the alcove and saw they'd closed the door. The wood shouldn't have been enough to mask their voices, but no matter how hard I listened, their voices remained muffled and unintelligible.

I decided to leave before someone else came through here and went back upstairs to my room.

I sat on my bed and thought about all the Goodleighs had said. *Murderous wretch?*

Were they talking about the deaths of my foster parents? I'd had nothing to do with their accidents, though it was easy to see why the Goodleighs and anyone else might think otherwise. Before my awakening, I wouldn't have considered the extreme odds of having so much misfortune preying on those around me. It meant someone was committing these foul acts for a reason. It was also no coincidence they occurred around the same time as my birthday. Unfortunately, I had far too little data to reach any sort of conclusion.

Secondly, why should I have provided the Goodleighs with the financial security to retire? They fully expected me to be sold at one of their auctions for an enormous sum. Because I hadn't lived up to expectations, my value had dwindled.

This train of thought took me across a great landscape of possibilities. For example, how did they procure their candidates? Did they scour childcare services for children with a certain potential and snatch them when they had the chance? Then again, how would they know the hidden potential unless they knew something of the child's parents?

The more I thought about that method, the more I realized how impractical it was. How could you directly observe the parents if they were already dead? Kidnapping a child would be far more practical since it would be easier to calculate their pedigree by studying the parents.

The Goodleighs had proven themselves capable of stooping to great lows for their own personal gain. Such tactics would yield a more reliable outcome. The missing variable, however, was what constituted an acceptable result. I didn't know what AP meant, but it seemed to be a primary measure of a child's worth.

I took out the phone. "Phone, are you capable of copying the contents of tablet devices?"

"This device can download data from another device. Would you like to see a tutorial?"

"Yes."

The phone projected a video showing how to initiate the process. I would have to activate the tablet's screen and then tell the phone to copy the contents. A pin password would be transmitted to the tablet. I would have to respond with the code before the tablet would allow its contents to be downloaded. This scenario was reliant on the tablet not having extra security enabled. It was possible I'd have to enter a password. Since the tablet screen had been on when I'd been in the office, I didn't know if it needed a password or not.

Another task remained—retrieving the carpet from the tree. According to the clock on the phone, I had another thirty minutes before Brickle unchained his hounds to guard the perimeter. I'd considered getting the carpet in the morning, but doing this mission under cover of darkness provided me a better chance of getting it inside.

I should do it now while I have time.

I tiptoed through the empty downstairs hallway, quiet aside from voices emanating from the dining hall where some staff were still finishing dinner. I opened the rear door and crept out beneath a starry sky.

A tall lamppost near the brown barn provided the only other light down the dirt road. A few stray grunts and oinks emanated from the direction of the pigpen. In the distance, the cows mooed. Keeping to the opposite side of the road from the lamp, I made my way through the darkness. Memory served me well and I found the closed gate to the sheep pasture without incident.

Once over the gate, I let the dim moonlight guide me in the direction of the trees at the center of the pasture. It took a moment to orient myself on the correct tree in the grove and I shimmied up to the nearest branches. I stopped in the lower branches to catch my breath and looked at the time on the phone. I'd used seventeen of my allotted thirty. Haste became a necessity if I was to make it back to the house on time.

I reached the rolled up carpet a moment later and tucked it under an arm. A chorus of bells announced the sheep moving away from my location. Time ticked past while I clambered down the tree. About twenty feet from the ground, my boot caught between two branches. I reflexively reached out with both hands to grab a branch, releasing the carpet. My fingers narrowly grabbed a small limb just in time to prevent twisting my ankle.

That was close.

Unfortunately, I had little time to catch my breath. Reaching back with the other hand, I gripped another branch and pulled myself upright, jerked my boot free from its trap. Within a couple of minutes, I reached the ground and looked for the carpet. It was nowhere to be seen.

I took out the phone and was going to use its screen as a flashlight but realized I could probably use its holographic capabilities to better effect. "Phone, illuminate this area."

A white sphere projected from the screen, casting the area in a dim light. A quick glance told me the carpet wasn't anywhere nearby. I looked up, thinking it might have draped across a lower branch. My breath caught in my throat when I finally spotted the rug drifting several feet off the ground near the base of another tree.

"What in the world?" I might have stood in stunned silence for another few minutes had not my senses immediately prevailed. I had precious few minutes to reach the house. Unless I took a shortcut and climbed the pasture wall, there was no way I'd make it before Brickle released the hounds.

I walked to the carpet and looked to see if it might simply be stuck in a branch, but the other trees had no limbs this low. I jumped up and grabbed the carpet. My fingers seemed to adhere to the surface while my feet dangled inches off the ground.

Struggling to pull myself up was an exercise in futility. My arms didn't possess the strength and my legs couldn't assist. I wished the carpet had been a few feet lower. As if on command, the carpet drifted lower and my feet touched the ground.

I'd read of flying carpets and once seen an old movie with them. Never in my wildest dreams had I thought they might actually exist. I should be utterly shocked. Instead, a part of me accepted it as a simple matter of fact, as if I already knew such magical wonders existed.

I willed the carpet to drop even lower until it was even with my knees. The carpet negated the necessity for me to hoof it back to the house. Why walk when I could simply fly? I climbed onboard. *Climb higher*, I commanded it. The carpet rose slowly into the air. I would have shouted with glee if not for the need to keep silent. A tree branch slapped against my face. I toppled forward, but my feet seemed glued to the carpet.

More limbs hit me. In my excitement, I'd completely forgotten to steer clear of the trees. I willed the carpet to descend and then directed it forward out of the trees. Controlling it seemed as simple as looking where I wanted to go and wishing it to do so. I badly wished I could practice all night. What could be more fun than flying free without a worry in the world?

Unfortunately, the Goodleighs checked on us at random times, usually after we were asleep. I had to enter the house through the back door since all the windows on the second floor were nailed shut.

Flying by the light of the moon, I took the carpet high enough to clear the trees near the pasture wall. The wind in my ears was the only sound it made as it swiftly flew toward the destination. Brickle called to the baying hounds as he went to their cages. I was nearly out of time.

Thankfully, the outside lights weren't on. I lowered the carpet to the ground. Despite the way it bonded to my feet, all I had to do was step off and the surface released me immediately. I supposed the bonding must be a safety feature to keep riders from falling to their deaths. I also noted that when I wasn't touching the carpet, it didn't respond to my commands. I wondered if I'd inadvertently commanded it to fly when I almost fell from the tree, or if it was designed to automatically levitate when unfurled.

The baying hounds drew closer. I willed the carpet to deactivate. It flopped to the ground. I rolled it up and slipped through the back door. The mingled voices from the dining hall and upstairs made it difficult to tell who was talking. I removed my boots and walked as quietly as possible toward the main staircase. I heard footsteps above and the conversation faded.

Avoiding the creaky second step on the stairs, I crept up them and peeked around the corner at the top. Mrs. Goodleigh walked with Ambria toward her room near the end of the hallway. When they passed my room, I sneaked from concealment and kept to the wall to minimize squeaks from the wooden floor.

A column jutted from the wall about halfway down. I ducked behind it just as the pair stopped outside Ambria's room. They spoke in quiet tones for a moment. Ambria laughed. She looked flush with excitement. The awful truth sickened me. She'd already been bought and paid for and her new owners would soon have her in their clutches.

Mrs. Goodleigh opened the door to the bedroom and they stepped inside, leaving the door ajar. I used the opportunity to creep to my door. Turning the doorknob slowly as possible made the click marginally quieter. I stepped into the room.

"Conrad, what are you doing?" Mrs. Goodleigh said.

I threw the carpet into the room and poked my head outside the door. "Apologies, Mother. I needed to use the toilet."

She stood just outside Ambria's door for a few seconds, her gaze tight. "I suggest you think of such things earlier." She motioned toward the bathroom. "Hurry and be quiet."

I nodded and went into the lavatory. After doing my business, I returned to my room just as Mrs. Goodleigh left Ambria's. My nerves stretched tight as a drum. If she came into my room, she'd see the carpet. Praying she didn't call for me to wait, I entered my room and closed the door. Quickly as possible, I grabbed the carpet, lifted my mattress, and unrolled it onto the metal frame. The door clicked the instant I lowered the mattress.

"Conrad, you know how rude it is to be noisy when others are trying to sleep."

As if she wasn't doing it right now! I let my shoulders slump and faced Mrs. Goodleigh. "I apologize, Mother. I drank too much water at supper."

She huffed. "Your lack of sense is a burden on us all, boy." Mrs. Goodleigh stormed from the room, slamming the door behind her.

"I suppose making noise is rude unless you're a grownup," I whispered. Adults had such ridiculous double standards. A part of me wished I could strike her unconscious, fly her high into the air on the carpet, and then drop her into the pigpen. I flinched. *Why am I thinking of such awful things?* My new intelligence apparently came with a murderous streak. The line of thought drew me back to Mrs. Goodleigh's earlier comment about me being a murderous little wretch. What if she was right? I had killed the crazy man in the sheep

66

pasture, proving I was quite capable of committing the deed and intentionally concealing the crime.

Sometimes bad things have to happen.

I took a deep breath to clear my mind. Now was not the time to question my sanity.

I had to escape this madhouse.

Chapter 9

The flying carpet was my salvation. I might be a murderous wretch, but at least I cared enough to help Ambria. *That means I'm not a heartless monster, right?* I couldn't just leave her here and consign her to a dark fate. It also behooved me to steal the contents of the tablet in the Goodleighs' office. While I might be able to steal it, I didn't want them to know I'd discovered their secret. If I took the tablet, they might decide to cover up their diabolical activities by any means necessary, including killing every orphan and burying the bodies.

These two conditions of my escape complicated things considerably. The flying carpet would make things easier, but first I had to find a way outside. With mine and Ambria's windows nailed shut, I couldn't simply slip out and fly around to her unless I decided to break the window. That would cause too much noise and alert the hounds.

I sat on my bed, closed my eyes, and conjured a mental image of the manor. It took me only a matter of seconds to find the first possible exit—a window at the far end of the upstairs hallway. I'd seen one of the girls cleaning it one day. She'd climbed a ladder to reach the glass. I'd seen her open it to clean the outside.

The vaulted ceiling peaked about twenty feet from the floor. I imagined flying the carpet through the window and circling around to the Goodleigh's office window. After confirming the office was empty, I would slip inside and close the window in case the hounds walked past. Once there, the phone would copy the tablet and I'd return to my room.

My eyes flicked open and I felt a grin stretch my lips. The plan was simple and it would work. The second phase, however, introduced a human variable. What if Ambria didn't want to go with me? She might not believe me, and showing her the documents might take too much time. I formulated a line of logic to use on her, detailing the documents and convincing her that escape was the only answer. I hoped it was enough.

The preamble to my escape plan was more difficult than I'd thought. It required me to wait until the wee hours of the morning, thus ensuring the others would be asleep. It was still early yet and I had a long time to wait. I considered setting an alarm on the phone and getting some much-needed sleep. Instead, I decided planning the logistics of this grand escape would be time well spent.

Getting out of the manor was one thing, but where would we go from there?

A location instantly came to mind. Levi Baker no longer needed his house. It would provide a good place for Ambria and me to live until we found something permanent.

"Phone, where does Levi keep the key to his house?"

"This device provides access to Levi Baker's house."

"How do I unlock his house?"

"Security parameters have restricted this information," the phone replied.

"How do I bypass security?"

"The following procedure will unlock security parameters: Facial scan of Levi Baker; verbal command to unlock security parameters. For more information, a helpful tutorial is available."

"Does Levi Baker have to command the phone to unlock the security?" I asked.

"Parameter was not specified."

"In other words, I could tell the phone to unlock security after it scans Levi Baker's face?"

"Yes. Would you like to view a tutorial?"

That didn't seem necessary. The task of disabling the security on the phone would be gruesome, but I saw no way around it. I needed some way to unlock Levi's house. Something told me simply breaking a window wouldn't suffice. If the man could control animals, had access to a flying carpet and a phone advanced far beyond anything I'd seen, surely his home had security measures I couldn't hope to bypass. I hesitated to think of what I'd seen so far as magic. If the phone contained such advanced technology, surely it meant the carpet and ability to control animals utilized science as well.

I ordered the phone to map the route to Queens Gate. As I zoomed out, I took note of my current location. The orphanage was at the end of an unlabeled road bordered by pastureland and forests northeast of the tiny town of Stapleton. The border between England and Wales was quite literally across a small paved road. According to the map, journeying to Queens Gate by car took three and a half hours.

Out of curiosity, I looked for another place.

"Phone, find the residence of Dr. Rufus Cumberbatch."

It took a few seconds, but the phone responded with a red marker to indicate the address. I had the phone project the map in a first-person view of the property and confirmed it was the correct estate. The doctor lived all the way down near St. Ives, nearly five hours away. A quick search of my memory told me that it hadn't taken the Goodleighs nearly that long to reach his house.

We'd left just after breakfast and arrived at the doctor's before noon. Our return to the orphanage saw us back around early afternoon. I knew with certainty my routine naps during those trips was no coincidence. Mr. Goodleigh must be skilled at hypnosis and somehow put me to sleep with that strange chant of his. It did not explain how we managed a long trip in such a short time.

The mystery would have to wait. I had more imminent dilemmas to solve.

After mapping out the route to Queens Gate, I noticed a row of small icons indicating various means of travel. The car symbol was obvious. Bus and train icons represented mass transit options. Two symbols were for those hardy enough to endure the distance on foot or bicycle, and yet another was by plane.

When I clicked on a set of ellipses, another menu dropped to reveal even more options. The first, an arch icon, was grayed out and wouldn't let me select it. The next showed the outline of a person riding a wavy line. When I clicked it, the wording on the map changed.

Via flying carpet, broomstick, or other airborne means.

Needless to say, the time estimate dropped considerably when the route changed from winding roads to a straight line in the air. A little red exclamation point beneath the icon description caught my attention. I touched it to reveal a strange warning.

Always follow Overworld guidelines for travel by nonstandard means. All flights via these methods are observed and strictly enforced by the Overworld Transportation Authority.

"Phone, what is the Overworld Transportation Authority?"

"The OTA monitors the use of non-standard transportation to prevent detection of the Overworld by normals. Using a large network of all-seeing eyes, the OTA is able to quickly find and apprehend violators."

"How do I avoid violations?" I asked.

"According to the OTA, keeping out of sight by use of camouflage or cloud cover is preferred."

I looked out the window and saw clouds blotting out some of the stars. I should be able to follow the rules. I had dozens of other questions to ask the phone, but realized the clock had just ticked past midnight.

Time for me to act.

I pulled the carpet from beneath the mattress and spread it on the floor. After practicing how to control it by moving up and down and circling the room, I deemed myself an able enough pilot to make this work.

My door opened with a faint creak that might as well have been rumbling thunder in the absolutely silent hallway. I waited several seconds, ear cocked for the sound of footsteps. While it wasn't totally unheard of for someone to get up and use the bathroom in the middle of the night, the Goodleighs made it plain they did not approve.

Rather than step into the hallway, I sat on the carpet and glided silently into the corridor, closing the door behind me. Heart in my throat, I levitated up to the ceiling and flew over the thick wooden rafters to the window. The latch opened and the window slid up noiselessly on greased rails.

Not daring to use any form of light, I peered into the outside gloom and guided the carpet up and over the pitched roof of the common room. Once on the other side, I hovered over the shrubbery in front of the office window I'd unlatched. Rather than descend, I opted to wait and listen for the sound of the guard dogs. Minutes ticked past, the susurrus of the breeze through the trees keeping me company in the lonely night.

Hands trembling, I took a deep breath. It did little to calm my nerves. I felt sweat trickle down my back. I had never done something like this before. A sense of exhilaration swept through me quickly followed by overwhelming apprehension.

What in the world am I doing?

I had no choice but to escape. Downloading the information on this tablet and saving Ambria were strictly optional. I was risking everything to help someone I barely knew. What did I plan to do with the information on the tablet—mount a later rescue or inform the authorities? Uncovering the Goodleighs' sins offered no security for my future. I nearly let cowardice convince me to fly for Queens Gate without a glance back at this sinister place.

A pain in my chest held me fast. Leaving Ambria to her fate seemed unimaginably cruel when I could save her. Through some uncanny circumstance, I'd been given the chance to do something worthwhile with my otherwise unremarkable existence. Perhaps this Overworld had authorities who could prosecute the Goodleighs if I gave them the evidence.

The memory of Ambria touching my hand melted the icy tension in my heart. She was my first and only friend. She had been kind to me even when I was too dull to appreciate it. Though I knew little of friendship, I realized preserving this fragile connection to another person was worth the risk my life and liberty.

That settled, my nerves unknotted and the shaking in my hands diminished. I had never been brave before. Hopefully, this would not be my first and last time.

The carpet dropped behind the thick shrubbery next to the dark office window. I pulled up on the frame. The window resisted but grudgingly slid up with a slight grating noise. I listened for several seconds before proceeding. Using only the light of the phone screen, I located the tablet. It had been moved to the other side of the desk. I swiped a finger across it and activated the screen.

A breath of relief escaped me when I saw the screen was not password protected. I unlocked the device with another swipe and commanded the phone to download the contents. As illustrated in the tutorial, the phone displayed a number that I had to enter on the tablet before the download began.

The first time estimate showed nearly three hours.

Biting back an exclamation of disbelief, I watched as the estimate dwindled to forty-five minutes. That was still a lot of time, but at least—

Muffled voices sounded outside the door.

Panicking, I hit *Cancel* on the phone screen. Nothing happened. I looked at the tablet and saw, *Attempting to cancel process*, on the screen.

The voices grew louder. Though I couldn't make sense of the words, I knew they belonged to the Goodleighs.

The words on the tablet screen vanished. I flicked off the screen and quickly crept back to the window. I stepped out onto the carpet and shut the window. Just as I finished, the door opened and the lights came on. *Up!* I commanded the carpet. It shot upwards right toward the overhanging eaves. I threw up my hands. *Stop!* The carpet halted, my head inches away from ramming into them.

My panicked breaths subsided. *That was too close!* I had no idea why the Goodleighs would be up at this hour unless they'd somehow been alerted to my absence. If that was the case, why would they go to the office? I noticed a light shining from the direction of the driveway and took the carpet toward it.

Mr. Goodleigh's car was parked in front of the door. He never left it outside at night, preferring to store it in the large garage just behind the house. I directed the carpet back to the side of the office window and peeked inside.

A little boy lay unconscious on the leather couch next to the desk. The Goodleighs spoke as they looked at him. I made out bits and pieces of the conversation through the thin windowpanes.

"...a fine addition. We'll introduce him tomorrow," Mrs. Goodleigh said.

"Agreed." Mr. Goodleigh stretched and yawned. "I'll put him in the secure bedroom for tonight." He tapped on the tablet, turned it off, and set it on the desk. He picked up the child and carried him from the office while Mrs. Goodleigh closed the door behind them.

I rose into the air and observed the driveway. A few minutes later, Mr. Goodleigh came outside and drove the car behind the house to the garage. I looked at the time on the clock and waited a full thirty minutes before going back to the window and making a second attempt.

Heart thumping, I opened the window and went inside. Once again, the phone began the download. I waited impatiently for it to finish, one finger on the cancel symbol. Sweat trickled down my forehead and anxiety churned my stomach. The download finally finished. I turned off the tablet and wiped the screen with my shirt to cover any smudges I'd left.

When I went to the window, I heard sniffing just beyond the shrubbery. I hardly dared move as one of the hounds rooted in the dirt. It finally lost interest and moved away, judging from the sound of its panting. I climbed aboard the hovering carpet and closed the window, then flew up over the roof.

This will be the most dangerous part.

If Ambria resisted or made a scene, she could alert the adults.

I went to the open window on the second floor and glided across the rafters. The hallway was eerily quiet aside from the occasional creak of wood as a stiff wind picked up outside. I went to Ambria's door and tested the knob.

Locked.

If she was asleep, I might be unable to wake her without knocking hard enough on the door to wake the whole house.

I gently tapped. Waited.

Nothing.

Once again, I tapped, a little louder this time.

A moment later, I heard footsteps coming toward the door. Ambria opened the door without bothering to be quiet. Her eyes flared when she saw me, and she opened her mouth to speak. I put a finger to my mouth and shook my head.

"Be quiet," I whispered.

"Conrad, what are you doing?" she hissed back. "You shouldn't be out of your—" At that moment, her eyes settled on the hovering carpet and her eyes went even wider.

I motioned her back into the room. She backed inside, mouth dropping open with astonishment.

"What—how?" She seemed unable to form a complete sentence.

I eased shut the door. "Ambria, you have to listen to me. You're in danger. The Goodleighs didn't find a family for you. They're selling you."

Ambria's nose wrinkled. "Selling me? What are you talking about? That's rubbish!"

"Quiet, please," I said.

She pushed down on the carpet with a hand then got on her knees and looked beneath it. "How are you floating?"

"It's a flying carpet." I held up my hand to ward off further questions. "Let me show you something." I took out the phone and turned it on. I pulled up the document detailing her sale and showed it to her.

She read it in silence, a look of pure horror drawing her mouth wide and wrinkling her forehead. Ambria dropped the phone with a loud thunk and backed away, tears forming in her eyes. "Why would they do this to me? I thought they were proud of me." Agony filled her voice.

I picked up the phone and put it in my pocket. "I don't know, but I'm leaving tonight and I want you to come with me." I tried to smile, but found it hard with my nerves twisted and ice cold apprehension solidifying in my chest.

"Come with you where?"

"I found a safe place, but we have to go now. Grab some clothes and change."

She stood still a long moment and then shook herself, as if reaching inside for inner strength. "I need to change out of my nightgown. Turn around."

I did so and waited what seemed an eternity. Had anyone heard her drop the phone? Was anyone coming upstairs to investigate? I heard no footsteps or the sound of voices outside the room and hoped the Goodleighs weren't at this very moment sneaking our way.

"I'm ready," Ambria announced.

I turned around and saw her inspecting the carpet dubiously. "Get on behind me," I said.

She did so and grabbed my waist. "Am I dreaming?" she murmured. "This can't be real."

I pinched her and she squeaked. "You're awake."

Ambria trembled. "I'm scared."

I nodded. "Me too." With that, I opened the door and glided into the hallway.

After closing her door, I flew the carpet up into the rafters and exited through the window at the end of the hall. I turned the carpet and closed the window. It would make an interesting mystery for the Goodleighs once they realized we were gone.

We're almost free.

Chapter 10

I remembered I still had to scan Levi's face and shuddered at the thought. I swung by the brown barn, scanned for any hounds and listened, but heard nothing.

"What are you doing?" Ambria asked.

"I have to get some stuff I buried." I got off the carpet and opened the barn door. "Be right back." I went inside, grabbed a shovel, returned to the carpet.

Ambria raised an eyebrow but said nothing.

It took a few minutes to fly over the wall and find the correct tree where I'd buried the dearly departed. I parked the carpet behind a tree so Ambria couldn't see what I was doing.

"Wait here, this should only take a few minutes."

She nodded mutely.

Using the phone to cast a dim illumination on the ground, I moved the sod and quickly dug on the side where Levi's head should be. A few minutes later, I felt the shovel hit something squishy and grimaced. Clearing away the dirt, I found the dead man. Worms squirmed around his face.

Shuddering, I scraped them and the dirt away with my hand until the man's pale face was clean as I could manage.

"Phone, scan Levi's face." I held the screen toward the corpse. A thin green light flashed across the face.

I heard a gasp and turned to see Ambria hovering over my shoulder. Her mouth opened and she drew in a breath. I dropped the phone and put a hand over her mouth, managing to mute the scream, but it still echoed. I heard a hound bay in the distance, soon joined by a chorus.

"Get on the carpet," I hissed. "Do it now!"

"He's dead! What happened to him?"

"No time to explain." I pushed her toward the carpet. "Trust me, Ambria, please."

She backed away slowly, horror contorting her face. "Did you—" A shudder ran through her body and tears pooled in her eyes.

"Please," I begged. I grabbed the phone and shoved dirt back into the grave. The baying of the hounds drew closer and closer. I didn't have time to conceal my crime and gave up.

Ambria sat on the carpet, face buried in her hands, body shaking with sobs. I climbed on in front of her and directed the carpet into the open field. The moment I cleared the trees, I flew us higher and higher. By the light of the moon, I saw the dogs pawing at the gate to the pasture. A large figure ran up behind them.

Brickle.

He thrust open the gate and yelled something at the dogs. They vanished into the trees.

Wasting no more time, I willed the carpet to fly in the direction of London. Ambria squeaked and gripped my waist as we shot off. The wind howled in my ears and blew my hair back. I wondered if the carpet came equipped to handle this, and tested a command.

Block the wind.

The gale abruptly ceased.

I let out a long breath. All strength seemed to leave me as relief melted my stressed muscles. I took out the phone. "Phone, unlock security."

"Facial scan of Levi Baker recognized. Security features are unlocked."

"Give me full access," I said. "Transfer ownership of Levi's belongings to me."

It surprised me with a flash of green, presumably as it scanned my face. "You now have full access."

"Can I unlock Levi's home?"

"Yes."

"Where did you get that phone?" Ambria leaned around me, eyes red, but curious.

I slumped. It was time for her to know everything. "Please don't hate me for what I'm about to tell you."

"Did you kill that man?"

"It was an accident—" I stopped. "Let me start from the beginning."

She sucked in a breath. "Okay, Conrad. I trust you."

I almost cried with relief. There was one person in this world who trusted me. One person who was my friend. "Thank you, Ambria." I swallowed a lump in my throat and thought about what to say. "Do you remember when I got in trouble for killing the bull and the boar?"

"Of course."

"I think it started that day." Figuring the carpet could fly straight without me facing forward, I turned around and began my story. I told Ambria how I'd gone from being stupid to smart and how Levi Baker commanded the sheep to attack me. I repeated the information the phone had given me and what I'd found on the Goodleighs' tablet. I told her everything. "After I downloaded the data on the tablet, I came to get you. You know the rest."

Tears pooling in her eyes, Ambria looked at me for a long moment. She abruptly gripped me in a fierce hug. "Oh, Conrad, you rescued me."

"I was scared out of my wits," I admitted. "But I couldn't leave you behind."

She kissed my cheek and sat back. "You think we'll be safe at Levi's?"

I nodded. "I hope so." The plan raised a question. "Phone, does Levi Baker live alone?"

"Yes," it replied in its monotone voice.

"What will we do once we're there?" Ambria asked. "How will we buy food and pay for utilities?" Her brow wrinkled. "How will we survive?"

"We'll find a way." The time on the phone showed three AM. I activated the map and saw we'd covered a third of the distance in the forty minutes it had taken to tell my story. The phone estimated another hour and a half to reach the building with the underground tunnel to Queens Gate.

"I've never lived…outside." Her small frame slumped, the former elation sinking in a sea of worry.

My heart tightened until it felt like a small hard rock in my chest. I had never lived on my own. I didn't know what it meant to work for my survival. Some of my fosters had jobs, but I'd never gone with them to work. I knew where to buy food and supplies, but where would I find the money?

I realized I might have the answer in my hand. "Phone, where do I find money?"

Phone replied. "Your account balance is two hundred and fifty-six thousand, four hundred and seven tinsel."

"Tinsel? Account balance?" How could I have an account balance? I didn't own anything.

"Tinsel is the currency established by the Overworld Conclave," the phone said. "Would you like me to repeat the account balance?"

"Where did the money come from?" I asked.

"I do not have access to that data."

It suddenly occurred to me how I had an account. "Was this account formerly Levi's?"

"Yes. Levi Baker authorized account transfer to your name."

"How much is tinsel worth in British pounds?" I asked.

"The current exchange rate is two point three seven pounds for one tinsel." The phone paused. "Would you like historical exchange rates or rates for other currencies?"

"No, thanks."

"You're welcome." The phone's monotone voice betrayed a hint of personality.

I wanted to tell Ambria the good news, but she had fallen asleep. Her long brown hair splayed across her face, hiding it from view. Her hand lay limp on my lap. I gently touched her hand. It felt so warm and soft. My heart seemed to grow back to its normal size.

I have a true friend.

We were not experienced with the world, but we would adapt. We had money. We hopefully had a house. Now all I needed was to find purpose. We were free, but what would we do with the rest of our lives?

I wanted to free the other orphans from the Goodleighs. I had all their data on this phone. Perhaps if I read it I could find out where the other children had been sent. A peculiar tingling sensation tickled my right eye and made it twitch. I blinked and squeezed my eyes shut, but it didn't seem to help. A moment later, the sensation vanished.

I'm so tired.

My body didn't want to be awake another minute. Seeing Ambria slumbering so peacefully tempted me to do the same. I looked at the phone to check the map when another of the strange thoughts sprang into my head.

Arcphone manufactured by Orange. Key competitor Magicsoft. Capable of storing hundreds of complex spells.

A sharp pain formed in my right temple while more facts about the phone circulated in my mind. The words finally ceased and the pain melted into relief. Whatever had happened to me the other day was starting again. I looked at the carpet beneath me, expecting this inner monologue to identify it, but the voice remained silent.

"How do I know these things?" I'd never heard of an arcphone and why would I think a piece of technology could store spells? Magic spells? I shook my head. *Doesn't make any sense.* A laugh burst from my mouth. Riding a flying carpet made even less sense, yet here we were. Something told me an open mind would serve me well. If Queens Gate was truly an underground city, it might hold more marvels than I could comprehend.

Ambria moaned and flinched in her sleep. I reclined next to her and put an arm on her shoulder. She relaxed and her breathing returned to a slow even tempo. Touching her comforted me in a way I'd never felt before. When Mrs. Goodleigh had once hugged me, it felt cold and impersonal. The only touching my foster parents had done was to spank or shove me when I didn't do something quickly enough.

My eyelids grew heavy and my body relaxed. Sleep wrapped me in the warm folds of her robe and pulled me under.

A loud beeping noise woke me.

I jerked upright and found the phone flashing beneath me.

"Collision alert," the phone said.

It was still dark and stars twinkled all around us. We were still far above the ground and in no imminent danger I could see. Several bright stars, however, seemed to be getting closer. A rumbling noise reached my ears. Drowsiness fled, replaced by abject fear as the white nose of a passenger jet appeared in the gloom.

Down, down, down!

The carpet dove at a sharp angle. The fuselage slid past just feet over our head. Its wake sent us spinning like a top. I grabbed Ambria, even though she was bound to the carpet as firmly as I was.

Stop!

I didn't know how else to control the spin. My desperate command didn't help. I willed the carpet to turn in the opposite direction of the spin. It finally slowed and stopped. I fought back a sick feeling in my stomach.

"Huh?" Ambria rose on one elbow and blinked her bleary eyes. "Are we there yet?"

I laughed hysterically.

"What's so funny, Conrad?"

It took a moment for me to catch my breath. When finally I could speak again, I told the phone to display the map. Once I'd fallen asleep, the carpet had continued on its path, but had curved south. *Unblock the wind.* A stiff breeze whipped my hair in a southerly direction. Without my guidance, the carpet had been blown off course ever so slightly and taken us close to Heathrow Airport.

Ambria looked at the map and back to me. "Well, are you going to tell me?"

"We almost hit a jet plane."

She gasped. "Conrad, you should be more careful. We wouldn't want to damage someone's nice jet."

I regarded her for a moment and saw the smile creasing her face. A chuckle broke free.

Ambria giggled. "That would be quite a surprise for a pilot if he ran into a pair of kids on a flying carpet."

"Like bugs on a windshield." I clapped my hands together. "Splat!"

Ambria grimaced. "Eww."

Her disgust only made me laugh harder.

Using the map, I made a course correction and took us toward the building on Bayswater Road right next to the Queensway subway station. Though it was still dark, our little detour had cost us more time and early morning traffic filled the roads. Using the buildings as cover, I flew the carpet over the roofs of tightly packed buildings to the destination marked on the map.

The entrance to the parking deck was a narrow entrance just a little way down from the entrance to the subway station. I check both ways for passing pedestrians or cars. The moment the area was clear, I landed the carpet, rolled it up, and tucked it under an arm. We stepped off and entered the tunnel. Black car exhaust stained the concrete walls and a musty odor tickled my nose.

A blue number one painted on the concrete support columns identified the first sublevel we reached. The map indicated we had quite a distance to go down. I saw lifts nearby and walked toward them.

"Maybe these will take us where we need to go."

Ambria looked around the parking deck. "Are you certain there's an underground city here somewhere? This looks normal to me."

Indeed, there were cars parked here as in any such garage. I shrugged. "I suppose we'll find out soon enough." I touched the down button for the lift. "Phone, is there a faster way to get down?"

"The hidden lift provides direct access to the way station," it replied.

Ambria and I looked at each other. I addressed the phone again. "Where is the hidden lift?"

The phone projected a large holographic arrow pointing to our left.

"Brilliant," Ambria said. "Phone, you are absolutely lovely."

"You are the wind beneath my wings," the phone replied.

We laughed.

As we reached the corner, the arrow rotated right. We followed the arrows like a compass and soon reached a dark corner behind a support beam.

There was nothing there. We'd reached a dead end.

Chapter 11

I looked at the blank gray wall. "What now?"

"Reach through the wall and press the button on the left side," the phone instructed.

I touched the wall and gasped when my hand went right through it as if nothing was there. I felt a bulbous button on the other side and pressed it. A few seconds later, a ding sounded and the wall vanished to reveal a brass carriage. The gate slid open, and after exchanging a look, Ambria and I stepped inside.

There were only two buttons in the lift—an up and a down. I pressed down. The gate slid shut and the wall reappeared. Without warning, the bottom seemed to drop out beneath us and the lift went into freefall.

Ambria screamed first, though my cries of terror followed right behind. We grabbed each other and held on tight as we plunged into the earth. A scant few seconds later, the lift slowed and the doors opened. A family of colorfully dressed people stared at us, the screaming lunatics in the lift.

We went silent, looked at the ground, and stepped off.

"Are you quite all right?" a young girl asked.

"First time," I admitted. "Apologies."

The presumed father spoke. "Don't worry, I screamed my first time too." He chuckled, and then we all enjoyed a good laugh.

"Have fun being scared," the girl said as the lift closed and shot into the air.

It was then I realized there was no shaft to guide the carriage, at least not until it reached a hole in the cave ceiling far, far above.

Ambria tugged on my sleeve. "Conrad, look."

I turned around and suddenly felt small as a fly. The cave extended in every direction and the ceiling seemed a mile high. A giant black arch encircled by a thick silver ring stood in the center. The floor was smooth, polished, and darker than night. A yellow glow illuminated even the farthest corner, though I couldn't see any source for the light.

A loud hum filled the cavern. The air within the arch crackled with electricity. When the throbbing sound hit a fever pitch, the air inside the arch split open, revealing a group of people on beautiful horses standing in a cavern similar to this one. The horses trotted through and went to a large stable filled with a menagerie of animals.

"Elephants." Ambria pointed toward the stable and then clapped her hands together. "Oh, Conrad, can we go look at them?"

Though the odd assortment of creatures was unusual, I hardly found them noteworthy enough to be the first element I inspected in this odd environment. "Sure," I said, and walked forward on unsteady legs, the carpet bundled beneath my right arm.

Hundreds of people filled the far side of the cavern. The large silver circle seemed to be off-limits. A painted yellow ring with red slashes seemed to confirm the theory. Whatever kind of power that arch used, it might be dangerous while in operation.

We went to the stable and walked around it. Elephants roamed inside a large pen right next to a small herd of zebras and horses. A young man dressed in dirty coveralls led a saddled giraffe from within the stable and stopped it next to a set of stairs. A woman with several shopping bags climbed onto the back of the giraffe, gave the boy a silver bill, and then directed her unusual mount toward the arch.

"I can't decide if these people are mental or brilliant," Ambria said. She gripped my hands and jumped in place. "Isn't it exciting?"

I was excited, confused, frightened, and absolutely ready to explore this place until I dropped from exhaustion. "It's too much to take all at once."

She giggled and kissed my cheek. "Wonderful, right?"

"Absolutely." I consulted the phone map and saw the line leading to a set of double doors a little ways behind us. "Why don't we find the house and rest? We can explore later."

She tore her gaze from the spectacle and nodded. "You're right." She rubbed her stomach. "I'm hungry."

I realized how hollow my tummy felt and agreed with her. "I need to find out how to withdraw money from the bank."

"We have money?"

I told her the good news. "We should be able to live off it for some time, unless the cost of living is high."

Her forehead pinched. "This was Levi's money."

"Yes." I wasn't sure if I should feel guilty or not. The man had wanted to kill me. I'd defended myself. *Yes, by sneaking behind and hitting him with a shovel.* "For better or worse, the money is ours now, Ambria. I don't know how to get more."

She hugged me. "I'm sorry, Conrad. I don't mean to be difficult." She took a step back. "I'm simply overwhelmed."

I smiled, unsure if I should give her a comforting touch on the shoulder, or keep my distance. I was new to friendship and didn't want to overstep my bounds. "Me too."

We walked through the crowd, our eyes wandering this way and that, our necks craning to take in the inexhaustible supply of oddities. A pair of men dressed like palace guards complete with large, black, fuzzy hats stood in front of the doors. They were such a spot of normalcy, I hardly even paid attention to them. When we approached, they stood aside and opened the doors.

My next step faltered at the sight before me. There was a world beyond the doors. A field of grass, a blue sky, and warm yellow sunlight. I turned to ask one of the guards a question and nearly choked on my own breath. His face looked like carved wood. His eyes were painted on. This was no man, but a wooden puppet!

Ambria shrieked and gripped my arm. "What are they?"

"No idea." I guided her quickly through the doors so we didn't make another scene. The puppets closed them behind us. "I think they're some sort of remote-controlled robots."

"They were creepy." Ambria blinked and looked up into the sky with pure bewilderment. "Aren't we underground?"

A gentle breeze disturbed that notion, but I nodded anyway. "They must have an artificial environment." The sun warmed my skin, and clouds drifted lazily across the sky. "It's very convincing though."

"It's amazing." She pointed to a gleaming building atop a mountain cliff to our right. "What's that?" Her finger abruptly shifted to the cliffs on the opposite side of the wide valley. "Look, there's a really huge building up there, too. What is it?"

A group of other people waiting at a nearby building looked at us curiously. What could only be described as a small pirate galley, complete with a Jolly Roger flag drifted through the sky and down toward the building on our left. A bright silver rocket ship jetted flames as it departed the building to our right and flew up toward the buildings on the cliff.

"I feel like such a tourist," Ambria said. "Absolutely everything here astounds me."

"Perhaps we should pretend not to be surprised," I said.

"I completely agree." Her eyes went huge again. "Oh, it's so lovely!" Ambria gazed adoringly at the city in the center of the valley. "What is that place?"

So much for pretending we're not tourists.

Though I could only see the fringes of the town, it looked very British. Thankfully, the schooling we'd received at the orphanage had included history. I remembered seeing pictures of buildings like this, but couldn't remember the time period.

The map on the phone pointed to the town directly ahead, so I assumed that was Queens Gate. Unfortunately, I saw no method of transportation to get us there. I stopped a man in blue robes as he rushed toward the pirate ship. "Sir, is there a bus we can take into town?"

His forehead pinched and he looked at me as if I were mental. "A bus?" He looked at the rug under my arm. "Just take your carpet, boy." With a huff, he resumed his march as the pirate ship docked with a wide deck atop the building.

I felt foolish for asking such a question. In a place where a flying pirate ship and a rocket were common means of public transportation, a flying carpet was probably ordinary. I leaned down to unroll the carpet on the ground.

"Look out!" Ambria shouted.

I looked back just as someone carrying a large stack of books tripped over me. Leather-bound tomes scattered everywhere. One of them bounced off my head and stars danced in my vision. When my senses cleared, I pushed up and saw a boy about my age giving the two of us a dazed look.

"You should look where you're going," Ambria chided. She leaned down. "Are you okay, Conrad?"

Though I felt a bump growing on the back of my head, I nodded.

"I'm sorry," the boy said. He pushed a mop of blond hair from his face and looked at us with sad green eyes. "I'm such an idiot." He pushed himself up and held a hand out to me.

I took it and let him pull me up.

He shook my hand vigorously once I was on my feet. "I'm Max Brimble."

With some effort, I freed my hand and nodded. "I'm Conrad." I hesitated to use the last name Levi had given me, at least until I confirmed it was my real name.

"I'm Ambria." Smiling brightly, she gripped his hand in both of hers and gave it a good shake.

"Are you students?" he asked.

Ambria and I looked at each other. "Students?"

He pointed up at the left cliffs. "At the university." Max looked at our clothes. "You certainly look like a couple of noms or is that the new fashion?"

"Noms?" I asked.

He frowned. "Don't you know anything?"

Ambria put her hands on her hips. "No, we don't."

He grinned. "I know everything there is to know about this place."

She held up a hand. "I hate to be rude, but we haven't had breakfast and need to go into town."

Max's face brightened. "Breakfast?" He began gathering his books. "I'm starving and I know a great place in town." He nodded toward the flying carpet. "Could you give me a ride to my uncle's house and then we can go eat?"

I looked at Ambria.

She shrugged. "Well, I suppose it would do us some good to have a know-it-all with us."

Max laughed. "Then let's go."

By the time we stacked the books on the carpet and secured them with a strap, there was barely enough room for the three of us. I let my legs dangle over the front of the carpet. Ambria sat behind me, and Max sat in front of his books. I eased the carpet forward, but the books seemed secure enough to go faster. Flying high, we zipped into town.

Tightly spaced row houses lined the outskirts of town. Quaint cobblestone streets boasted ornate houses of all shapes and sizes. Two massive domed buildings claimed the center of the city and a clock tower reminiscent of Big Ben loomed above them. It all seemed like the glorious reproduction of an era long past mixed with the new. People dressed in a wide variety of clothing walked below. Old-style horse-drawn carriages rolled through the streets, though many of them actually had no horses pulling them.

"Queens Gate is lovely," Ambria said, her warm breath on my ear. "I'm so glad we escaped, Conrad." She squeezed her arms around my chest. "I'm so grateful to you."

"You're welcome." I wasn't sure what else to say.

"Ooh, take a left here," Max said.

Since we were flying over the city, I wasn't sure how much of a left I needed to take. "Hard left?"

He pointed to a road leading toward the outskirts of town. I followed it all the way to the end where a small cottage nestled against the towering cliff face.

"This is my Uncle Malcom's house," Max explained as I landed the carpet. "I'll just run these books in if you don't mind waiting."

A middle-aged man with a crop of white-blond hair emerged from the cottage. He wore a loose gray robe and held a crooked stick in his hand. "Who are these people, Max?"

"Friends from school." He got off the carpet. "This is Conrad and Ambria."

Malcolm gave us each a hard look. "Don't look very savory."

"I just need to run my books inside," Max said. He took one stack and entered the house, returned, and took the rest. All the while, Malcolm stared at the two of us as if we might sprout claws and fangs and attack him.

Max came outside and rubbed his hands together. "I'll be back later, Uncle Malcolm."

"Don't let those two get you into trouble." Malcolm narrowed his eyes at us. "Looks like you picked up a couple of beggars."

Admittedly, our plain gray work clothes did look rather lowly, but it seemed mean for the man to make such assumptions about people he didn't know. I felt a strong urge to get off the carpet and confront him. To get in his face and challenge him to call me a beggar again. *How dare this lowlife insult me?*

I felt my fists clench and looked down at them. *Why am I so angry?* It reminded me of the other evil impulses I'd felt. The mood abruptly faded and I felt like myself again. I didn't remember having such a touchy temper during my idiot days.

Max climbed onto the carpet. "Just follow this road back to town and take a left at the end."

I did as instructed, keeping the carpet just high enough to fly over the other traffic. Following Max's instructions, we soon arrived at what could only be described as a large wooden egg with windows and a wide deck on the second story.

A sign dangling by chains on the front porch bore the name of the place—*Chicken Little.*

Ambria crooned. "How adorable."

"Best breakfast in town." Max hopped off the carpet.

I suddenly realized I'd forgotten something. "Where can I withdraw money?"

"Ah, over here." He led us down the street to a tall black building with golden trim. "Miser Bank."

"Why don't you two go into the restaurant?" I said. "I'll just be a moment."

"See you there," Max replied.

Ambria raised an eyebrow at me then turned and followed our new companion.

Once they were out of earshot, I queried the phone. "How do I withdraw money?"

"You may enter the building and speak with a teller, or use the crystal ball."

I noticed a crystalline sphere on a pedestal and approached it. "How do I use this?"

"Place a hand on the crystal ball," the phone told me. "Then you may request a withdrawal."

I did so. A light flashed in my eyes. *Welcome to Miser Bank,* said a voice in my head. *How can we help you?*

I had no idea how much money breakfast would cost or what other expenses we might incur, so I asked for a large sum. "A hundred tinsel, please."

Authorized. A section of the pedestal opened and a wad of silver currency emerged. I took it and rubbed one of the bills in my hand. It felt smooth and light as silk, but was stiff enough to keep it neatly stacked with the others. I shoved the money in my pocket and went to Chicken Little.

Max and Ambria waved to me from the second-story deck.

"Come on up," Max called down cheerfully.

I went inside. Patrons crowded the tables. Many were dressed in the sort of robes that seemed to be favored by the locals of this strange town. The odor of pancakes, bacon, sweet pastries, and more delighted my nose. My stomach reminded me with a growl that it was every bit in need of delighting as my nose. I walked up a set of stairs that curved with the egg-shaped building and joined the others at the table.

"The blueberry walnut pancakes are my favorite," Max said.

My mouth watered so much at the thought of pancakes, I had to keep it closed so I didn't drool.

The prices seemed reasonable relative to what I'd seen in the outside world, though I'd rarely been invited to eat out with my foster parents. I'd had plain pancakes a few times, and had once even enjoyed leftover bacon before the family dog snapped it up.

When the waitress came, I ordered pancakes, bacon, eggs, orange juice, and even coffee.

"How do you want your eggs?" she asked.

I stared at her blankly. "I don't understand."

"Scrambled, sunny-side up, over easy, over medium, hard, poached—"

"Sunnyside up sounds good." I smiled and looked at the lovely clear weather overhead.

"Got it." She turned to Ambria and took her order. Ambria ordered her eggs scrambled.

"You two sure eat a lot," Max said after he ordered. He grinned. "I like you already."

The waitress delivered our drinks a moment later. Ambria and I took sips of orange juice and sighed in unison.

"I could drink this all day," she said.

"It's so good," I agreed.

Max's forehead wrinkled. "You two act like you've never had a proper glass of OJ. Where are you from?"

I choked on my next sip and coughed. *What do I tell him?*

Ambria smiled brightly. "What were all those books for, Max?"

He made a face. "School. I'm preparing for the entrance exam."

"High school?" she asked.

His frown turned to slack-jawed confusion. "A what school?"

"What's the name of the school?" I asked.

"Ah." His eyes brightened and he pointed toward the top of the cliff in the distance. "Arcane University."

"Arcane?" I blurted before I could stop myself.

Instead of giving me a suspicious look his eyebrows rose as if lift by realization. "Ah, yeah, I forgot they were thinking of renaming it to Overworld School of Magic or Arcane Academy." He pshawed. "Of course, then it would be too close to Science Academy."

Ambria and I exchanged wide-eyed looks.

I decided to be partially honest. "Max, I have to admit we're new to Queens Gate and there's a lot we don't know."

He didn't look concerned. "Oh, that's all right. A lot of people go to the other magic schools and are completely shocked when they get here." He gave us a conspiratorial look. "How about I give you a tour after we eat?"

Though I hadn't slept much, I found this new environment invigorating. There was so much to see and explore. It was also time I accepted a fact I'd tried to avoid.

Magic exists.

Chapter 12

I'd tried to rationalize Levi Baker's control over animals as science, and explained away the flying carpet in a similar manner. Even this underground city complete with sun and sky defied scientific explanation. Unless Max was delusional, there were several schools devoted to the study of magic, and even a university here in Queens Gate.

Ambria and I were ignorant of this underground society. I wasn't sure if that could put us in danger, but didn't want to take the chance.

"A tour would be great," I told Max.

The food came a moment later and I dug into it with abandon. The food was so rich, so delicious, I felt full after eating less than half. My body had grown accustomed to plain, tasteless foods over the years. I reigned in my enthusiasm and surrendered. Ambria ate even less than me, though she obviously enjoyed it just as much.

"I wish my tummy was bigger," she complained. "I hate the thought of wasting so much food."

"Where do you live?" Max asked as he swiped a final slice of pancake through a puddle of syrup.

"At our cousin's," Ambria said.

"What's his name? I know a lot of people here in town."

I wanted to stop her from answering, but didn't know how to do it without alarming Max.

"Levi Baker," she replied.

Max's nose wrinkled. "Oh. I don't know him personally, but I've heard he's absolutely mental."

"Mental?" Ambria said.

I thought it described the man perfectly.

"He used to be a teacher at the university, but I heard he did some bad things and they kicked him out." Max tilted his head. "If he's your cousin, does that make you two brother and sister?"

Ambria and I looked nothing alike. Adding another layer of fiction on top of this would only make it harder for us to keep our lies straight. Besides, if we were related, we'd have to come up with parental names and weave a tremendous background story.

I shook my head. "We're orphans. Ambria and I have been friends a long time, and her cousin invited me to come here too."

"Why'd she say 'our' cousin then?" he asked.

"My mouth was full." Ambria crossed her arms. "Really now, are you the sort of person to nitpick every little thing?"

Max put up his hands in surrender. "No, not at all. My uncle always says I'm too curious for my own good." He looked down. "I'm sorry to hear you're orphans." His frown brightened into a smile. "I have a huge family. You're both welcome to come to my house."

What would it be like to have a family? A sharp pain pierced my chest and I fought back a wave of tears. Cora had been the closest to a mother I would probably ever know.

"That would be wonderful," Ambria said. "Where do your parents live?"

"They live out in the country a ways." He didn't expand on whether he meant England or here in Queens Gate.

Outside of the restaurant, the cliff loomed in the distance. "Should we take the carpet up there?" I asked.

Max nodded. "It'll be faster than waiting on a shuttle."

"By shuttle, do you mean the pirate galley and the rocket back near the entrance?"

"Yep. One goes to the university and the other to the academy." He pointed to another silver rocket flying far above the town. "There are two shuttles that go back and forth between the schools."

We climbed aboard the carpet. I flew it up toward the ledge of the cliff. From this height, the valley looked like a huge green bowl with trees and sheep dotting the countryside like cotton. Dirt roads led to large manors and thatched cottages. Far in the distance, the underground realm ended in a solid wall of rock rising all the way into the sky where it met with the other two mountains forming the valley.

"We're so far up." Ambria's arms tightened around my waist.

I looked down and felt dizzy. We were on level with some of the clouds, probably a mile above the ground with only a thin carpet between us and a terrifying fall. It was with some relief we crested the rise and flew over solid ground. An expanse of tall trees lay before us.

Willing the carpet higher, I took in a magnificent sight. A white castle stood proudly in the center of a large complex of buildings. Four round towers pierced the sky, with roofs shaped like arrow tips. Someone had carved intricate images of people into the stone, each one with an unfamiliar symbol beneath it. Something about the symbols tickled my brain, but I couldn't recall where I'd seen them before.

A crystalline dome covering an oval building to the right of the white castle sparkled in the sun. Stone buildings several stories tall rose to the left of the castle. Wide pathways wound between them and across the verdant grounds. An even more imposing structure that looked like a massive stadium loomed behind and to the right of the complex.

A thick, black iron fence wound the perimeter of the campus. It looked shiny and new when compared to the aged buildings behind it.

Max flourished his arm across the scene. "Welcome to Arcane University."

"It's breathtaking." Ambria's eyes glistened. "I've never seen anything like it."

"Let me give you the tour," Max said. He pointed toward a snow-capped mountain rising behind the university. A thick, black forest ringed the peak. "That's the Dark Forest. You don't want to go in there."

"Why not?" I asked.

"Well, there's a giant beast called the tragon that lives in there." Max held his hands wide, as if demonstrating the size of the creature. "It's as big as a tyrannosaurus rex and can breathe fire like a dragon."

Ambria gave me a look of pure disbelief. "If you say so, Max."

"It's true!"

"I believe you," I said. At this point, I could believe anything he told me.

"It's also where most of the monsters were sent after the war." He shuddered. "I've heard there are giant toads with teeth that could tear a man apart and mutated insects big enough to ride lurking inside the forest. Don't even get me started on the laserphants or the frogres."

"Laserphants?" Ambria asked.

"Yeah, elephants that shoot lasers out of their eyes." He wiggled fingers next to his eyes as if shooting lasers. "Pew, pew, pew!"

I hesitated to ask him about the war. Being new to Queens Gate was one thing, but ignorance about something large as a war would only expose us as frauds.

Ambria's lips peeled away from her teeth. "Where did these monsters come from?"

Furrows formed in his forehead. "The Overlord, of course." Max shrugged. "I guess we're all kind of young to remember the war, but it seems like it's the only thing they talk about in Overworld history class."

I diverted the conversation to something safer. "Tell us more about the university."

"Sure. Why don't we get something more comfortable to fly around on, though? My legs are getting cramped on this tiny carpet."

Resuming our flight, I took us toward the tall iron fence, intending to fly over it.

"No, wait!" Max tugged my sleeve. "We need to get our security charms from the gate guard." He pointed toward a small shed near the gate. "If you try to fly over the fence without one, the shield will knock you silly."

I hastily amended our direction and halted at the shed.

A man in a distastefully bright green robe put down a novel and came out to us. He looked at Max. "You already have a charm."

"Yes, sir. My friends need them."

The man took out a slender wooden rod and ran it over Ambria. He pursed his lips. "A fourteen. Very nice, very nice." He did the same thing to me and shook his head sadly. "Poor boy. I hope you have the smarts for Science Academy." Before I could say a word, he pressed the rod to my chest and uttered a few words. I felt a tingle in my chest. He repeated the procedure for Ambria.

"Oh, how odd," she said.

"You may proceed." He turned for his shed, stopped and looked at Ambria. "I've only seen one other person higher than a fourteen and that was Nigel Davenport himself." The guard picked up his novel and dropped back into the chair.

"Can we walk a bit?" Max asked, holding a hand to his back as if he had a knot in his muscle. "That carpet isn't designed for three people."

I rolled it up and tucked it under my arm. "Sure."

When we passed through the gate, Max grinned at Ambria. "I didn't know you were a fourteen. That's amazing!"

I suddenly remembered where I'd heard that number in reference to her. It was something the Goodleighs had mentioned.

He glanced at me. "Are you going to Science Academy, or are you just staying in town with Ambria?"

I didn't know how to answer that question. "I don't know yet."

"Well, the entrance exams are in a month. You'd better study hard if you want to apply."

"How exactly do the tests work?" Ambria asked. "And how much does it cost to go to school here?"

"I can't believe you weren't contacted by the school with an AP that high." Max shook his head slowly. "If you do well enough on the entrance exam, you might get a scholarship. The cost varies drastically depending on your potential, your elementary performance, and so forth."

"Can you start from the beginning?" I asked. "We don't know anything about the school system."

"You mean, you never even attended a magic school at all?" Max looked flummoxed.

"As orphans, we didn't have many opportunities," I said. "We attended a normal school."

Understanding replaced his confusion. "Ah, you went to a nom school." He shuddered. That's awful." Max started walking again. "Overworld schools all follow the same path. Core school starts around age five. You learn reading, writing, math, and all the basic skills for five years. After graduating core school, your AP is measured. The early bloomers who show potential at age ten can qualify for neophyte training at Arcane University."

"I hate to sound totally ignorant, but what is AP?" Ambria asked.

Max grimaced. "You two were practically raised as noms, weren't you?"

Judging from the earlier reference, I knew he must be talking about normal, non-magical people. Since he didn't seem overly concerned about our pedigrees, I reasoned it might be safe to be more honest with him. "I'm afraid we were."

"Tragic." He led us into a courtyard surrounded by the apartment buildings and sat down on a bench. "AP stands for arcane potential. It's the magical equivalent of your SP. AP is important for admission to the university, while SP is the primary measuring stick for Science Academy."

"SP means science potential?" I asked.

Max nodded. "Scientific."

My forehead pinched. "How is that different from IQ—intelligence quotient?"

It was Max's turn to look puzzled. "You must be talking about a nom term because I've never heard it."

"It's how noms measure intelligence," I said. "You take a written exam."

"Noms and their reliance on written testing." He sighed.

Ambria tugged on Max's sleeve. "Back on the topic of the school system, what happens to those children who don't qualify for neophyte school at the university?"

"Ah, they continue to learn other real-world skills that will serve them in case they never show any arcane potential." Max held up a finger. "However, if students display remarkable intelligence, they can be probed for SP and perhaps gain early admission to Science Academy, provided they pass the entrance exam."

"Probed?" I didn't like the sound of that. "Do they poke you with a stick like they do for AP?"

Max blinked a couple of times. "Oh, the stick is called a wand." He shook his head. "No, they have a machine that measures your intelligence." He shivered. "I don't much care for the academy. They're all sorts of strange."

Ambria smirked. "I think everything here is strange."

"Of course you do. You were raised as noms." Max gave us a sympathetic look. "Don't you worry. I'll make sure you know everything you need." He continued explaining. "If someone hasn't shown arcane potential by the time they're thirteen, it's highly unlikely they'll ever have it. Most of us manifest it by age twelve." He jabbed a finger at his chest. "I developed right after I turned eleven, but it was too late to apply for the university that year."

"What's your AP?" Ambria asked.

"Eight." He waggled his hand. "Even if you have a low AP, you can still raise it with a lot of hard work. My older brothers already raised theirs by three points. My sisters don't seem to care as much."

The conversation Dr. Cumberbatch had with Mr. Goodleigh made more sense now. This should have been a special birthday for me. In a way, it had been, I supposed. I'd become smarter and my vision had improved, though that had probably been due to the blow to my head and not because of my birthday.

It was no wonder the Goodleighs were so disappointed in me. I'd just turned twelve and had absolutely no potential at all. Ambria had blossomed right on time. It was evident she fit into this new world we'd stumbled into and that I had no place here. With my newfound intelligence, I might be smart enough for Science Academy. Even if I wasn't, this new life was far better than the old one. There were probably plenty of opportunities for noms here.

"What's the entrance exam like?" Ambria asked.

"There are two parts to the test—arcane and science. Even if you're only interested in the university, you still have to take the science portion." He took out a small scroll and unrolled it. "This is the basic list. You can read through it and ask me if you have any questions."

Ambria took it and ran a finger down lines and lines of text.

"I'm ready to see more of the campus," I said. Since I wouldn't be taking the test, there was no sense in reading it.

"Sure!" Max stood and walked toward a small shed. He tugged on the door. When it failed to open, he looked up and down the path and then swiped a small gem over the handle. The door swung open, revealing wall-mounted racks filled with old brooms. "Grab one and we'll take a tour the easy way."

Ambria and I looked at each other then back to the brooms. Max fetched one, turned it sideways, and released it. It hovered in place. The broom handle supported a leather seat similar to the ones used on bicycles. Metal stirrups protruded from the bottom of the saddle.

Max hopped on his and looked at us expectantly. His forehead wrinkled when he saw our confusion. "Oh, yeah, guess you haven't seen these before." He patted the handle. "They fly."

Ambria took one, held it out, and let go. It fell to the ground with a clatter.

Chuckling, Max got off his ride and picked up the fallen broom. He pointed to a notched section near the front of the handle. "Give this a squeeze and it activates the hover spell." He demonstrated and let the broom hover. "These are real simple models—self-stabilizing and all that so you don't have to work to keep yourself upright." He nudged the broom. It wobbled then righted itself.

I took one for myself. It was a bit heavy to hold. I squeezed the notch. The broom went light as a feather and levitated when I released it. I mounted it as I would a horse. The broom bobbed as if floating on water before settling into place. Using the leather straps behind the seat, I secured the rolled-up carpet to the broom.

Ambria climbed on hers as well and giggled. "This is amazing." She gripped the notch. "How do you—" The broom shot forward. Her laughter turned to a shriek as her ride streaked toward one of the dormitory buildings.

"Pull back on the notch!" Max yelled.

Her forward momentum turned vertical as the broom jetted nearly straight up.

"Back, not up!" Max shouted.

The broom looped upside down, flipped right-side up, and then looped again, curving upward in a zigzag pattern. Ambria's desperate screams faded as she climbed higher and higher. I jumped on my broom. As my hand gripped the notch, a strong sense of déjà vu hit me. *I've ridden one of these before.* The strange controls suddenly seemed quite familiar.

I twisted my hand on the notch and the broom took off. I pulled up on the handle and it climbed straight up. Thanks to Ambria's erratic flight path, I caught up to her quickly. Just as she looped backward and the broom righted itself, I grabbed her wrist.

She looked at me with wide, terrified eyes.

"Let go!"

Her white-knuckled grip didn't relent. Seeing only one alternative, I pushed her wrist hard, causing her hand to twist on the handle. The broom eased to a halt beside mine.

"Conrad!" Ambria released the broom and reached to hug me.

"No!" I shouted back. I didn't want her to lose her balance and fall off.

She suddenly seemed to remember how high we were and gripped the broom handle with both hands.

"Take a deep breath," I told her, and followed my own advice. My heart thumped so hard in my chest, I thought it might fly out.

Max flew up to us, eyes wide. "Are you okay?"

Ambria gave him a cross look. "Max, you nearly got me killed."

He looked down. "I'm sorry. I should have explained better." His features brightened with a grin. "It looked like fun, though."

I couldn't help but laugh. Ambria relented and managed a weak chuckle though her face was white as a ghost.

"I must have looked so silly." She put a hand to her chest. "Perhaps you should tell me again how to control this thing."

Max looked at me. "Where did you learn how to fly so well? Are you sure you've never seen a flying broom before?"

"I'm sure." I had no idea how I'd taken to it so naturally. It was just like when I knew what the carpet was without having ever seen one. I should have been happy. Instead, I felt a little scared. An unknown part of me was slowly revealing itself and I had no idea what else lay in store.

Chapter 13

After practicing the broom controls for a few minutes, Ambria announced herself ready to take on the world—or at least the university campus.

We flew over the castle first. It stretched for acres. Gargoyles lined the towers and roofs. I pointed out the odd symbols carved into the walls. Max explained they were Cyrinthian symbols, a language used by Arcanes to craft spells. In this case, they were charmed to protect the castle in case of attack.

"That's the library," Max explained as we flew over the oval building with the crystal dome. "I'll be spending a lot of time in there for sure."

I saw tiny figures walking on the floor far below and people riding flying carpets up to the terraces jutting from the walls.

Next, we flew over a colorful garden filled with flowers and hedges trimmed into likenesses of people and various animals. At the center, a bush shaped like a unicorn reared on hind legs, its horn pointing majestically into the sky. I didn't understand how it was possible to so meticulously craft a plant into something so intricate.

"This used to be the candy garden, but it was destroyed during the war." Max twisted his lips wistfully. "They figured it was healthier to replace it, I guess."

"A garden of candy?" Ambria looked doubtful. "I don't see how it's possible to grow sweets like plants."

"Magic, remember?" Max nodded his head toward the large arena behind the garden. "That's Colossus Stadium. They used to hold the Grand Melee there, but someone built an Obsidian Arch there during the first war and they haven't demolished it yet."

"First war?" Ambria asked. "How many wars have happened?"

"Two." He paused for a moment. "Oh, that's right. I guess you wouldn't know about them, would you?"

"I suppose you can tell us all about them later." Ambria took off for the stadium. "I'd like to see everything else first."

We flew over the stadium and looked down at rows upon rows of seats. It looked as if it could seat thousands. Tattered banners hung from wooden poles all around the top level. Dirt and broken stone occupied the benches, and large black marks in various sections gave it a war torn look. Patches of grass poked through the mostly barren turf. In the center rose a tall, black arch like the one I'd seen in the cavern.

That must be an Obsidian Arch.

There was so much to learn about this place, but I preferred to save the questioning for later. Seeing so many new things was like savoring the wonderful pancakes I'd had for breakfast. I couldn't possibly consume all the new information at once.

A large, grassy meadow ran behind the university and all along the Dark Forest. On the opposite side of the stadium lay another field guarded by tall stone walls. A thick patch of woods bristled in the middle. Beyond those rose the ruins of a mansion. It looked as if something had demolished its right wing.

"Those are the Fairy Gardens," Max said. "The house back there used to be where the Arcanus Primus—the head of the Arcane Council—stayed when he was visiting. They never got around to repairing it, though."

"Fairies?" Ambria clapped her hands. "How wonderful! Can we say hello to them?"

Max chuckled. "Fairies don't exist. That's just what the place is called." He pointed to the woods in the center of the estate. "There are dryads, though, and the Lady of the Pond lives in the water there."

I thought back to fairy tales I'd read. "Aren't dryads fairies?"

Max pressed his lips together. "Technically, I suppose they are, according to nom folklore." He shrugged. "They don't have wings and they're pretty, but they sure do have an evil streak from what I've heard."

"Can we see them?" Ambria asked.

"If we go in there, the Lady of the Pond might stop us. She doesn't like trespassers." He rubbed his stomach. "Besides, I'm starving. Let's go get some lunch."

"You're hungry again already?" Ambria crossed her arms. "I feel like I just ate."

Max ignored the comment. "Let's go down to Queen's Gate. We can take the brooms there."

Ambria puffed out her lips. "But I want to see the dryads."

I wasn't exactly hungry yet either, but my backside was tired from sitting on the broom all this time and my throat felt dry. "Let's save it for another time."

We flew the brooms down to Queens Gate and landed in a cobblestone plaza. The bronze statue of a young man with angel wings and demon horns stood in the center. He wore a confident smirk on his face and seemed to be looking down at passersby. The statue might have been more impressive if not for the buildup of grunge and graffiti marring the marble base and the statue itself.

The placard on the bottom read: *Justin Slade, Savior of Eden.*

Eden. The name jolted my brain.

I see Justin Slade and a dark-haired girl entering a white arch veined with obsidian. He leads an army of people in blue cloaks and skin-tight black armor. "Now is the time, Serena," I whisper. "Let them enter and shut it down."

A short, blonde woman smiles at me. "It will be my pleasure."

"Conrad?"

I jerked back and realized Ambria was tugging on my sleeve. "What—where?"

"You zoned out," Max said. "What happened?"

I stared up at the statue and shook the fuzz from my mind. "It was really odd. For a moment, I thought I saw that man leading an army into big white arch."

"What do you mean you saw him?" Max raised his eyebrows.

Ambria peered at me as if I might be mental. "I think your blood sugar might be low."

I shook my head. "No, I actually saw him with a dark-haired girl and an army. There were people in blue cloaks and black uniforms following him."

104

"You must have seen the documentary," Max said. "Justin Slade did lead an army through an Alabaster Arch. He was taking them to fight a war in another realm called Seraphina. A day after they went through, someone sabotaged the Alabaster Arch network and took it down completely. Nobody's been able to get it activated since, and that's been about six years ago."

"Another realm?" Ambria gazed into the distance. "Do you mean there are other worlds?"

"Several of them." Max seemed quite pleased to have even more stories to tell us. "Let's go eat." He pointed to a towering stone building shaped like a humanoid. "Golem's Gourmet has great fairy pies."

Ambria's eyes widened. "We're going to eat itty-bitty fairies?"

Max grinned, but said nothing more no matter how she badgered him for an answer.

Fairy pies, as it turned out, were similar to stuffed pizza, except they contained bits of mushrooms from the fairy gardens, which made me feel light as air. As I ate the last bit of my pie, it seemed as though I could fly without the aid of a broom.

After we paid, Max led us upstairs to the top of the golem's head. "Watch this!" He leapt toward the courtyard nearly five stories below. Ambria screamed and tried to grab him, but he was out of reach.

Instead of splatting on the ground, Max floated slowly down like a feather. "Jump!" he called up to us.

Ambria gripped my hand. "I hope those fairy mushrooms don't wear off quickly."

Laughing, I ran toward the edge of the roof, Ambria in tow. With a squeal, we leapt. We floated, light as dandelion seeds, flipping head-over-heels and drifting slowly toward the ground.

"Again, again!" Ambria said the moment our feet touched the ground.

Max raced us back up the stairs to the top of the building. This time, we joined hands in a circle and jumped. Kicking our feet, we were able to float in one direction or another. By the time we landed, I felt gravity pulling down on me again.

"Aw, I feel heavier already," Ambria said. "I suppose the mushrooms don't last long."

"Not the small amount they put in the pies," Max said. "The cook once told me the Lady of the Pond limits how many mushrooms they can harvest, so they can only put a little bit in each pie."

"What next?" Ambria asked.

It wasn't much past noon, but I felt exhausted. It seemed hard to believe only yesterday Ambria and I had been prisoners at the orphanage. She'd gotten some sleep, but I really hadn't rested much. We hadn't even been to Levi's house yet. I didn't dare ask Max to join us without making sure the place was clear.

"I think it's time we went to Levi's," I told Ambria. "I'd like to get cleaned up and rest."

Her face fell, but she nodded. "I suppose we should since we haven't been there yet."

"If you'd like, I could grab some board games and bring them over," Max said. "I've got Unicorn Alley, Chesstle, and some cool card games."

"Uhm, maybe tomorrow," I said, perhaps a bit too quickly. "I'm not sure how Levi would react to us bringing a guest so soon."

"True, he is a bit of a nutter from what I've heard." Max grimaced. "I'm sorry, I shouldn't say that about your cousin, although if he is too odd, feel free to come stay with me."

"At your uncle Malcolm's?" Ambria shook her head. "I don't think so. He seems a bit mental himself."

Max waved off her concern. "He's not very nice, but he'd eventually forget you were even there. Besides, he'll be at work all night."

She laughed. "Bad memory?"

"Awful," Max said.

"Do we need to return the brooms?" I asked. Even though flying was fun and made the trip shorter, I didn't want to go up the mountain and back.

"Uh, you can return them tomorrow," Max said. "The university lets students borrow them for a few days at a time."

I held out my hand to him. "Been a pleasure, Max."

He shook my hand. "Same, Conrad."

Ambria gave him a nod. "Perhaps we'll see you tomorrow."

"I sure hope so." Max gave us a grin, hopped on a broom, and took off.

I took out the phone and looked at the map.

"He certainly seems nice," Ambria said. "Perhaps we should tell him everything. He could probably help us fit in better."

"Hmm." I gave it some thought. "Let's get to know him better first."

Ambria climbed onto her broom. "I still can't believe we're in such a magical place." She squealed. "It's exciting, isn't it?"

I looked at our brooms and realized Max had taken off with the one that had my carpet strapped to it. It appeared we'd definitely be seeing him again. "Yes, exciting."

"You don't sound very excited." Ambria gave me a concerned look. "Are you feeling okay?"

I boarded my broom and set off toward Levi's house. "I keep getting these weird feelings."

Ambria flew alongside me. "Like the vision at the statue?"

I nodded. "When I got on the broom, it was like I already knew how to fly it."

"Maybe you should visit a doctor. Seeing things is certainly not normal."

A shudder ran through my shoulders. "I don't think I can." A cold sweat dampened my forehead. "When I think of doctors, I think of Dr. Cumberbatch and what he did to me."

"I'm sure the ones here are much better." Ambria gave me a stern look. "I won't let you lose your mind, Conrad. We need each other if we're to survive."

I knew she was right, especially since I controlled the money. "Maybe Max can help us find a good doctor."

"You trust him enough for that?"

I nodded. "Yes. All I have to tell him is that I'm feeling sick."

"True." She waggled her broomstick, guiding it back and forth in a wavy pattern along the empty street. She looked up at a building with the portrait of a man's face painted on the side. The man's eyes were crossed and he wore a tall pointy hat. "This city might be nicer than anything I've seen, but it looks run down in places."

I read the words beneath the man's portrait. *Ignatius the Idiot. He's a puppet not a leader.* "Phone, who is Ignatius?"

"Please narrow your parameters," it replied.

I obliged. "Who is Ignatius in Queens Gate?"

"There are three people by that name. Of note is Ignatius Creed, Primus of the Arcane Council."

"Please tell me more about him," I said, turning a corner as directed by the map.

"Ignatius Creed took office four years ago. According to his public speeches, his primary focus is reuniting the Overworld Conclave and maintaining the rule of law." The phone continued to detail Creed's time in office, but I lost interest and cut it off.

We passed by a small square with a restaurant shaped exactly like its name: The Copper Goose. A little ways past that, we reached Concord Avenue. The row houses here were at least three stories tall and constructed of brick. Ornate staircases decorated with marble statues of animals led to wooden double doors. Every staircase had a different animal. There were lions, elephants, horses, rams, and even mythical beasts like griffins and manticores. Similar statues decorated the windows and in some cases, each corner of the roofs.

One twenty-five Concord Avenue had glowing red bird statues perched on the ends of the handrails and on ledges at the top corners of the window frames.

"Phoenixes," Ambria said, stopping to touch one. "How lovely." She jerked back her hand. "It's warm!"

I put a finger to it and felt the heat. "Brilliant."

Despite the grandiose statues, the houses on this road had seen better days. Wooden shutters hung loose, the doors looked weathered and aged. Patches and cracks showed on the brick, and the paint had faded and peeled in places. Street artists had added decorations of their own to the sides of the houses, giving it a very ghetto look.

"This used to be a nice neighborhood," I said.

Ambria looked up and down the street. "This isn't the only place that used to be nice. It feels like Queens Gate is only a shadow of what it used to be."

I walked up to the front door. "Phone, unlock the door."

The phone emitted a beam of light into the keyhole. There was a click, and the door creaked ajar. My mouth dropped open at the mess inside. Stacks of newspapers and books crowded all but a narrow path. I stepped inside, flicked a light switch. Flames flickered on in candelabras hanging in the hallway and foyer.

A wooden staircase brimming with piles of paper ran up the wall to my right. Another room filled with junk lay beyond it, and yet another similarly occupied room was to my left. Straight ahead, the hallway ended in a door.

"How awful." Ambria stepped up beside me and pinched her nose. "It smells like mold in here."

"This man was a packrat." I stepped carefully through the narrow path and went up the stairs, turning on the light switch as I did. Flames burned in wall-mounted sconces. Soot and grime dirtied the glass and reflectors.

Ambria followed me. "He could certainly use a maid."

"More like a bulldozer." I reached the top of the staircase and turned right, activating the lamps as I did. The room at the end of the hallway was empty of everything but a bed and a nightstand. The attached bathroom boasted a large clawfoot tub with a hand shower.

Ambria stared at the tub longingly. "I know what I'm doing tonight."

"Don't hog it," I said with a smile. "I could use some relaxation too."

There were two more bedrooms side-by-side in the middle of the hallway. Each looked nearly identical to the first with four-poster beds and luxurious bathrooms. One of them held a number of books and newspapers though not as many as we'd seen downstairs. Apparently, Levi had only recently begun to stack them in here, judging by the dates on the papers.

"Look at this." Ambria held up a newspaper so I could see the front.

The *Overworld Daily* was printed in large block letters across the top. Just beneath it was a story someone had scribbled over in red ink, and then written *NO!* in large letters across it. The headline read, *Court Denies Reparations to Overlord Victims*. I peered closely at the headline, but the words were blotted out by the madman's pen strokes.

I glanced at the date. "This was nearly a year ago."

"What a nutter." Ambria dropped the paper back onto the stack. "Well, at least two bedrooms are clean."

I went back into the hallway and entered the last door. When the lamps flickered on, the light revealed a huge montage of images covering nearly every inch of the wall. A web of red yarn ran from needles stuck in a map of the United Kingdom. In the center of it all was a huge photo circled with red ink. Beneath it, messy handwriting proclaimed, *I found him!!!*

"My god, Conrad," Ambria breathed. "That's you."

Chapter 14

"What in the world's going on here?" Max said from behind me and Ambria.

The two of us jumped and shouted at the same time.

"What are you doing here, Max?" Ambria pushed him back. He tripped and sat down hard on a stack of newspapers.

"Ouch." Max gave her a hurt look. "I took the wrong broom. Soon as I noticed it had your flying carpet on it, I looked up the address to this place and came by to drop it off." He stood up and pointed to the montage on the wall. "I think it's time you explained to me why your picture is on that wall of weird and why it says 'I found him'."

"I don't know." It was the truth, but I knew it wouldn't stop his questions. Unfortunately, I couldn't come up with an explanation.

Ambria stared at me in silence as if attempting to formulate an answer of her own.

"Well?" Max said. His eyes narrowed. "Why would Levi be looking for you, Conrad?" He looked suspiciously at Ambria. "Are you really related to Levi or did you just make that up?"

Before I could stop him, he pushed past me and into the office. He walked along the wall and let out a long whistle. "Whoa, these articles form a timeline stretching from the first war to the second war and all the way to now." He stopped a third of the way. "This must be when the *Overworld Daily* was forced to close, because there's a big gap in dates."

I let out a resigned sigh. "Max, please tell me about the wars."

He gave me a wary look. "I want the truth, Conrad."

"I don't know much." I looked at Ambria. "We came here looking for the truth."

Max walked to the left end of the wall. "Six years ago, Justin Slade led the allies to victory over Daelissa, an evil Seraphim who wanted to conquer Eden. The first war was called the Second Seraphim War."

"What is Eden?" Ambria asked.

He waved his arms around the room. "The place where mortals live is called Eden. There are other dimensions we call realms. Seraphina is one them and that's where the angels—Seraphim—live."

"Angels?" Ambria blanched. "We were in a war with angels?"

Max wrinkled his forehead. "You've got to forget everything you learned as a nom. The Seraphim are totally different than the biblical ones."

The orphanage hadn't given us a religious upbringing, but we'd been taught about various religions. I clamped down on my surprise and continued where Max had left off. "After the war, you said Justin Slade led his army into Seraphina to fight another war, but someone sabotaged the gateway and stranded him there."

"That's right." Max took a couple more steps down the wall. "The Second Seraphim War tore apart the Overworld Conclave. Justin and his allies had only just started to piece the government back together when they left to help with the war in Seraphina."

"How irresponsible," Ambria said. "They should have finished here before leaping off to another war."

"I guess they never thought they'd be trapped in another realm," Max said.

"What happened next?" I asked.

"Well, with thousands of Templars, elite Arcanes, Daemos, and other allies out of the way, a new underground organization led by Cyphanis Rax, one of Daelissa's former allies, seized power. Before Cyphanis could declare himself ruler, he was murdered. A man named Victus and his wife, Delectra, took control."

Templars? I imagined men in shining armor. I had no idea what he meant by Daemos, but didn't want to bury him in questions. "Was Victus a magician?" I asked.

Max laughed. "Don't ever call an Arcane that. It's a terrible insult." He pressed his hand to a newspaper with the headline, *Victus Declares Himself Overlord.* "Victus was a powerful and brilliant scientist. His wife was a powerful Arcane."

"A scientist?" Ambria rumpled her forehead. "How could a scientist be powerful?"

"Well, since you two are obviously even more normal than you let on, I'd bet you've never seen what an Overworld scientist is capable of." He shivered. "Victus—the Overlord—created mutated animals to fight for him, not to mention his robot army."

"Robot army?" I was astounded. "It sounds like something out of a mad scientist movie."

Max traced a finger along the wall and stopped. "Well, now I know why Levi was so mental. Cyphanis Rax was his father."

"What?" I walked over to the newspaper and read the headline. *Cyphanis Rax Murdered!*

Cyphanis and Kara Rax were found dead in their home today. Though their son, Levi, was away in France, their daughter was home at the time and is missing, presumed dead. Due to Cyphanis's imminent rise to power, speculation is rampant that this was an assassination.

Red ink filled the margins all around the story, one word predominant: *WHO?* It was easy to see where Levi's descent into madness began. He'd lost his entire family in one blow.

"Why is his last name Baker?" Ambria asked.

"I'm sure he changed it." Max gave her a wan smile. "Cyphanis Rax wasn't much more popular than the Overlord."

Despite the awful tragedy, I still didn't understand how all of this connected to me.

Max continued. "Once the Overlord took over, he dismantled the Overworld Conclave and set up rules to make sure every Arcane and scientist was registered so he could keep an eye on them." Max looked away from the wall. "There was one thing they hadn't counted on."

Ambria sat on a wooden stool and looked at Max, her eyes rapt with curiosity. "What was it? Tell me!"

"Justin Slade's younger sister, Ivy, hadn't gone to Seraphina with the others because she was in Australia and was supposed to join with the army at a later time." Max shrugged. "I don't know all the details, but she found out that the Alabaster Arches weren't working and came to Queens Gate. The Overlord set a trap and almost killed Ivy when she arrived. After that, she built a resistance of her own and fought him."

"Was she powerful?" Ambria asked.

Max nodded briskly. "Ivy is a Seraphim. She's way more powerful than any Arcane alive. Even so, she needed help to defeat an army of mutant animals, robots, evil scientists, and Arcanes."

I found a headline a few more steps down. *Ivy Slade Defeats Overlord.* There were several such headlines, each one about a different battle. The last battle had been fought at Queens Gate.

"After Ivy beat their army, the Overlord and his people scattered everywhere and went into hiding." Max leaned against the wall and faced us. "They finally tracked down the Overlord and his wife, but before they could arrest them, the pair committed suicide."

Ambria gasped. "How awful."

"That's not the worst of it," Max said. "They had a little boy nobody knew about who was with them when they died."

"Did they kill him too?" Ambria's eyes filled with horror.

He grimaced. "No. Victus and Delectra killed themselves with poison right in front of the boy."

"What terrible people." She huffed with disgust.

"And the boy?" I asked. "What happened to him?"

"A group of healers took custody, but they were ambushed. The kidnappers took him and the bodies of Victus and Delectra." Max pointed at another newspaper headline. *Overlord and Delectra Dead!* He began to read the article. "Victus and Delectra Edison were declared dead today—"

My heart solidified to ice in my chest. "Edison?"

Max nodded. "The boy had been missing for years." Max looked directly at me. "Until now." He jabbed a finger at the photo. "The boy's name was Conrad Edison."

If Max had hit me over the head with a pipe, he couldn't have gotten a stronger reaction. My knees went to jelly. I wobbled and felt my rear end hit the floor. I lost my breath and began to hyperventilate.

Ambria rushed to my side and hugged me. She looked at Max. "How can you be sure? Maybe Levi was wrong."

He shrugged. "Maybe. I guess we'd have to read all his notes to find out."

Their words sounded fuzzy and it was hard for me to concentrate. *My parents were evil people. Maybe that makes me evil. Maybe that's why I killed Levi and why I want to hurt people.* I thought of the phone and wondered if Levi had put his research on there. I took it out. "Phone." My voice sounded weak. "Do you have information about Conrad Edison?"

"There are twenty-two documents on this device about that subject," it replied.

"Please display them."

The screen flickered on and showed a picture of two dead bodies with a distressed boy standing between them. A man in robes stood next to the boy, a wand in his hand. I noticed an icon that said *Play* and touched it. The video projected into the air.

The boy cried as the man waved the wand over him. The man crouched and waved the wand over the bodies. He stood and nodded. "This is definitely their child," he said to someone off screen. "I believe he's four or five years old."

"Why isn't he talking?" asked a woman, presumably the one recording the video.

"He's traumatized." The man touched the boy's forehead. "He'll need immediate treatment to avoid any long-lasting damage to his psyche."

A familiar voice spoke. "I'm here to retrieve the bodies and the boy."

The man with the wand nodded. "Let me finish the preservation spell on the bodies first, Rufus."

Ambria and I exchanged shocked looks.

"Dr. Cumberbatch?" I said.

The video stopped and the projection vanished.

"What was he doing there?" Ambria asked.

Max turned to the wall and ran his finger down an article. "According to the story about the boy being stolen, Rufus Cumberbatch and two other Arcanes were knocked unconscious. When they came to, the bodies and the boy were gone. They never found out what happened to them."

"Why would they take the bodies?" Ambria said. "That doesn't make sense."

Max shrugged. "The victors wanted to display the bodies in the council hall here in Queens Gate so everyone could see the Overlord and Delectra were definitely dead." He peered again at the article. "They suspected sympathizers took the bodies to keep that from happening."

"Gruesome." Ambria shuddered. "They couldn't bring them back to life, could they?"

"Nah." Max's lips peeled back. "Necromancy doesn't work like that. They'd just be animated corpses."

I flicked the screen to the next document. It was another video. When I played it, it showed the boy's face changing over time with an age displayed below. When it reached eleven years, there was little question the boy looked like me. Try as hard as I might, I couldn't remember witnessing my parents committing suicide in front of me. I couldn't remember much of anything from that long ago. Closing my eyes, I tried to recall the day I arrived at the orphanage. It was like trying to catch a mosquito buzzing around my ear—definitely there, but out of reach.

Max looked from the projected image to me. "I'm beginning to think Levi has it right. You're the son of the Overlord."

I couldn't disagree.

The next several documents were pictures of me at the orphanage, some of them taken up close. I saw the Goodleighs next to me in one of the images. They seemed to be talking to someone. Judging from my age in the pictures, these images had been taken within the past few months. I thought hard, but couldn't remember meeting Levi. I remembered my last foster parents picking me up. Before that, I vaguely remembered another man who'd visited and spoken with me, though the Goodleighs had turned down his offer to take me. I remembered the man touching me. I remembered his face. It looked nothing like Levi's.

I scrolled past the picture and a text document appeared in the air. There were a bunch of numbers and symbols that didn't make sense, but at the bottom it read:

The hair sample is an exact match for the Edison boy.

Max and Ambria stared at me.

It suddenly seemed as though I couldn't get enough oxygen. My heart filled with dread. I went to the next document, another video.

Levi Baker's deranged face filled the air. "I've found him. Years of tracking down leads. Months investigating the Goodleighs and Rufus Cumberbatch. It's finally paid off. The boy is every bit as murderous as his parents. It seems all his foster parents die in horrific accidents, or meet some other terrible fate." He burst into maniacal laughter for several seconds. "When the boy returns to the orphanage, I will find him and slaughter him like he deserves. The Overlord's bloodline will die!" His eyes grew dark and fierce. His lips peeled back from his teeth. "My family will be avenged."

"Levi Rax was absolutely mental," Ambria whispered.

Max sat cross-legged on the floor across from me. "Did Levi come for you?"

I nodded numbly. "Yes, he tried to kill me by mind-controlling animals."

"Ooh, that's so illegal. Animal rights activists would tear him up on the spot." He stopped talking and stared at me. "So, what happened?"

"I ran away. Then I realized he would keep coming for me, so I snuck up behind him and tried to knock him out with a shovel." I felt Ambria's grip tighten on my shoulder. "I hit him too hard and now he's dead."

Max's eyes grew wide. A smiled curled his lips. "He tried to end the Overlord's bloodline, and instead, you ended his." He chuckled. "Wow, that's irony for you."

"Irony?" My voice trembled. "It's murder, Max! A man is dead and you're laughing about it."

He held up his hands in defense. "No, it's not funny that Levi is dead, it's just so bizarre how it ended for him. C'mon, you've got to see the black humor in that." He paused, raised an eyebrow. "Is it too soon?"

Ambria shoved him in the chest and sent him falling over backwards. "You're an awful person, Max!"

Max lay spread-eagled on the floor. "I suppose I am. My parents are awful people, so I guess that makes me just as bad."

Mirthless laughter burst from my mouth. "I think my parents have yours beat, Max."

"What makes your parents so terrible?" Ambria asked him.

Max sat up and dangled his arms over bent knees. "My father wanted to become Primus, but Ignatius Creed beat him in the election."

"Wanting to become a leader doesn't make you evil," Ambria said. "Leaders want to help people."

"Not my father," Max said in a scoffing tone. "He thinks it's his birthright since we're related to Alexander Tiberius, one of the original founders of the Arcane Council."

I squeezed my eyes shut and pressed my hands tightly over them. *We are individuals. Our parents don't make us evil. We have a choice!*

Cora and I enter a grocery store. This time, she purchases our food. Now that Bill is dead, we have money. She squeals with delight as we unpack the groceries at the apartment.

"Why are you happy, Mum?"

She laughs. "We don't have to steal anymore, son. We're free."

I'm not sure what she means. "Free?"

"Free to make better choices. We have money and don't have to be afraid anymore."

"Did Bill frighten you?" I ask.

Cora nods and wipes a tear from her eye. "From now on, we are what we make of ourselves."

I felt someone shaking me and opened my eyes.

Ambria looked sad and concerned. "Are you okay, Conrad?"

I pushed to my feet, squared my shoulders, and took a deep breath. "We are what we make of ourselves." I pulled Ambria to her feet and then offered a hand to Max. He gripped my hand. I pulled him up and gave each of them my sternest gaze. "Our parents don't make us what we are." I jabbed a finger into my chest. "We do."

A wide grin spread across Max's face. "You're right. Our parents might be stupid, but we don't have to be."

"Speak for yourselves," Ambria said brightly. "Although I never knew my parents, I'm certain they were very nice and sweet people. That's why I'm so wonderful."

Everyone burst into laughter.

The more I thought about choice, the more I thought about the Goodleighs and Rufus Cumberbatch. What they were doing was about as wrong as it could be. We could prove that we were good by *doing* good, and I knew exactly where to start.

We would shut down Little Angels Orphanage and free the children.

Chapter 15

I announced my plan to the others.

"What a wonderful idea!" Ambria clapped her hands and did a little dance. "Those evil people must be stopped."

Max grimaced. "How are we supposed to take on criminals like that? Are they Arcanes? What if they kill us?"

I'd already thought about that. "Let's talk to Ivy Slade. I'm sure she'd be willing to help us shut them down."

He shook his head. "I forgot to mention that Ivy went looking for a way to bring her brother and the others back from Seraphina. She vanished and hasn't been seen for years."

I felt my smile fall. "Are there any authorities who might help us?"

"Not really." Max looked up in thought. "The Templars in Eden are spread really thin since most of their legions went with the army. The Custodians took over some of the Templar duties, but there aren't enough of them to police the Overworld and clean up any supernatural scandals." He sighed and clapped me on the back. "It was a noble idea, Conrad, really it was. We just don't have any practical way to pull it off."

Ambria deflated. "Surely there's some way to do it."

I looked at the phone. "I copied all of the information about the Goodleighs onto this device. Maybe there's something on there we could use."

"Information is great," Max said, "but it won't help us fight grownups."

Ambria put her hands on her hips. "I'm sick of your negativity, Max. Why don't you propose something positive for a change?"

He hemmed and hawed for a few seconds. "Well, we have flying brooms, and I know a couple of spells that might help."

"What about a cloak of invisibility?" Ambria asked.

"No, but I've heard of Templar armor that can camouflage you."

The last thing we need is to wear heavy metal armor. I was about to comment when Ambria spoke.

"Excellent." Her frown vanished. "Let's get some."

He looked down. "I don't know where to get any, and even if I did, we'd have to steal it from people who are probably a lot more dangerous than the Goodleighs."

I sighed. "We don't have to rush into this. Let's take time to formulate a plan and gather supplies."

Ambria nodded. "I agree."

"Me too," Max said.

"Well, since we're not rushing off to rescue orphans, I have another plan." Ambria looked toward the hallway. "Let's clean this pigsty."

"I need to go study," Max said. "Why don't you—"

Ambria grabbed his arm. "A good person would help his friends."

He gave her a look of surprise. "Friends?"

She smiled. "Of course. You might just be a foolish boy, but if I can be friends with Conrad, I suppose I can be friends with you."

I snorted. "You make me feel so special."

Max abruptly gave her a hug. "I'll gladly be your friend." He turned to hug me, seemed to think better of it, and held out his hand.

I shook it. "To friends."

He beamed a smile. "Friends."

Ambria gave us a cross look. "Well, now that that's settled, let's figure out how to clean up this mess."

A few hours later, we'd only managed to move the junk from the foyer to the street curb.

Ambria stared doubtfully at the sidewalk where we'd put everything. "Are you certain someone will collect it?"

Max threw up his hands. "Yes. The gnomes love trash. Rumor is, they can spin it into gold, but someone else told me they actually turn garbage into water."

"Gold sounds much better," Ambria said.

"I suppose. Gold isn't worth much in the Overworld."

My stomach rumbled loudly. "Where do you recommend we eat?"

Max pointed down the road. "The Copper Goose is a good spot and they have a great selection of Nutter Beer."

Ambria stuck her nose in the air. "I'm too young to drink and so are you, Max."

He chuckled. "It's not real beer, silly. It's made by Mr. Nutter."

The name brought back a memory of the normal world. "I had a Mr. Nutter's angel biscuit a few days ago."

"Oh?" Max looked surprised. "I didn't realize he was selling to noms now too."

"Let's go," Ambria said. She went inside and got her broom.

The rest of us followed suit. We flew down the street and parked at the goose-shaped building I'd seen earlier. The interior smelled delicious. I ordered lycan stew, which the server assured me contained no lycan whatsoever. Ambria ordered fish, and Max had a chicken pot pie.

When the server brought us our Nutter Beers, I gave mine a dubious look. It looked dark and thick. Max took a long sip. "Ah, tastes like almond pie."

"Mine tastes sweet." Ambria smacked her lips. "It reminds me of some walnuts and honey I once had."

I sampled it. A warm, soothing sweetness filled my mouth. It tasted pleasantly earthy with a nutty undertone, though I really had no basis for comparison. "Very good," I admitted.

After eating, I paid for 'Ambrias meal and mine and noted I only had about forty tinsel left. While we probably had enough money to survive on even if we spent fifty a day on food, it didn't seem like the most frugal use of our resources.

As we flew back toward the house, I asked Max if there was a grocery store nearby.

"Sure, there's several." He pointed behind us. "I'd recommend Bartelby Brothers."

"We'd have to cook." Ambria didn't look excited by the prospect. "We haven't even cleaned out the kitchen yet."

Max harrumphed. "Cleaning that dump is going to take forever."

"Not with our new friend helping," Ambria said sweetly.

"Oh, I'll help." Max arched an eyebrow. "I'll use a fire spell on all that paper."

A bell chimed in the distance. Max flew his broom up above the rooftops and looked toward the clock tower in the center of town, a large blue moon highlighting his silhouette. Ambria and I followed him.

"Almost curfew," he said. "I suppose it's time for me to go home."

I tensed at the thought of being forced indoors just like at the orphanage. "What happens if you don't go inside?"

"Nobody makes you go inside, but it's definitely safer." Max looked at the streets below. "Without the Templars around, the vampires have gotten bolder, and they come out at night to feed on blood and party."

My stomach went tight at the thought of such supernatural horrors walking the streets.

Ambria squeaked. "Vampires?"

He nodded. "Just stay inside and you should be okay."

"Enough talk. I'm going inside now." Ambria flew her broom to the door, hopped off, and went inside.

"I'll see you tomorrow," Max said.

I waved goodbye and watched him fly swiftly away into the darkness. For a time, I hovered in the night air, observing the moon and trying to spot other oddities. The knowledgeable voice in my head told me this place wasn't on Earth, but even it didn't know where this pocket dimension existed. The city center glowed in the distance like a hearth. Further from the core, the city darkened. Our particular street had only a few working street lamps. Most nearby houses remained unlit despite the pitch black pressing in from all sides.

I wondered if they were abandoned, or if perhaps vampires lived there. Requiring no light, they might be watching me right this very moment. A shudder took me by surprise.

"Conrad, why are you still out?" Ambria called from the front door. "Come inside this instant."

I did as instructed and carried the broom up the stairs where Ambria waited. At the top, I tripped on a bundle of newspapers. They tumbled down the stairs, causing the other stacks to topple like dominoes, leaving a nearly impassible mess.

Ambria groaned. "Ugh! As if this place wasn't already a disaster." She regarded it for a moment and sighed. "We'll just have to clean it tomorrow."

"I'm sorry." I leaned down to pick up some of the loose papers, but Ambria stopped me.

"Tomorrow, Conrad." Her voice was stern.

I nodded. "Yeah. Tomorrow."

"I'm going to bathe and sleep." She hugged me and kissed my cheek. "Thank you again, Conrad. Sweet dreams." She entered her room and closed the door.

A yawn made my jaw crack. I decided to skip a bath and, after putting the broom in a corner of my room, fell into bed. Sleep met me a moment later.

I woke up, the hairs on my arms standing on end. Pale moonlight filtered through the sheer curtains. A pair of glowing green eyes met mine. Fear gripped me and I froze in place. A dark form rose and stood outlined by the window. Triangular ears twitched atop its head. Despite the dim light, I realized this creature looked like a walking cat. A tail twitched as it came toward me, eyes narrowing to slits.

"Go to the doctor," it said with a purr.

"The doctor?" My voice emerged in a squeak. I felt like a mouse waiting for the pounce that would end my life.

The cat glanced toward the door. "They're coming. You must go." It turned toward me and padded to the edge of the bed. It leaned forward, eyes blazing like emerald embers. "Free yourself. Release the curse!"

I flailed. My eyes flicked open and saw only a dark room. I quickly turned on the lamp next to the bed and looked around. I was alone. "Was I dreaming?" It was the only explanation that made sense.

Muffled conversation rose from downstairs. I quickly doused the light and crawled out of bed, careful to keep the frame from squeaking. I tiptoed across the floor, praying the hardwoods didn't creak. A light shone through the crack at the bottom of the door. It looked faint enough to emanate from downstairs, or so I hoped. Slowly twisting the doorknob, I eased open the door and crouched.

The voices grew clearer. Though I couldn't hear what they were saying, I recognized them at once. The Goodleighs were here!

Thankful for the cover of the bundled newspapers and magazines, I crept forward on hands and knees a little way before peeking over them. The downstairs light was on. I saw Felicity and Marcus—the days of me calling them Mr. and Mrs. Goodleigh were over. The pair stared with disdain at the mess on the stairwell.

"I doubt anyone lives here now," Felicity said. "This *sty* isn't fit for pigs."

Marcus sniffed the air. "Must and mold." He turned to her. "Doubtful the children came here even if they had the means."

"Levi, no doubt, had magical means of transportation." Felicity peered around the room. "If the children found it—"

"*If* they found it, why would they come here?" Marcus propped his chin on a fist. "No doubt Levi divined Ambria's lineage and came after her."

Ambria? Why would they think she had anything to do with Levi's appearance?

"She must have enlisted Conrad's help to kill him."

Marcus dropped his arm and shook his head. "I find it hard to believe that frail boy could have killed him."

"A shovel to the back of the head is cowardly but effective." She pursed her lips. "Perhaps if we brought Brickle, he could sniff around this place and determine the truth."

Marcus seemed to consider it. "That's a capital idea, Felicity. If anyone can track those rascals it would be him."

"I don't intend to let that valuable girl slip through our fingers." Felicity kicked over a stack of papers. "It's probably only a matter of time before Conrad kills her."

"I doubt the boy would do that. He prefers killing foster parents." Marcus turned for the door. "Let's return home and arrange for Brickle to visit this derelict."

Felicity stepped toward the kitchen. Her lips curled up with disgust as she brushed against a newspaper stack. She vanished down the hallway beneath us and called back to her husband. "The basement door is blocked."

"Are you even certain it's the basement door?" Marcus asked.

"It's the most logical place." She grunted. "People keep their secrets locked up inside basements. I'd like to have a look before we leave."

He sighed. "Let's have Brickle move the rubbish out of the way while he's here. We'll come back and look."

There was a loud thud, like someone kicking at something. "I'd just as soon burn this place to the ground."

"Let's go. It's late, and I don't want to get caught by a roving gang of vampires."

I heard a click and looked down the hall from me. Ambria poked her head out of the doorway, eyes bleary. She opened her mouth to speak.

I hastily put a finger to my lips and shook my head.

Her forehead pinched.

Waving my hand frantically and pointing at the floor, I motioned her to get down. Marcus spoke in an admonishing tone to his wife. Drowsiness fled from Ambria's eyes as recognition ignited fear. She quickly dropped to her knees and eased shut the bedroom door behind her.

The Goodleighs broke into an argument about entering the basement. Felicity finally won.

"This is a foolish waste of time," her husband growled. Several grunts and thuds later, a door clicked open.

"A closet?" Felicity's voice rose.

"Yes, a closet." Marcus's voice dripped with anger. "Let's go."

"Perhaps it's that door," she said.

I heard a squeak and a scuffle. Marcus dragged his wife down the path between the newspapers, ignoring her rude remarks as she resisted. They vanished outside, and the door slammed shut behind them.

Ambria's eyes froze wide with terror and her face blanched pale as a ghost's. For the eternal space of several minutes, we said nothing, neither of us hardly daring to breathe in case the wicked pair returned.

I finally broke the silence. "I don't think it's safe to stay here after tonight."

She crawled over to me and gripped my arm painfully tight. "How did they find us?" A large tear formed in the corner of her eye and trickled down the side of her nose.

I bit my lower lip and thought about it. The Goodleighs had found Levi Rax's body after my poor attempt to conceal it. They seemed to recognize the man, most likely because of his infamous father, Cyphanis. The only part of the conversation I hadn't understood was why they thought Ambria could be the reason for his appearance at the farm.

"When I scanned Levi's face, I didn't have time to hide his body again." I winced as her fingernails dug into my skin. "They knew who he was and probably looked up the address."

"How did they get in?"

I shrugged. "Probably magic."

"Where will we go?" She asked in a frantic voice.

I pried at her fingers. "You're hurting me."

Ambria flinched as if suddenly realizing how tightly she held me. "I'm sorry, Conrad, but I'm scared."

Her fingernails left little indentations in my skin. I rubbed my arm and thought about what I'd heard the Goodleighs say. "Have you ever seen Levi before?"

Her forehead wrinkled. "No. Then again, all I saw was his awful-looking corpse."

Taking one last glance at the door, I decided the Goodleighs were gone for the night and stood. "Come with me." I entered my bedroom, Ambria close on my heels. I picked up the phone. "Project a current image of Levi Rax." An image of the deranged man flickered in the air. "Take a good look."

She tilted her head one way then the other. "I've never seen him before."

"The Goodleighs seemed to think Levi was there for you and not me."

"I have no idea why."

An obvious solution came to mind. "Phone, search documents for Ambria."

"Two documents found," the phone replied and listed them.

The first document was about Ambria's sale. The second was labeled *Ambria Prospectus.* Both had been downloaded from the Goodleigh's tablet.

"What's a prospectus?" Ambria said.

I shrugged. "It has the word prospect in it, so maybe it's about why someone would want to buy you."

Her lips stretched into a grimace. "That's awful. I can't believe they would sell children."

127

I opened the file. The first line identified her as *Prospect 257*. The next line made us gasp with astonishment.

Chapter 16

Prospect Name: Ambria Rax.

"That's not my name!" Ambria wailed.

I read the next paragraph entitled, *Prospect Outlook*, aloud. "As the daughter of the powerful Arcane, Cyphanis Rax and his wife, Kara Beckinsale, Ambria has the potential to be a formidable Arcane when she comes of age. Both of her parents had pure and powerful Arcane lineages and both were of above average intelligence. Her older brother, Levi, has proven himself quite capable at Arcane University. We suspect Ambria will also prove powerful with the proper training.

"In addition, Cyphanis demonstrated he was a ruthless and clever manipulator, willing to do whatever it took to move to the top. Ambria's temperament has shown she will be much the same as him in that regard. This makes her the perfect candidate for assassin or gladiator training, though her flexibility will allow her to fit many roles."

"Gladiator? Assassin?" Ambria's lips curled with disgust. "They wrote about me like I'm a sheep for sale on the market."

"Probably because that's all we are to them." Out of curiosity, I found and displayed my prospectus.

"Yours looks just as rosy as mine." Ambria took it upon herself to recite it. "The name Victus Edison is almost pedigree enough for his son, Conrad. A renowned scientist, Victus was an innovator of new technologies and the first novice at Science Academy to build a battle bot that won the Grand Melee.

"His wife, Delectra Moore, was the perfect Arcane complement to Victus's scientific genius. A descendant of the great Ezzek Moore, her magical resume is simply too long to list. Together, they were the pair that overthrew the Conclave and ruled the Overworld.

"Given time and maturity, we're certain Conrad will live up to his parents' reputation. He will be as adept with science as with magic and provide the buyer with a powerful asset. Pairing him with the optimal mate will give the owner control over a bloodline that could win them the world."

I shook my head slowly. "I think they overestimated my abilities."

Ambria patted my shoulder. "I'm glad neither of us matches our descriptions." She laughed.

I didn't see much humor in the situation. "What's funny?"

"Well, I was so certain my parents were good people." She sighed. "I suppose my parents were just as bad as yours and Max's.

"My parents were the worst of the lot." I closed the holographic document and put the phone on a dresser. "Cyphanis might have been ruthless, but from what Max told us, he used politics to get what he wanted. My parents killed anyone who got in their way."

Ambria slumped to the floor. Tears welled in her eyes and she broke into sobs. "Oh, Conrad, this is awful. We can't live here anymore, our dead parents were evil, and we'll probably be hunted by the Goodleighs for years." She wiped her nose with the back of her hand. "What are we to do?"

My lower lip trembled so I pressed my mouth into a tight line to keep it under control. Anger smoldered deep in my heart. Ambria and I had been brought into this world by bad people. We'd been kidnapped and imprisoned by the Goodleighs for most of our lives. We had very little experience with the outside world. The home of the man I'd killed was supposed to have been our sanctuary. Instead, it would soon be visited by Brickle.

We could leave, but if Brickle brought his hounds, he'd discover in no time that we'd been here. That would only renew the hunt. Queens Gate would no longer be safe. My fists tightened. I imagined taking a knife and plunging it into Brickle's heart. Watching him fall to the floor and bleed until his last breath rattled from his chest.

Do it! Kill him!

I sucked in a harsh breath and the image fled.

130

"What are you thinking, Conrad?" Ambria looked at me with red eyes.

"About what to do next."

"Perhaps Max can help us hide that we were here," she said. "I'll bet he knows a spell that could cover our tracks. Maybe we could stay at his uncle's for a while."

I didn't want to stay at his grumpy old uncle's house. I wanted to stay right here. That was when I realized this situation might actually be much better than we thought. We'd wanted to save the other orphans by raiding the orphanage. As discussed, it would mean fighting against Brickle, his hounds, and the Goodleighs, not to mention the other staff. But if Brickle came alone with only one hound, we might be able to capture him.

"Do you still want to free the other orphans?" I asked.

Ambria nodded. "Of course." She stood and regarded me with confusion. "What does that have to do with this?"

"We'll capture Brickle. With him out of the way, it makes the task easier."

"What?" Her voice rose an octave. "Are you mental? We'd need an army to take him down." She looked me over. "Conrad, you're thin as a stick. How do you think you could capture a big brute?"

"We make a trap." Ideas brewed in my head. "We need to search this place thoroughly. If there is a basement, it might be the perfect place to trap and imprison him."

Ambria pressed a hand to her cheek. "You *are* mental!"

I shook my head. "No, I'm not. If this plan is going to work, we need to start preparing tonight."

She stared at me with big round eyes for several seconds. Finally, she drew in a breath and huffed. "Well, let's hope this plan of yours doesn't get us all killed."

I felt a smile on my face.

A wry smile lit hers as well. "Why are we smiling, Conrad?"

"Because we've decided enough is enough." I squeezed her shoulder. "We're fighting back." I didn't know how much time we had before Brickle arrived. He might be here first thing in the morning, or later in the afternoon. Since it took several hours to make the trip from Queens Gate to the orphanage even on a flying carpet, I felt I could safely assume we had three or four hours at minimum. Since

Brickle would probably have to wait until the Goodleighs arrived back at the orphanage before he could leave, we might have double that time.

"I'm so tired, Conrad." Ambria yawned. "I was wide awake and frightened to death when the Goodleighs were here."

"That was an adrenalin rush." I fought off a yawn. "It's normal to feel tired after being so scared."

"Do you think it's safe to sleep?" Her dark hair framed large concerned eyes.

I nodded even though I didn't think sleeping was in our best interests. Brickle could be here by morning. The best thing to do was stay up all night and prepare our defenses, but Ambria looked so tired, I kept those thoughts to myself. "Why don't you get some sleep?" I told Ambria. "I'll make sure everything is locked up tight."

She nodded groggily. "Thank you, Conrad." She went back into her room and closed the door.

I looked at the mess on the stairwell and finally decided the only way downstairs was by sliding down the wooden rail. I straddled it and used both hands to brake my descent. After reaching the bottom, I went to the closet Felicity had opened. Dozens of robes hung beneath a shelf with a stack of twigs and branches on top.

Strange place to keep firewood.

I looked closer and realized the twigs were actually broken and cracked wands and staffs. I tugged a bundle of papers to the doorway and stepped onto it so I could see the shelf better.

Wand and staff breakage seemed very common judging from the number of those discarded. I picked up a couple of wands that looked whole and realized they had cracks running lengthwise or splintered ends. Some wands were gnarled and crooked while others had once been perfectly straight and polished until some accident landed them in the trash heap. All of them bore strange symbols etched into the wood.

I noticed labels affixed to many of the magical instruments, the handwriting too messy to read, or faded from time. Those I could read bore names. It was only after reading several of the names that I began to suspect the true origin of these wands. *These people are dead.* I wondered if Levi had killed them.

A notebook lay to the left of the stack. I'd paid it no heed at first, but its proximity to the wands drew my attention. I opened it and found a title above a list:

BOOK OF THE DEAD
Those killed by the Overlord will forever be remembered
I shivered and dropped the book.
This closet is full of bones.

In a fit of rage, I swiped the shelf clean of the wands and watched them clatter to the floor. A wooden box the color of cinnamon landed on my foot, though not hard enough to cause pain or injury. When I flipped open the top, I found red satin cloth enfolding two unblemished wands. I inspected the labels on the handles: *Mother, Father.*

These must have belonged to Cyphanis and Kara. Kara's ebony wand bore a straight polished handle before curling into a three-ring spiral and ending with straight tip. Cyphanis's pure white wand ran perfectly straight from end to end. Magical runes etched in gold lettering decorated both wands.

I decided to take the wands. Perhaps Max or Ambria could make use of them. As I folded the satin cloth, I noticed something scrawled in faded ink on the back and spread it out.

Betwixt and between shall the entrance be seen.

The rest of the sentence was too faded to read.

The entrance to what? I didn't have time to solve the mystery so I bundled the wands into the cloth and stuffed them into my back pocket.

Since the closet held nothing else of immediate interest, I navigated my way down the crowded hall to the kitchen. It looked nothing like the kitchens I'd seen, aside from a sink. There was no stove, no oven, and no refrigerator. I opened the pantry door. Small black shapes squeaked and raced past my feet. I yelped and jumped back from the wave of rats.

I'd seen plenty of rats in the houses where I'd lived. One set of foster parents had made me crawl around a narrow space beneath their house to place rodent traps. A family of poisonous spiders beneath the house hitchhiked on my clothing, probably as I pulled myself through their webs. When I climbed out from under the house, the spiders had leapt from my clothes and bitten my temporary parents, killing them within minutes.

While I didn't particularly like rats or spiders, I'd learned that both had a knack for getting into places, no matter how secure. As the last rat scurried away, I followed it through the kitchen and into a utility room of sorts where piles of robes, shirts, and pants lay atop a table.

The rat ran beneath it and vanished into the wall. I stopped and stared at the dead end. There were no cracks in the baseboards, nor holes in the wall. Moving the ironing board to the side offered me no better of a view. Pressing my hands to the wall yielded no other clues. I knocked on the wall. It felt just as solid and sounded no hollower than the other sections I tested.

Another rodent scuttled between my feet. When it reached the wall, it seemed to squeeze beneath it despite the miniscule seam between baseboard and floor. Running my fingers along the seam, they detected a much wider crack than what I saw. In other words, my eyes were lying to me, much like they had at the hidden lift that took us to Queens Gate.

Illusion.

The thought came from my mysterious reservoir of information. I accepted this hint as fact, but it brought me no closer to seeing what the illusion concealed. I suddenly remembered the writing on the cloth. Since the cryptic message had been with the two wands, the logical conclusion meant peering between the wands would reveal a hidden entrance.

A bit smug with myself, I pulled the wands from my back pocket and held them up vertically, one in each hand. Looking between them revealed nothing. Frowning, I switched the wands around. Still nothing. Holding them horizontally didn't help either.

"Betwixt and between shall the entrance be seen," I chanted, thinking perhaps it was a spell.

I went from feeling smug to insecure about my intelligence. *I was so stupid before, I'm probably just average now with delusions of grandeur.* I shoved the wands back in my pocket and knelt next to the wall. I felt all along the invisible crack. My fingers caught on something metal just a few inches from where the rats had vanished. I

134

pressed against it but it didn't budge. A firm pull dislodged the metal with a click. The wall flickered and subtly changed.

The invisible crack at the bottom became visible. Small seams outlined the shape of a door. Unfortunately, the door didn't open. A small round hole was where a doorknob should be. I put a finger inside and tried to pull open the door, but couldn't get a firm grip. I took Cyphanis's wand from my back pocket and pushed it into the hole, intending to use it as a lever. A latch clicked and the door swung open. I looked at the wand with astonishment.

The wand was a key.

Cool dank air blew across my face bringing with it an earthen odor. Stairs carved in rock led down a dark tunnel. I felt along the wall and found a button. Pressing it ignited torches in sconces all along the descending corridor. Uncertain what lay below, I crept down the stairs silently and into a roomy basement. Three shelves towered before me, laden with a variety of scrolls and bottled liquids.

A bundle of silvery chains hung from a nail protruding from the end of the closest shelf. When I pulled at the chains, I realized it was actually a net with a string of slick rope laced through the links.

I strode around the shelves, found another row of shelves, and behind them, a wall of bare rock. It took me quite some time to rummage through the items on the shelves.

The simple labels on the bottled liquids did little to betray the purpose of their contents. Someone had gone through the trouble of molding the bottles into interesting shapes. The container labeled *Iocaine* was shaped like a small bald man while another liquid named *Fluxus* occupied a warped and distorted flask. A bottle shaped like a head with wide bugging eyes held a fluid named *Insanity,* while a heart-shaped vessel bore the name *Vitus*. I didn't dare pull the corks from the bottles. For all I knew they might be poisonous.

One shelf had been divided into smaller compartments, each one containing a scroll with a bit of ribbon holding it shut. The scrolls varied in size as did the color of the ribbon holding them closed. I pulled out one with a green ribbon in the hopes that indicated it was safe, and gingerly untied the binding. Three large symbols glowed dim red on the parchment. Small script at the top of the page presumably translated each symbol into English along with instructions for drawing on the ground a circle with a pattern of lines crisscrossing it.

The instructions didn't tell me what purpose this diagram achieved, but I knew better than to recite the words. I rolled the parchment and tied it closed, then opened one with a yellow ribbon. This one was far more specific and had a picture of a man holding out his right hand as a fireball erupted from it. The written instructions echoed the illustration.

It's a fireball spell! "Brilliant!" I unrolled more scrolls and soon realized the ribbon color indicated the spell's function. Yellow was for offensive spells—fireballs, freezing fields, lightning bolts, and even gales of wind.

Brown ribbons signified defensive spells like protective barriers. Hex scrolls bore blue ribbons. These spells transformed the targets into harmless creatures like frogs and rabbits, though only for a limited time, according to the instructions. I used the phone to make a list of the color-coding and the spell types. The only scrolls I couldn't decipher were those with green ribbons.

Once I finished organizing the scrolls my eyelids were so heavy I could hardly keep them open. I doused the downstairs light, pulled myself back up the stair railing, and fell into bed the second I reached it. Physically, we were no match for Brickle.

As I drifted toward sleep, I still dared feel hopeful about our chances. These magic scrolls might prove the difference between victory and death.

Chapter 17

Ambria woke me up bright and early. "Conrad, get up! We have to set traps for Brickle."

I forced myself to climb from beneath the warm covers while Ambria paced nervously at the end of my bed.

"I found some scroll spells that should help us." I told her about the basement and the treasures I'd found.

"That's great, Conrad." She paused uncertainly. "Maybe we can split them up so we each have a few."

A knock sounded from downstairs. We carefully made our way down the railing as several more impatient knocks sounded. Just as I was about to open the door, a cautious thought drew back my hand. *What if it's Brickle?* Then again, if it was him, why would he knock? I looked through the peephole and saw Max glaring at the door.

Relieved, I opened it.

"About time," he said in a grumpy voice. "I was beginning to think you were still asleep."

Ambria grabbed his arm and pulled him inside. "Shush, Max. We've got something important to tell you." She told him about our late night visitors and about the company we expected.

Eyes wide, Max backed toward the door. "You want to capture a grown man?" He shook his head. "There's no way. I might know a spell or two, but nothing that would help with kidnapping someone."

"We found scrolls in the basement," I explained. "Some of them are for shooting fireballs and others turn people into animals."

He stopped. "Really?" Confidence asserted itself on his face. "I know a thing or two about using scrolls. My uncle keeps some around to chase away strangers and squirrels since he can't—uh, he hates people and animals."

"What a nice man." Ambria rolled her eyes.

"Maybe you can help me, Max." I motioned them to follow me and took them into the basement. The chain net caught my eye and it gave me an idea. "I think if we can lure him down here, we could rig that net to fall."

Max inspected it. "Hmm, it's made of silver and reinforced with diamond fiber." He touched the slick rope woven into the links and held the bare tips where they extended beyond the chain. "Just touch the ends and they'll bind together." He demonstrated by pressing together two strings. They wove into each other. He held it up. "Try to pull it apart."

I tugged as hard as I could but the diamond fiber wouldn't part.

"Let me try, Conrad." Ambria took it. "This looks weak as yarn." She had no better luck breaking it than I did.

Max traced his finger across the string and it parted. "If we use it to tie him up, we'll have to make sure he can't reach the seams or he might be able to open it himself."

"You mean to say he can simply touch it and free himself?" Ambria rolled her eyes. "What good is that?"

"Well, you could use blood." Max acted as if he were pricking his finger. "That way only the person who's blood is on it can open it."

She grimaced. "I'm not cutting myself for that."

"I'll do it," I said. "I just need a knife."

"Eew." Ambria shuddered.

I led them to the scrolls and showed them how the color-coding worked.

Max was as puzzled as I was about the ones with green ribbons. He read one and said, "Maybe we should draw one of these diagrams and have it ready just in case."

"The circle looks like it might be a magical trap. I'll bet the spell imprisons whoever stands in the circle." Ambria grinned. "I love to draw. I'll find something to write with."

"Try using this." Max reached toward a shelf and grabbed a piece of chalk.

"Perfect!" She looked around on the floor. "Where should I put them?"

I looked up at the wooden rafters and walked to an open area a few feet from the stairwell. "We could put the net up there and rig it to fall when we lure Brickle down." I pointed to my feet. "Draw a diagram here."

"How large should it be?" she asked.

I shrugged. "Big enough to hold Brickle."

"In other words, huge." Ambria curved her arms as if holding a big wine barrel.

"Let's figure out how to set up the net," Max said.

He and I looked around the basement for some way to secure the net that would allow us to release it.

"What's that cloth in your back pocket?" Max asked as we rummaged around.

I took out the wands and the cloth and showed him what it said.

"Cool." He held up the wands and looked between them. "Did you find anything?"

I shook my head. "I thought it was a way to find the basement door, but it didn't work."

He held them up and looked around the basement.

Ambria dusted off her hands and stood up outside a completed diagram. "Will you two work on the net? We don't have time for you to play around with the wands."

"I've got an idea," Max said. He handed me a wand and flourished the other. "My mom has a spell she uses to hold paintings on the wall. Maybe it'll work on the net."

"Ooh, I want to see a spell." Ambria clapped her hands.

Max took the cloth and held it against the side of a shelf. "Hold that there, Conrad."

I pressed a finger to keep it in place. Max stepped back, flicked the wand, and said, "*Affixiato!*"

My hand flattened against the shelf. I tugged but couldn't budge it. "What did you do?"

He twisted his lips. "Oops, I think the spell hit your hand instead of the cloth."

"Well unfix it," I said.

Max touched a finger to his chin. "Let me just remember the counter-spell."

Ambria groaned and pressed a hand to her face. "Oh, Max."

He gave her a sheepish grin and turned back to me. "This should do it." Narrowing his eyes toward my hand, he flicked the wand. "*Defixiatio!*"

Nothing happened.

Max waved the wand again. *"Unfixiato!"*

My hand remained firmly glued to the shelf.

"I'm sorry, my mother doesn't take down paintings very often." He sighed and paced in a circle. He stopped and held up a finger. "Ah, I remember." He turned, flicked the wand up, back down, and then pointed it at my hand. *"Disruptus!"*

My hand came free and the cloth fluttered to the floor. Sighing with relief, I picked up the cloth.

"Why can't we use that spell to pin Brickle to the wall?" Ambria asked.

"It won't work on thick objects," Max said. "I might be able to do it to a hand, but not his body." He gave us a serious look. "My big brother tried to do it to me once and it didn't work."

Ambria's forehead wrinkled. "That's not very nice."

"Like I said, my family isn't very nice." Max tweaked the end of the wand between two fingers. "They have worse spells they like to test on live subjects, so I try to stay out of their way."

"Can I cast a spell with the wand?" Ambria asked.

"That depends on if you can aetherate."

Her eyebrows rose. "Aetherate? What does that mean?"

"If you hadn't been stuck in nom schools, you'd know what it is." He gave her a smug look and crossed his arms. "Arcanes have to fill up with magical energy which is called aether. Aetherating is what we call it when you're energizing yourself with aether."

"Is it hard?" I asked.

Max shook his head. "Nah, not really once you've done it a couple of times. It's kind of like learning how to wiggle your nostrils or making your tongue and eyes do this." He stuck out his tongue and made it roll up then crossed his eyes.

Ambria crossed her eyes and stuck out her tongue, but couldn't seem to make it curl up. I tried to mimic them but failed to cross my eyes or roll my tongue.

Max burst into laughter. "You two look mental."

140

"As if you didn't too." Ambria puffed out her lower lip. "Tell me how to aetherate!"

I held up my hands. "Let's save the aetherating lessons for later. Right now we need to finish setting the trap."

"Boo." Ambria sighed. "Guess I'd better draw more circles."

"Let me get something to stand on so I can hold up the net," I told Max. "Then you can attach it."

He pointed to a wooden box in the back corner. "That should work."

I gave him the other wand to hold onto while I walked over to pick up the crate. Thankfully, it wasn't very large or heavy and I was able to cradle it in my arms.

"Whoa! You gotta see this." Max stared between the wands at the back wall.

I stopped behind him and looked. One section of the rock wall was covered in lines of strange symbols that weren't visible unless you looked between the wands. "What do they mean?"

Max shook his head. "I'd have to translate. I guess it's a spell to open a hidden passage." He turned to me with a delighted grin. "Maybe there's buried treasure behind the door."

Exciting images of pirates and chests overflowing with gold lit my imagination. I walked to the diagram Ambria had drawn and set the crate in the middle then returned to Max. "You really think there's treasure back there?"

Ambria stamped her foot on the ground and drew our attention. "Why are you two dreaming about buried gold when we've got work to do?" She huffed angrily. "Give it a rest and finish the trap!"

The thud of a door slamming shut echoed down the stairwell.

Mouths open, eyes wide, we looked at each other. Without another word, I hopped onto the crate and pressed the net in place.

"Affixiato," Max whispered in a loud voice after flicking the wand.

The net flattened against the rafters and hung there. I grabbed the crate and moved it out of the way. We waited and waited for another sound from upstairs, but all remained silent. My stomach tightened with anxiety. Had that noise been Brickle, or something else? Another minute passed and still no noise. I crept up the stairs and stopped at the door. I felt warm breath on my neck and turned to see Ambria and Max right behind me.

I motioned them to return downstairs but they shook their heads. Repressing a sigh, I settled for a stern look before tiptoeing across the kitchen and to the hallway. The front door was closed and didn't look as if anyone had battered it open. I heard a faint noise and held my breath. It sounded like someone sniffing. I padded down the hallway to the foyer and the sound became much clearer.

The sniffing stopped. The only sound I heard was my pulse banging in my ears. The railing above me creaked. A massive figure leapt the railing and thudded to the floor with a loud crash. Lips bared in a feral grin, Brickle rose from one knee, all seven feet of him.

"There's my little runaway rats." The huge man cracked his knuckles. "Didn't think you could escape Brickle, did you?"

I was so frightened I couldn't move. Ambria let out a little squeak.

"These are my friends," Max said. "My father is a very important man and he won't let you take them."

"Shut your little pipsqueak mouth, boy." Brickle took a step forward and punched a fist into his hand. "Or else I'll send you home with a broken face."

"Run!" Max shouted.

I wanted to run but my legs felt weak as jelly. I staggered back. Ambria cried out and grabbed my arm tight. Off balance, we both fell to the floor as Brickle advanced.

"Affixiato!" Max shouted.

Brickle's left foot stuck to the floor. He tugged and jerked, muttering dark words. Max grabbed my arm. "Run, you idiots!"

My body finally responded. I jumped up and pulled on Ambria. She responded like a sack of potatoes at first but abruptly screamed and scampered away toward the kitchen.

"Think you've stopped me?" Brickle growled. "Not even close." His facial hair thickened and his chest muscles burst through his shirt. Dark black claws sprouted from his shoes until they split at the seams to accommodate massive paws. Within seconds, Brickle was no more. Instead, a giant wolf stood in his place. Oddly, it still wore a pair of shredded work pants. The beast fell to all fours.

A terrified scream exploded from my throat. Max's cry joined mine and we hurtled down the hallway back toward the basement.

"He's a lycan!" Max shouted.

I looked over my shoulder just as the wolf tore loose a large plank of wooden flooring still magically glued to its foot. With a howl, it lunged forward. The plank caught on the sides of the hallway and jerked the massive beast to a halt. Fangs flashing, saliva drooling from its black lips, it tugged its hind leg hard. The wood splintered and broke. Max and I ran yelling through the kitchen, the sounds of crunching plaster and breaking wood close behind.

We stumbled down the stairs. Max tripped and I fell over him. We rolled down the rocky steps, grunts of pain bursting from us at each impact and landed in a heap at the bottom.

Ambria held a scroll in one hand. "Move!" she shrieked. "Run!"

I rolled and clambered to my feet, turned and pulled Max up after me. We raced to the first set of shelves and grabbed scrolls from the floor.

The wolf bounded through the doorway. Muzzle wide, eyes like burning red coals, it leapt for Ambria. She shouted the strange words from the scroll and thrust her hand toward the wolf as it leapt for her. Green light enveloped the beast. Just as its jaws snapped at her throat, the wolf vanished, and a large green frog smacked off Ambria's face and plopped on the floor. She staggered back. I quickly ran forward and booted the frog toward the diagram she'd drawn.

Instead, it slid across the floor and smacked against the wall to the right. Green light flashed and the wolf reappeared, its head facing the wall. It stumbled, turned this way and that until it found us. It glared malevolently, fury in its eyes. Max chanted and flung a fireball at the wolf. Still a bit stunned from its time as a frog, it didn't move in time and the orange flaming sphere slammed into its hind section. The creature—Brickle—spun from the impact. Smoke rose from its fur and with it the foul odor of burning hair.

Brickle recovered more quickly than I could have imagined, the flames on his hide flickering out. Before I could read the words from my scroll, he leapt. I dashed out of the way just in time. The huge wolf smashed hard into the shelf and toppled it over. I ran toward the stairs while the others scrambled in opposite directions.

The beast's head swung to the side and caught Max hard. He flew through the air and hit the ground with a loud thump before sliding into the wall. My heart seemed to lodge in my throat as I watched the monster prowl toward Max, tongue lolling, a wolfish grin revealing the teeth that would soon tear my injured friend to shreds.

Chapter 18

I didn't know where I found the courage, but I ran up behind Brickle, gripped his tail, and gave it a good hard tug. He spun around. A paw slashed at me, tore through my shirt, and grazed my skin. I fell backward with a shout. Brickle howled and snapped his jaws hard enough to amputate a limb. My muscles turned to water. I couldn't coordinate my legs or make them move fast enough as the wolf raised a massive, padded paw and slashed it toward my chest.

Ambria cried out the words from a scroll. A sheet of ice slammed into the wolf and froze him into place. Brickle's eyes blazed. The ice cracked. It wouldn't hold him for long. I used the slight pause to regain my wits and kicked my feet against the floor to push myself backward. The ice shattered. I threw up my arm as shards pelted me. Unbearable weight crashed onto my chest. I felt hot, rancid breath on my face. I looked up at the jaws of death.

This is it. I'm going to die.

Ambria chanted again. The wolf vanished in a flash, replaced by a large fish with sharp teeth. Mustering all my willpower, I gripped the slimy thing and tossed it toward the diagram. This time, it landed just inside the circle.

Ambria grabbed another scroll and recited the words. "*Daema xhe ceanas incorpiro!*"

A loud boom echoed in the small room. Green flames leapt from the lines in the diagram and a black blob seemed to tear itself from the earth just as the fish morphed back into the wolf. The blob sprouted a dozen or more legs, resembling a huge spider. A horrific screaming face pressed against the inside of the abdomen as if trying to escape.

The wolf backed away, the fury in its eyes morphing to absolute terror. Hackles raised and growling, it tried to escape, but the circle

145

confined it. The black creature spun to face the wolf. With an ear-piercing screech, it lunged. Brickle's claws raked the creature. His jaws clamped onto one of the legs, tearing it loose. Dark ichor spurted from the wound. The two monsters burst into a frenzied melee. Blood sprayed and the wolf yelped pitifully.

Somewhere in the mix, Brickle transformed into humanoid form but with a wolf's head. "What have you done!" he shouted. His snarls turned to yelps and half-human screams. "Help! Help!"

With a hair-raising chitter, the monster's abdomen opened like a giant mouth while its legs thrust the screaming Brickle into the maw. The mouth snapped shut. I heard muffled cries pleading for help. The sides of the blob bulged, its prey punching, kicking, and flailing desperately. The movements abruptly stilled.

A moment later, the monster belched. A jumble of bones fell from its mouth and onto the floor. It turned to face us. This time the humanoid face seemed to be smiling.

"*Zo jakini.*" It screeched with laughter.

Ambria screamed and screamed and screamed. The scroll fell from her limp hands as she backed away from the horror, her throat sounding raw with agony and terror.

I heard retching and looked behind me. Max heaved and threw up on the floor. The scraping of nails on the floor drew my attention back to the monster. It screeched a chitinous leg across the floor while the face inside the abdomen leered at me. The flames in the diagram flickered. The air around the circle shimmered as if the prison was losing power.

With a smile, the creature spoke again. "*Xhe jakini.*"

I knew with certainty it planned to eat us next once it escaped. I raced for the scroll and picked it up. There were more symbols written at the bottom of it. I quickly read the pronunciation instructions and recited them. "*Daema xhe ceanas deincorpiro!*" The monster shrieked. Flames danced in the diagram and thick black tar bubbled within the lines. The liquid spun like a vortex and drew the screeching monster down into the earth.

With a brilliant flash, the tar and the monster vanished. All that remained were the smoking lines in the diagram and an awful stench like rotten eggs—that, and a pile of lonely bones.

Almost as an afterthought, the silver net dropped onto Brickle's remains with a loud rattle.

I dropped the scroll and gaped at the awful sight.

Ambria gripped me in a desperate hug. "Conrad," she sobbed. "What have we done?"

Max, pale-faced, sweat dripping down his forehead, shambled to my side as if he could hardly move. "I know what the green scrolls do now."

My throat felt so tight I could hardly breathe, but I managed to croak a word. "What?"

"They summon demons."

"Demons." The word escaped my throat in a harsh whisper. A flood of images rushed through my mind's eye. I saw people screaming as monsters of pure nightmare devoured them or sucked a smoky substance from their bodies. I saw a woman with a cruel smile on her face as she chanted these creatures into being. I heard one word over and over again—*Daema*.

"I don't know how to break the trance." Max sounded as if he were down a long tunnel far from me.

"Water certainly didn't work," Ambria replied.

The basement blurred into focus. My eyes felt incredibly dry though my hair felt wet. I squeezed shut my eyelids and held them like that for a few seconds.

"Conrad, are you okay?" I felt Ambria's hand touch my forehead. "You just stood there for nearly fifteen minutes. We thought you'd gone into shock."

"I almost went into shock," Max said. "I've never summoned a demon."

"I'm the one who summoned it." Ambria's voice cracked. "Does that mean I'm cursed?"

"Of course not." Max sounded exasperated. "I know my parents have summoned demons plenty of times and they're not cursed."

I cracked open my eyelids and blinked a few times. "I think my parents used demons to kill people."

"How would you know?" Max asked.

Blinking out the dryness in my eyes, I shook my head. "When I was in the trance, I saw all these visions of them doing just that."

"How could you see visions of things when you weren't even alive?"

My gaze flicked to the pile of bones and I quickly looked away. "I don't know. Maybe I saw it when I was younger. I've seen a lot of strange stuff lately." I told them about the frightening nightmare with the shadowy creature in my bedroom and how it seemed to know the Goodleighs had arrived at our doorstep. I told them how I seemed to know things someone my age shouldn't know, like the scientific classifications of animals. "It also explains how I was able to fly that broom so well without any practice."

Ambria looked at me as if I might be crazy.

Max, however, pursed his lips and nodded matter-of-factly. "It sounds like someone put a spell on you." He put a hand over his stomach. "Let's talk about it over food. I'm starving."

"Are you serious?" Ambria put a hand over her mouth. "I completely lost my appetite. The thought of eating makes me queasy."

"I'm a growing lad," Max said. "I need to eat, demons or not."

I wasn't all that hungry, but couldn't stand to be in this place a moment longer. "Let me get changed."

Ambria grabbed my shirt and looked at the torn fabric. She lifted it, revealing thin red lines where the wolf's claws had grazed me. "Brickle was a werewolf, wasn't he?"

Max nodded. "We call them lycans."

"Did he infect Conrad? Will he turn into a werewolf at the next full moon?"

He burst into laughter. "I don't know where you got that idea. Being a lycan isn't contagious. You're either born that way, or you have to convince an alpha wolf to turn you."

"So he's not going to howl at the moon?" Ambria looked a little disappointed.

"No, but he might start lifting his leg to pee."

Max guffawed. Ambria belatedly giggled. I wanted to laugh, but I felt so grim and sad after the visions of people who might have been my parents killing people with demons. They'd been awful people. Now I'd helped kill someone with a demon. That made me just as bad as my parents.

After Ambria and I cleaned and changed clothes, we went to Chicken Little for a late breakfast and sat on the second floor near the

148

door to the balcony. By then, I'd somewhat recovered my appetite. Even Ambria ordered biscuits and tea. As we ate, she told Max about the startling discovery of her parents.

He stopped in the middle of chewing a mouthful of pancakes. "You're the long-lost daughter of Cyphanis Rax?"

She gave him a disapproving look. "Don't talk with your mouth full, Max. It's impolite."

He took a gulp of orange juice and repeated his question.

"Yes, silly. I'm Ambria Rax."

Max grimaced and looked around at the crowded restaurant. A man and woman at a nearby table regarded us with strange looks.

"Keep your voice down," Max hissed. "You really don't want everyone knowing you're related to Cyphanis."

Ambria's forehead pinched with worry. "Oh, I suppose you're right." She dropped her biscuit and buried her face in her hands. "Why did our parents have to be such gruesome people?"

I rubbed a hand on her back, hoping it might comfort her. Instead, she started sobbing softly.

A man in worn gray robes walked up to our table. "Maxwell Tiberius." He said the name like an accusation.

Max looked up at him. "Who are you?"

"Wigston Hodges." The man scratched his scruffy beard and gave a mirthless laugh. "Figures you wouldn't recognize me, boy. When Cyphanis was in charge and forced some of us to leave Queens Gate, your father stole my family heirlooms."

"Oh." Max tilted his head slightly. "Now I remember you. You blamed my father for a lot of stuff, but you never proved anything."

The man snarled and leaned forward. "He was one of Rax's toads, you little rat. Everyone knows he and his cronies robbed me and others blind because we didn't support him."

Max made a face. "Your breath stinks, and you look drunk. Why don't you leave me alone?"

The man raised his fist into the air and shouted, "Your father left me destitute!"

Ambria had stopped crying and stared at the man. I noticed most of the other patrons watching the spectacle. Some of them gave Max unkind looks and grumbled. Not a one of them offered to help.

"There's the old coot!" someone shouted from across the room. Two older boys with white-blond hair dashed across the room. It took me only a second to realize they were identical twins. Their eyes settled on Max.

One spoke. "Well, little brother, it looks like old man Wigston was about to throw you over the balcony."

Max made a face. "No he wasn't."

"I can and I will!" Wigston shouted. He swung a clumsy fist at the first twin and missed by a wide margin.

The second boy laughed and booted Wigston in the backside. The older man plowed into our table. Food flew everywhere. Ambria shrieked. I jumped back and tripped over my chair.

"Get him Rhys!" shouted the second boy.

The first boy took out a wand, waved it in a pattern, and said, "*Impellatus!*"

Wigston doubled over with a loud "Oof!" He stumbled out of the door and flipped backward over the balcony railing.

"*Constrictus,*" said the second boy, flicking the wand at Wigston. The iron railing wrapped around the old man's foot a split instant before he plunged to the hard cobblestones below.

The boys chortled and performed an elaborate handshake.

Max stood and gave them a horrified look. "What have you done?"

"Saved your hide, you little mouse." Rhys pinched Max hard on the cheek. "You're lucky Devon and I saw that piece of garbage skulking around here."

"Help!" Wigston called as he vainly tried to pull himself up. "Please, someone."

The people on the second floor looked toward the balcony, but not a one of them made a move to aid the old man.

Rhys and Devon crossed their arms and smirked at the other patrons.

"Nobody wants to help the little old man?" Rhys said in a condescending tone.

"You people are just awful," Devon added. "I'm glad *I* don't need your help."

"Cowards." Rhys turned to Max and shoved him hard into the wall. "So this is what you've been up to." He looked at Ambria and me. "I guess you found some little friends."

Max strained against the older boy's grip, but couldn't move. "Yeah, so what?"

Devon put on a hurt face. "We feel like you're avoiding us, little brother. Your brothers and sisters miss you."

"Well, I don't miss you." Max's face turned red as he struggled.

Rhys released him and turned to me, hand extended. "I'm Rhys. Pleased to meet you."

I wasn't sure how to respond, but shook his hand anyway, flinching in anticipation of the older boy squeezing my hand too hard or doing something equally mean. "I'm Conrad."

He shook it politely and turned to Ambria. "Pleased to meet you, milady." He took her hand and kissed the top. "Please do let us know if our little brother causes you any trouble."

Devon followed Rhys's example, remaining every bit as polite. "Max is very troubled," he said. "Whatever you do, don't believe a word from his lying mouth."

The entire time this went on, Wigston pleaded for help until his voice grew hoarse. The two boys ignored him while the other patrons returned to their meals.

"Well, we must be going," Rhys said. "We're racing today."

Max's angry expression softened. "Really? Where?"

"Why should you care?" Rhys gave us a cool look. "You have new friends, Max. Go play dolls with them."

Max frowned but said nothing more. His brothers smirked. Though they both looked like copies of each other, I noticed Rhys had a freckle on his right cheek while Devon had one on his left. A vision flashed through my head and for a brief instant, I saw little twin toddlers looking up at me while a lovely woman with long, blonde hair smiled down at them. The image faded just as Rhys and Devon entered the stairwell and left.

"I don't like your brothers," Ambria said. "Not one little bit."

"At least they're not as bad as my sisters." Max shuddered. "Well, I guess we'll have to order more food."

"More food?" Ambria put her hands on her hips. "You're not getting another bite until you rescue that poor man from the balcony."

"I don't know how," Max said in a whining voice.

I looked at poor Wigston and wondered if anyone else would free him. I certainly didn't know how to unbend the metal railing wrapped around his ankle. I realized with a start that the man's boot was slowly slipping off his foot. If we didn't do something, he'd fall headfirst to the street.

"Stop bickering," I said to Ambria and Max as they argued about Wigston. "He's going to fall."

"What?" Max rushed to the balcony. "I don't know if I can hold him up."

"Maybe we both can." I looked down and saw Wigston's robe hanging over the man's face like an upside down dress, flashing striped boxer shorts and a pale gray-haired torso. While it looked rather comical, I knew now wasn't the time to laugh.

"Get away from that man," said an imperious voice.

I turned and saw a thin man with long, black hair glaring at us. He wore black robes and a dour look on his face.

"But he's about to fall," I protested.

The man took out a wand and waved it in a tight, concise pattern. Without saying a word, he flicked his wand. The metal railing straightened and Wigston fell with a loud scream.

Chapter 19

Ambria cried out and rushed to the railing. Max and I looked over just as Wigston thudded into the center of a huge cushion sitting below. Feathers flew in all direction and the man lay motionless. A moment later, he groaned and sat up.

I turned back to the man in black. "Where did that cushion come from?"

"I conjured it," the man said, lip rising in a sneer. He turned his cold, gray eyes to Max. "Your brothers think they can do whatever they wish, boy." He leaned closer to Max. "Maybe you do too."

"No, sir," Max said in a quiet voice.

The man straightened. "One day your parents won't be around to protect you." A smile curled his lips. "What a wonderful day that will be." He turned and left.

Ambria slumped against the railing and wiped tears from her eyes. "I think I'm done for the day." She pressed a hand to her chest. "My heart can't take more excitement, Conrad."

I sat down next to her and nodded. "I know what you mean." I looked up at Max. "Who was that fellow?"

Max found a plate of biscuits that had miraculously survived the incident and began buttering one. "That's Professor Gideon Grace." He tore into the bread and sighed as if it were the best food he'd had all day. "He doesn't like my family one bit."

Ambria gave him a hard look. "I thought your last name was Brimble."

Max hardly paused as he ate. "Nah. I just told you that because I didn't want you to know my real last name is Tiberius."

"And why not?" Her voice rose sharply.

He looked wistful. "You never heard of my family because you were raised like noms, but I didn't know that." Max swallowed. "I was afraid you might not be my friends if you knew my real last name."

Ambria sniffed. "Now that I know you're a big liar, maybe I won't be your friend anymore."

He looked down. "I didn't want to lie, but I was afraid you wouldn't give me a chance."

She threw up her hands. "Will you stop eating that stupid biscuit so we can leave?"

Max looked up, hope in his eyes. "Does that mean you're still my friend?"

Ambria rolled her eyes. "Yes. But you'd better not lie to us again."

I certainly understood why Max had lied to us. Wigston had attacked him just because of something his father might have done long ago. Professor Grace's disdain for Max had only underscored how difficult life was on my new friend.

"I'm still your friend too, Max." I stood up.

A man in dark blue robes hesitantly approached the table. Wringing his hands, he surveyed at the mess. "Mr. Tiberius, I'm so sorry about what happened. On behalf of Chicken Little, please accept my sincerest apologies. I'll make sure to ban Wigston from the restaurant from now on."

Max puffed up a little. "That man attacked me and my friends. Look what he did to our breakfast."

"I'll have a new meal prepared at once," the man said. "Let me get the servers to fix your table as well."

I almost protested, but my stomach rumbled. I hadn't really had a chance to eat before the interruption. I saw Ambria's face clouding with anger and grabbed her arm to ward off an explosion. She looked at me, eyebrows pinched together.

"That will be satisfactory," Max said.

The man bowed and left.

"How could you let him apologize for something your brothers did?" Ambria hissed.

"Wigston probably would've attacked me anyway." Max shrugged. "Besides, I'm starving."

Ambria's shoulders stiffened and her face turned pink. "Conrad, I can't believe you're going along with this."

I looked away. "Sorry, but I'm really hungry too."

She let out an exasperated groan. "Fine. You two idiots go ahead and eat. I'm going back to the house."

Before we could protest, she stormed away and down the stairs. I looked over the balcony and watched her fly away on the broom. I also noted the large feather cushion was gone along with Wigston Hodges.

"Girls are so hard to please," Max said.

"Yeah." I didn't know enough about girls to construct an educated opinion. Close as Ambria and I had grown over the past couple of days, I still hardly knew her. It was difficult to believe we'd only spoken a few times before escaping from the orphanage. "She's been through a lot. I think she's having a hard time adjusting."

Max watched as two servers finished cleaning the floor and set the table and chairs upright. "I suppose anyone who was raised like a nom would have that sort of problem if they moved to a place where magic is normal."

"Or a place where a giant killer werewolf is eaten by a black spider demon."

He shivered and turned to me. "This morning has definitely been *pretty* crazy."

I lifted an eyebrow. "Crazy? It's been absolutely insane, Max."

"Oh, yeah. I guess since you've never seen lycans or demons, it would've been pretty shocking."

Max was excellent at understatement, or else he'd seen so many bizarre things that they didn't bother him as much as they should. Fresh food arrived. Max and I sat down and dug in. Despite the incredible amount of pancakes on my plate, I managed to eat most of them along with all the bacon.

Max polished off his French toast and started on an omelet. I sat back and tried to clear my mind of the day's events. It was impossible.

The more I thought about Brickle, the more worried I became. How long would the Goodleighs wait before coming to investigate his disappearance? What would we do when they came?

Max dropped his fork and burped. "You look scared, Conrad."

"I'm worried about what comes next when the Goodleighs search for Brickle."

"We'll handle them the same way."

I flicked my eyes his way. "With a demon?"

Max shrugged. "If we have to. At least that way they won't bother you anymore."

It also meant we could free the rest of the orphans. My heart grew heavy as lead and I felt sick to my stomach. I was responsible for two deaths in two days. Ambria hadn't said a word about it, but I'd killed the older brother she'd never known. *We're murderers.* A lump grew in my throat.

A server came by the table. "We're very sorry for the disruption earlier." She put down the bill and a brown bag. "We hope you'll enjoy these complimentary fairy cakes." She offered us an uneasy smile and left.

"Brilliant," Max said. He showed me the bill. The balance was scratched out with the word *Complimentary*. "We got to eat free!"

I smiled. "Spectacular."

"I guess it's like a belated birthday gift." Max chuckled. "Happy birthday, Conrad."

"Happy birthday, Conrad!" Mum puts a cake in front of me.

I'm so scared for her, I can hardly breathe. I know with certainty, she'll die soon, just like the others. But it's my birthday and she's still alive.

Cora ruffles my hair. "Blow out the candles, son."

I take in a deep breath and release it, snuffing all the candles.

"Yay!" She claps her hands. "Did you make a wish?"

"Yes." I wished for her to be my mother forever.

She hands me a fork. "Let's eat."

I grab her hand and hold it to my chest. "I love you, Mum."

She sits next to me, tears welling in her eyes. "You've never told me that before."

I can't tell her it's because I know she'll go away like everyone else. But no matter how I try not to love her, I can't help myself. She is the only person in this world who's cared for me.

"I love you too, son." She hugs me and kisses the top of my head.

156

Max and I walked downstairs and got our brooms. My guilty conscience seemed to grow heavier with every step. I wanted to punish the Goodleighs for what they'd done to us and other children, but I didn't want to kill them, especially not with a demon. *I'm not a murderer. The other deaths were accidents.* That rationalization seemed to lighten my conscience a fraction.

Max stuck his broom in a corner of the foyer next to Ambria's. I took my broom and the bag of fairy cakes up to my room since I wasn't hungry enough to eat them right away and then came back downstairs. We heard noises from the basement and went downstairs to find Ambria cleaning up the basement, though she stayed well away from Brickle's bones.

"Pick those up," she said in a terse voice the minute we arrived.

For some reason, the bones didn't disgust me. I'd helped Brickle butcher animals on the farm many times. Ironically, it had prepared me for something so awful as this. I moved the chain net, found a box of plastic bags on one of the shelves, and put the bones inside it. I left the bags on the curb where we'd put the other trash the day before. As Max promised, the other rubbish was gone.

Back in the basement, I saw Max holding up the wands and peering at the wall with the symbols.

"Can I hold your arcphone?" he asked.

I took it out and handed it to him. "Do you have one?"

"I used to, but my brothers took it." He handed me the wands. "Hold them up."

I did so. Max positioned the phone between the wands. "Phone, scan the wall and translate."

The phone traced the wall with a wide beam of light. "The inscription reads, 'My enemies will feed the sins of the past.'"

Max frowned. "How do we open the door?"

"Unknown."

He gave me back the phone and took the wands. Standing a foot from the wall, he held the wands to either side of the hidden door and moved them up and down. "I think that little arrow symbol might open it."

Ambria stormed down the stairs. "What are you two doing? I need help cleaning upstairs."

"We're solving a mystery," Max said. "Aren't you the least bit curious about what's behind this wall?"

She crossed her arms and looked at the symbols. "A little, I suppose."

"Why don't you keep looking at it?" I told Max. "I need to speak with Ambria."

He raised an eyebrow. "Sure."

I walked over to Ambria. "Can we go upstairs?"

"Is something wrong?" she asked.

I nodded. "Yes."

Her eyes grew worried. "It's the Goodleighs, right? They'll come find out what happened to Brickle."

"That's part of it." I motioned toward the stairs. "But there's more."

Ambria jogged up the stairs ahead of me.

Once we reached the top, I found it very difficult to speak. "I—I have to apologize."

"For what?" She looked genuinely confused.

"Ambria, I killed Levi—your brother and we never talked about it once we found out who your parents were."

Her face fell. "You didn't know he was my brother and neither did I. He was a stranger to me."

"Does that matter?" I squeezed shut my eyes. "I *killed* him."

She gripped my hand painfully tight. "Of course it matters, Conrad. You didn't mean to kill him, but he certainly wanted you dead." She kissed my cheek. "It was self-defense."

I looked down. "It still feels like murder."

"Conrad, look at me."

I forced my gaze to meet hers.

"I don't blame you for what happened, just as I hope you don't blame me for what happened to Brickle."

"None of us knew that scroll summoned a demon."

"You saved my life. You saved Max from Brickle." She smiled. "You are a *good* person, Conrad."

I hear Mum crying through her closed bedroom door and go inside.

"Why are you crying?" I ask.

"I can't tell you, Conrad." Cora wipes her face with a tissue and manages a smile. "Why are you still awake, sweetie?"

"Please tell me why you're sad." I squeeze her hand. "Please!" I want to make her feel better.

"I'm a bad person, son." She looks away. "I'm awful."

I think back to the night with Bill and, despite my dull wits, realize how he ended up at the bottom of the stairs. "Did you push Bill?"

Her eyes widen and fill with more tears. Like a dam bursting, she collapses on the bed and sobs. I lie next to her, wishing I could do something to make her feel better.

"You're a good person, Mum."

Cora stops crying and looks up at me. "How can you say that?"

"Good people sometimes have to do bad things." I smile.

She smiles back. "You're the best son a mother could wish for."

"You're a good person too, Ambria."

Her cheeks turned pink. "I'm very glad you feel that way, Conrad." Her lips flattened, though her eyes still smiled. "Now, let's get ready for the Goodleighs. This time, I want to be better prepared."

"No more demons?"

She laughed. "The Goodleighs deserve to be eaten by a demon, but I'd rather not see something so horrible again."

"Me either." I walked into the hallway. The destruction left by Brickle stopped me dead in my tracks.

The wolf had scattered and shredded the stacked newspapers all down the hallway. Slats protruded from the plaster walls like broken ribs. White dust covered everything.

Ambria sighed. "It'll take us months to clean this mess."

It would likely be only a matter of days before the Goodleighs came to investigate Brickle's disappearance. There was no way we could restore the hallway in such a short period of time. Then again, why did we need to clean it at all? "We should leave it looking this way."

"Are you really so lazy?"

"Of course not." I kicked a stray bit of plaster. "The Goodleighs will think Brickle tore this place apart looking for us. If we clean it, they'll be suspicious."

Ambria pursed her lips, looking from me to the debris. Finally, she nodded. "I suppose you're right. How long do you think it will be before the Goodleighs come?"

"A few days."

"I got it!" Max shouted from downstairs. "I opened the door!"

Ambria and I exchanged a glance and rushed downstairs. Sure enough, Max stood in front of a dark hole in the wall. We ran over to join him.

"What's inside?" I asked.

He shrugged. "I don't have a light."

A rumbling noise echoed from somewhere down the tunnel. Ambria shivered and backed away from the opening. "We shouldn't go in there. There's no telling what's inside."

"Aw, you worry too much." Max dug through some items from the fallen shelf and held up a white marble. "A glowball." He flicked it into the air. The tiny ball blazed into light and floated over our heads. Max headed toward the dark passage with the glowball hovering over a few feet above and in front of him.

Despite the light source, Ambria didn't look convinced. "If you're stupid enough to go first, Max, then I'll wait right here."

He stuck out his tongue. "It's called being brave, not stupid."

"It's only called being brave if you don't get yourself killed." She backed away another step. "Well, go on." Ambria motioned toward the door. "Let's find out whether you're brave or stupid."

Max laughed. "Fine." He entered the door and vanished around a corner.

Just as I went to follow him, he began screaming horrifically.

Ambria cried out. "Oh, no! Max! Save him, Conrad!"

I ran toward the opening and nearly plowed into Max as he came back around the corner, laughing hysterically. "I really got you good."

Red-faced, Ambria marched over to him and slapped him on the chest. "Max, I will kill you myself if you do that again."

Still laughing, he held up his hands to defend himself. "I just couldn't resist."

"What's in there?" I asked.

"Just a tunnel." He shrugged. "I couldn't see very far inside."

"We should be preparing for the Goodleighs, not exploring dangerous tunnels," Ambria said.

"Why do you think it's dangerous?" Max asked.

She stared at him for a moment before answering. "The sign on the door telling us to beware the sins of the past makes it pretty obvious, wouldn't you say?"

"He probably stole a lot of money and stashed it there," Max said. "Stealing is a sin."

A part of me agreed with Ambria. The tunnel might lead somewhere dangerous and exploring it would take time we needed to set traps for the Goodleighs. On the other hand, why had Levi hidden this door? Perhaps he'd stored powerful magical weapons inside— weapons we could use against the Goodleighs. Admittedly, I was also very curious to take a look. "I think we should explore it."

"Really, Conrad?" Ambria gave me a disgusted look. She released a long sigh. "Fine, let's go." She retrieved a few scrolls from the floor. "I'll bring these just in case."

"Not a bad idea," Max said as he scooped up a few of his own.

I took a couple of offensive spells, several hexes and motioned to Max. "Lead the way."

He nodded and went back into the passage.

Stepping through the hole, a tall wide corridor to the right greeted me. The stone wall separating this passage and the basement was only a few inches thick. The path sloped down at a gentle angle. We followed the tunnel for several minutes before reaching a dead end.

"Well that's disappointing," Max said as he looked around. "So much for your dangerous tunnel theory."

"Maybe a rock will fall on your head," Ambria said.

"You'd like that wouldn't you?" He blew out a breath. "I can't believe there's nothing down here."

I might have believed my eyes, but the rumbling noise I'd heard earlier had grown steadily louder. "What do you suppose that is?" I asked.

"What is what?" Max asked.

"That noise."

Everyone went silent for a moment.

"It's just air," Ambria said.

"Or maybe noise from the city above," Max added.

I didn't know how far we were below the surface, but it didn't seem likely noise from the city would sound like that down here. I pressed my ear to the wall at the end of the tunnel and listened. A slight vibration in the stone tingled against my skin and the noise definitely seemed louder. My gaze settled on markings on the wall perpendicular to this one.

I motioned the glowball in that direction. As it drew closer, it revealed words burnt into the surface of the rock. There was also a small hole to the left. I almost tested it, but quickly changed my mind. For all I knew, something might live inside it.

Ambria peered at the words. "Yohan Picadoris, Clive Burwell, Anthony Wiener." She looked back at us. "It's a list of names."

I pointed out slashes in some of the names. "Some of them are crossed out."

"I recognize some of those names," Max said. "They were supposedly allied with the Overlord and then flip-flopped after he was dead. My father was friends with a few."

"Look at the wall between the wands," I told Max. "Maybe there's another hidden entrance. Maybe Levi kidnapped the crossed-out people and imprisoned them down here."

"You think so?" He took out the wands and looked around, but the wall looked just as blank as before. "Nope." Max turned toward the other walls, but found nothing there.

Ambria made a clicking sound with her tongue. "Let me hold the straight wand."

He gave it to her. She took it to the hole next to the names and pushed it in just as I had on the secret door to the basement. The wand flashed white and something metal clanked. The wall slid to the side with a loud grating noise. The rumble I'd noticed earlier turned into a much more distinct sound—one that I immediately recognized without layers of stone muffling it.

It was the sound of something breathing.

Chapter 20

Max stepped into the new area and motioned forward. The glowball rose higher and drifted inside a large open area. A giant silver bolt anchored an equally massive chain in the rock floor. The glowball drifted higher, growing brighter as it did until it penetrated the darkness beyond the chain.

A giant mound of shiny green skin reflected the light.

Ambria gasped. Max stumbled backwards. I felt rooted to the ground with fear.

The skin quivered as if it sensed the light. Two giant legs and arms unfolded from the mound. Back facing us, the creature rose, chain clinking. I wanted to turn and run as quickly as I could, but couldn't make my legs respond.

"What is that thing?" Ambria screamed.

The creature spun. Standing at least ten feet tall, it might have looked like a giant man with green skin except for its awful frog head. Bulbous parietal eyes blinked. The skin beneath the neck bulged like a balloon, quickly contracted, and a loud croak erupted from the mouth.

Beautiful. A sense of pride swelled my chest. *Wait, why am I proud?* I shook my head and the feeling vanished.

"It's a frog ogre—a frogre!" Max shouted, pronouncing the word with a long O.

I see large glass tanks all around me. Horrific half-formed creatures float within. Some are humanoid. I see elephant fetuses, and creatures that look half-human and half-beast. I turn and look at a lovely woman standing by my side. She smiles. "Soon, my love. Soon."

The vision flickered away, replaced by the chained monstrosity and a piercing pain in my head. The frogre croaked and lunged toward

163

us. The chain snapped taut, keeping the creature at bay even as hands the size of my torso grasped for us.

Ambria fell backward though the frogre couldn't possibly reach her from twenty feet away. I helped her up.

"We're safe," I told her.

"What if the chain snaps?"

"That's silver laced with diamond fiber," Max said. "No way it can escape."

Eyes bugging, Ambria made a retching sound.

At first, I thought the sight of this awful hybrid made her sick to her stomach, but then I followed her gaze to items scattered on the floor behind the frogre. I saw a human skull. Beyond it were items of clothing and more bones.

Max gagged. "I think Levi fed humans to this thing."

"His enemies," I said in a horrified voice.

"What a monster." Ambria shuddered. "My brother was beyond mental."

The frogre croaked and jerked at the end of its chain again and again until dark blood welled beneath the collar.

Max seemed to overcome some of his earlier fear and stepped closer to the monster. "Come and get me, you ugly thing." He picked up a rock and threw it.

The rock bounced off the creature's face. In a heartbeat, the frogre lunged toward Max, but fell far short of its goal.

"Stop teasing it," Ambria said.

"Why?" Max asked. "This is one of those evil monsters the Overlord made to fight his war. We should find a way to kill it."

"It's just a mindless creature," Ambria said. "It can't help being what it is. Didn't you say most of his monsters were imprisoned in the Dark Forest? Maybe we could find a way to get it there."

Max rolled his eyes. "Yeah. How are we supposed to do that?" He stepped closer to the monster, picked up another rock, and threw it hard. It hit the frogre in the snout.

Something long and pink flashed through the air. Max howled as the frogre's tongue snatched him by a leg and dragged him into the frogre's open maw.

It happened so fast, I almost couldn't believe it.

Ambria cried out.

Max's howl of surprise turned to an agonizing scream as his feet plunged into the monster's mouth. He grabbed the edge of the frog mouth and held on for dear life. Somehow, I had the presence of mind to remember the scrolls I'd brought along. Grabbing the first one from my pocket, I unrolled it and cast a hex at the frogre.

The huge frog-man beast vanished, replaced by a furry brown bunny sitting inside the metal collar. Max flopped to the ground next to the rabbit. The bunny hopped toward him. Yelping like a hurt dog, Max scrambled to his feet and ran toward us, the bunny hopping behind him.

"Oh my god, it's free!" Ambria shouted.

"Kill it!" Max shouted. "Kill it now!"

Ambria stared at the small animal as it hopped our way, cute little nose wiggling. "But it's just a little bunny. I can't do it."

I took out an offensive scroll but couldn't find the willpower to burn the rabbit to a cinder.

"Well, if we're not going to kill it"—Ambria gripped my arm—"Run for your lives!"

I abruptly remembered the time limit on the hex just as it expired. The brown rabbit exploded back into the lumbering form of the frogre. If the monster hadn't been disoriented from the abrupt change in physiology, it probably could have killed one of us instantly. Instead, it staggered to the side and fell over the pile of bones.

We turned and fled. The thud of giant feet sounded behind us seconds later. We raced through the small doorway into the basement. The frogre croaked and rammed into the stone frame. Its body was too broad to fit, though if it had half a brain it might have turned sideways to squeeze in. It pounded against the wall over and over again. Cracks ran through the rock and the basement ceiling began to crumble.

Ambria grabbed Max and me by the arms. "Don't stop running, you idiots!"

The frogre's tongue lashed out, barely missing me and sticking to the shelves right next to us. The shelf fell over with a crash. Bottled potions scattered across the floor. Miraculously, only one of them broke, sending foul-smelling, black smoke into the air. The wooden shelves turned black and began to crumble the instant the smoke touched it. As the smoke rose into the support beams, they too began to disintegrate.

"It's a rot potion," Max said. "This place is going to fall apart."

I backed toward the stairs and stumbled over several glass vials that had fallen in my path. I noticed the bottle labeled *Iocaine*. The image of a bald man choking to death flashed before my eyes. Without knowing why, I reached down and grabbed the potion before turning and running after my friends who were already at the bottom of the stairs.

Wooden joists groaned and creaked as support beams affected by the rot potion disintegrated. The kitchen dropped into the basement with a roar. The hallway fell apart all around us as the floor beams bearing the structural weight collapsed.

"Grab the stair rail!" I shouted.

We leapt for the railing and grabbed it as the floor beneath us plummeted into the basement sending a cloud of dust and old newspapers into the air. A loud croak sounded below us and a pink tongue shot from the dust, narrowly missing my backside. Adrenalin and fear boosted my strength. I pulled myself over the railing, grabbed Ambria's arms, and pulled her over after me. Max shouted in a panicked voice and I quickly saw why—the frogre's tongue had latched around his shoe.

"Help me," I told Ambria.

Together, we pulled on Max's hands but were unable to free him. The frogre's tongue was too strong and sticky. I tried to kick the tongue, but my foot wouldn't fit through the balustrade.

Ambria pushed me to the side. "Don't be stupid, Conrad." She reached between the balusters and untied Max's shoe then twisted it off. His shoe vanished with a loud *thwap!*

White-faced and sweating profusely, Max wriggled over the railing and onto the stairs. Just then, the stairs began to shake. I looked toward the front door, but the foyer dropped into the basement with a deafening crash leaving a huge gap we couldn't possibly leap. We had nowhere to go but up. When the house collapsed, we'd have nowhere to go but down.

We ran into my room. I tugged open a window and looked down. The cobblestone street seemed a very long way down and probably was, considering the bottom floor of the row house had such a high ceiling. Jumping was an option, but we'd likely break our legs or worse.

"Your broom, Conrad." Ambria grabbed the broom and thrust it into my hands. "We can all ride it."

Max shook his head. "No way could it support more than one person. It'd drop like a rock."

"Maybe we can take it one at a time and send the broom back up."

Once again, Max shook his head. "It just won't work, at least not fast enough to save everyone."

Mind racing, I came up with several options and discarded them immediately. We didn't have a rope, and the bed sheets wouldn't be long enough to reach the ground. We might be able to tie the bed sheets onto the broom so someone could lower themselves several feet toward the ground and drop. Then we could use the bed sheet to pull the broom back to the window for the next person.

I was about to mention that possibility when the house shook so violently, I knew we had only seconds to escape. My eyes settled on the brown bag I'd brought up earlier and inspiration struck. I grabbed the bag and handed everyone a fairy cake. "Eat these fast!"

"Conrad this is hardly the time to—oof!" Ambria's sentence cut off as I stuffed the cupcake into her mouth.

Max's eyes widened. "It's got fairy mushrooms. Brilliant!" He swallowed his in one gulp.

I crammed one into my mouth and chewed like a madman. The floor shook. The walls crumbled and fell. We'd run out of time. I jumped onto the broom and motioned the others on after me. Ambria gripped me tight and Max squeezed on behind her. The broom sagged toward the floor. The hardwoods cracked down the middle, shooting splinters all through the air. My arm stung as the slivers found my skin. Suddenly, my insides felt light and fluffy.

The floor dropped. Ambria shrieked. Max yelped. The broom sank, slowed, and began to gain altitude. With a horrific groan, the ceiling split down the middle and the entire room cracked open like an egg. The remaining walls fell away from us. Dust and bits of rubble rained on my head.

We broke into violent coughing fits. When the air cleared a few seconds later, there was nothing left of the house except a large mound of rubble filling what had once been the basement. The adjacent row houses were missing the walls that had joined them to this house, leaving them open to the elements.

"Well, at least the frogre is dead," Max said with a sigh of relief.

Ambria squeezed my waist. "It must be buried alive."

"Buried alive," I whispered, thinking it was a horrible fate for anyone, even a frog-ogre hybrid.

Max chortled. "Brilliant idea with the fairy cakes."

"It was very clever," Ambria said. "For a boy."

Despite the weight-reducing effect of the fairy mushrooms inside the cupcakes, the broom struggled to maintain altitude.

"I don't think there's enough mushrooms in the cupcakes to last long," Max said. "We'd better land."

I directed the broom toward a clear section of street. People peered from windows or stood in the street staring as the few standing walls in Levi Rax's house crumbled.

A giant green fist burst through the rubble. People screamed and scattered. Another hand plowed free of the rubble and gripped the edge of the road. Broken wood and stone exploded like shrapnel as the frogre burst from the wreckage. Its froggy face looked calm as ever, but its feet stomped the cobblestones hard enough to crack them. The skin beneath its throat bulged like a huge balloon, constricted, and unleashed a loud screeching croak that made my hair stand on end.

The frogre spun our way, eyes widening as it recognized its prey. *Ribbit!*

Ambria's arms tightened around my waist. "Get us out of here, Conrad."

I spun the broom away from the frogre and urged it to top speed. A pink tongue lashed out, cracking the air like a whip and narrowly missing us. The broom grew more sluggish and sagged toward the ground with every passing second as the fairy mushrooms wore off. We outpaced the enraged frogre chasing us down the street, but for how long?

People scattered before us, diving into shops and fleeing in all directions.

"It's a frogre!" someone shouted.

A woman's voice rang out. "A frogre is on the loose!"

"Dear god, what is that thing?"

"Let me try a spell on it," Max said. He chanted. I looked back as he thrust out his arm. A fireball burst from his palm and smacked into the frogre's face. The creature croaked. Its skin looked slightly blackened, but otherwise undamaged.

"Why didn't it hurt it?" Ambria asked.

"It has really tough skin." Max shook his head. "I don't think we can kill it with these spells."

"We've got to find somewhere safe to hide," I said. "We're getting too heavy for the broom."

"Oh, man," Max groaned. "I think Chicken Little skimped on the mushrooms for the cupcakes."

"It's no wonder they were complimentary," I said.

We were a couple of blocks ahead of the frogre, but the broom had slowed enough that the monster was gaining. A plaza opened up before us, the familiar form of the Copper Goose just across the way. People bustled about, doing their daily business, and eating at the various restaurants located around the square. The frogre thudded into the plaza and shattered the calm in a heartbeat.

Men, women, and children cried out and ran for their lives. An old man, a full head taller than the other people around him, remained standing in the sea of chaos. His wrinkled face remained calm. He looked from us to the frogre, as if assessing the situation, then produced a thick wooden rod and shook it. The rod flicked out to a long crooked staff with a large shimmering stone cradled by the wood at the top.

He slammed the staff on the ground, shouted a word, and aimed at the frogre. Jagged bolts of lightning flashed out at the beast. The frogre unleashed a high-pitched squeal and faltered. Max and Ambria cheered. But the monster pushed against the crackling energy like someone fighting a stiff wind. The spell looped back on itself and hit the tall man's staff. He jerked backward, long silvery hair flying free from beneath a knitted cap.

My friend's cheers turned to cries of despair.

"He can't kill it," Max said. "We're doomed."

"Shut up, Max," Ambria commanded. "You're not helping anyone with that attitude."

"Should I be happy that we're about to be eaten?"

169

The broom chose that moment to dive toward the ground as the fairy mushrooms wore off and our combined weight overwhelmed its ability to stay aloft. We hit the ground with loud grunts. The broom broke in half on impact. I rolled on the hard cobblestones and came to rest on my back at the tall man's feet. A big lump in my pocket pressed against my backside.

He looked down at me. "I do so hate fighting frogres. Terrible, terrible nuisances." He reached down and tugged me to my feet.

I ran to Ambria and helped her up while Max clambered upright. Ambria still had several scrolls stuffed into her pockets, but I didn't think they'd do any good. I reached into my back pocket and withdrew the iocaine potion. I didn't know what it did, but we were out of options.

I uncorked the bottle and ran toward the frogre as it closed to within striking distance with its tongue. Just on cue, the pink tongue lashed out for me. I threw the bottle and ducked. The tongue latched onto the bottle and whip-cracked back into the frogre's mouth. Unsatisfied with this meager offering, it whipped its tongue toward me. I tried to run, but it was too late.

The sticky pink flesh wrapped around my foot and dragged me toward my doom.

Chapter 21

I gripped a jutting cobblestone and held on for dear life. The frogre's tongue was so powerful that the force threatened to pull off my leg or my arms, whichever gave out first.

Ambria shouted and ran toward me. "Don't give up, Conrad!" She grabbed my arm and pulled.

Max raced over and helped her. "We'll save you!"

The old man shot another spell at the monster's tongue. The frogre squealed, but didn't release me. The man threw down his staff and grabbed my torso. Our screams and shouts mingled together as we fought and fought. But it was all for nothing. The monster was too strong. My fingers slipped from the cobblestone. My friends' feet slipped. In an instant, we all slipped and slid toward the gaping maw.

"Just let me go," I yelled. "Let me go and run!"

"Never!" Ambria shouted. "I will never let you go!"

"I won't either," Max said, face red and sweating. "I'll punch this monster from the inside if I have to."

The old man chuckled. "Well, it would seem this frogre is about to get a mouthful."

I heard a terrible keening behind me and twisted so I could look. The frogre's head darkened from green to a deathly shade of purple. The awful sound turned to a choked screech. The frogre stiffened and toppled toward us. Max shouted in dismay and leapt to the side as the massive beast thudded a few feet from where he'd been.

Its froggy eyes turned milky white and thick black fluid trickled from its mouth. The long tongue blackened.

"Curious," the old man said. He stood and peered closely at the dead creature. "What was it you threw into its mouth?"

"An iocane potion," I said.

171

He stroked his long beard. "Impressive. Iocane potion is extremely difficult to brew, and rather volatile during the mixing stage." His eyes wandered over the three of us. "None of you look old enough to be advanced potions students."

Max's eyes suddenly widened. "Headmaster Galfandor, I didn't recognize you." His face turned pink. "I—uh—well, I'm not advanced."

"It was mine," I confessed, not wanting Max to get into trouble with the headmaster.

"You can simply call me professor," Galfandor said. "I reserve such tedious formalities for official business." He looked back at the frogre. "What I am more concerned about is why one of the Overlord's abominations was running amok in Queens Gate."

"It burst from a house." Ambria pointed back the way we'd run. "We don't know what it was doing in there."

Max nodded enthusiastically. "Yeah, we just ran for our lives."

"We were studying potions," Ambria added. "That's why Conrad had that iocane potion."

My skin felt tight from the web of lies my friends were weaving around us. On the other hand, we couldn't tell Galfandor we'd been living in Levi's house. That would only lead to question after question until they discovered his disappearance and murder.

"Very quick thinking, Conrad." Galfandor held out his hand. I raised mine slowly. He gripped it tight and shook. "If you've already managed to concoct a working iocane potion at such a young age, I'm sure you'll do wonders at Arcane University." He paused. "I assume you're all applying for the upcoming semestrial?"

Max tugged on his shirt as if it might be on too tight. "Yes, professor."

"You must be a Tiberius." Galfandor tapped his chin. "The youngest, Max, if I had to guess."

"Y-yes, sir." Max responded.

"And you, young lady?"

"Ambria." She curtsied. "A pleasure."

"Likewise." Galfandor looked at the growing crowd around the dead frogre. "Very impressive indeed." He put an arm on my shoulder and took me aside. "Conrad, I am unfortunately, quite pressed for time right now, but I would like to invite you and your friends to dine

172

with me tonight. I am very interested to know more about where this creature came from."

Doing my best to keep my hands from shaking, I nodded. "Of course, professor."

He pulled back and gave me a strange look. "Curious," he muttered.

I wanted to ask him what he meant by that, but something drew away his attention.

Galfandor waved over a small group of stern-looking people dressed in skintight black uniforms. "Good day, Templars. Would you see to the disposal of this frogre?"

Templars? These people weren't wearing metal armor or carrying shields as I'd imagined when Max first mentioned them. They did wear swords slung diagonally over their backs and I noticed a cross emblem on the collars of their uniforms.

One of the Templars nodded. "Of course, Headmaster Galfandor. Can you tell us where it came from?"

"This young man can give you all the information you need." He smiled kindly at me. "I must be going. Though I was blessed with some excitement, I am now rather late for a meeting with the university deans."

The Templar nodded. "Of course, sir."

Galfandor squeezed my shoulder. "I will see you tonight, five-thirty sharp, Conrad."

"Okay," I said in a weak voice.

The old man walked into the crowd. It parted before him and closed behind after he passed. The people didn't even seem aware they were moving out of his way and I wondered if he'd used a spell.

The Templar's face grew stern after Galfandor vanished. "Where did the frogre come from?"

I almost blurted the precise address, but quickly stopped myself. "Just down the road a ways. We were on a walk when this house collapsed and that monster flew out of the debris and chased us."

The man waved over my friends. "I'll need your names."

"I'd like to see some identification first," Ambria demanded. She crossed her arms and stared at the man.

His comrades gave him amused looks while he regarded her with confusion.

"Our uniforms should be all the identification you need, young lady."

Ambria didn't relent. "What's your name?"

"I'm Stave, head of the Templar Guard in Queens Gate." He crossed his arms and narrowed his eyes. "Your turn."

She nodded as if satisfied. "I'm Ambria, this is Max, and Conrad." She pointed a finger to each of us in turn. "I'm afraid we really don't have much more to add to the story. The monster chased us here. Mr. Galfandor saved us and killed it." She pointed down the street in the direction of Levi's house. "If you walk down there a little way you'll see the house."

Stave spoke again. "I'm afraid—"

"I'm afraid we're late for a study session, Mr. Stave." Ambria brushed her hands together as if cleansing herself of the matter. "We really must be going."

The man looked as if he wanted to detain us, but finally nodded. "Don't leave town just in case I have more questions."

"Of course, officer," I said.

He squinted, confused. "Just Templar is fine, young man." Stave turned on his heel and headed toward the dead frogre, the others following in a neat line behind him.

Ambria gripped Max and me by the arms and practically dragged us away from the crowd. When we'd walked around the street corner, she sighed. "That was close."

Max's forehead wrinkled. "Close?"

"We can't have those Templar people linking us to Levi's house."

He raised an eyebrow. "Why not?"

She released an exasperated breath. "If they investigate the house, they'll figure out Levi is missing. They might find out he's dead and then we'll all be tied to his death, and probably Brickle's."

"That's a lot of ifs. *If* they excavate the place, they'll find all the bones in the tunnel and figure the frogre ate him." Max turned to me. "What do you think?"

"I think you're both right." With the excitement over, I became aware of a piercing pain in my temples. I pressed my hands to the sides of my head.

"Are you all right?" Ambria asked.

"Headache." I wondered if it was the same headache I'd had after first seeing the frogre and remembered the vision. "When I first saw the frogre, I had a weird daydream."

"Not a great time to be daydreaming," Max said.

"What was it about?" Ambria asked.

"I saw a laboratory with all these big glass tanks." Closing my eyes helped me remember the details better. "There were elephants growing in them, and these awful fetuses that looked like someone attached half a baby onto a goat." I opened my eyes and the headache slowly faded, as if remembering was the cure.

Max's eyes flashed with alarm. "Oh, man. You just described Overlord minions."

"I did?"

"Yeah." His lips peeled back. "The baby-goat hybrid was one of the really awful ones, from what I've read and seen in the war records. There were all sorts of monsters, but the Overlord's foot soldiers were mostly bistaurs—kind of like centaurs but with bison hind ends instead of horses."

"How awful." Ambria made gagging noise. "He actually took human babies and melded them with animals?"

Max shrugged. "Nobody knows exactly how he did it, or at least if they do, they're keeping it top secret." He jammed his hands in his pockets and scuffed a shoe against the pavement. "The best explanation I heard was that he and Delectra mixed science and magic to create these things from scratch."

"I hope he wasn't stealing babies." Ambria's face reddened. "That would be the most evil thing in the world."

"Not the most evil," Max said. "There are plenty of other eviler things."

"Oh, really?" Ambria crossed her arms. "Please, inform me."

I closed my eyes and let their conversation fade away. My head felt much better by now and it helped me think. Realizing my parents created such abominations sickened me, but that wasn't my most pressing concern. Instead, I wondered how I could remember the laboratory in the first place. Had I been in the room with my parents? Had I witnessed them plotting and planning their takeover? I must have, because there was no other explanation.

I'd obviously been old enough to remember such things, and yet, unless the memories spontaneously popped into my mind, I couldn't make myself recall anything. "Is it possible to make someone forget their past?"

Max and Ambria stopped their argument about evil things and looked at me blankly for a moment.

Max spoke first. "Yeah, sure. A skilled healer can repair memories or hide them from you. I guess anyone who understands mind manipulation could do it."

"Why do you ask, Conrad?" Ambria put a hand to my forehead. "Are you feeling strange?"

"I think my parents wiped my memories of them. I think that's why I've been remembering all this weird stuff." I smiled at Ambria. "I'm feeling better though, thanks."

She removed her hand and pinched her eyebrows. "That's awful, Conrad. Maybe they didn't want you to remember the terrible things you saw when you were little."

"It's hard to imagine Victus and Delectra caring about anything or anyone but themselves," Max said. "If they wiped your memory, there's probably a good reason for it."

"But he's their son," Ambria protested. "Of course they loved him. They didn't want him to be scarred for life so they took away the bad memories."

Max scratched his head and gave me an uneasy look. "I don't want to make you mad, Conrad, but all the stuff I read in history class about the Overlord was plain terrible. He killed a lot of people and didn't care about anything but power."

I put a hand on his shoulder. "I know. If they'd cared about harming my mind, they wouldn't have made me go inside that laboratory with them. Just remembering that place makes me feel sick." I didn't dare tell them it had actually made me feel proud and happy. If my parents had mind-wiped me, they'd done it too late. Only a sicko would feel happy about creating monsters out of innocent animals and humans.

I blew out a breath and leaned against the storefront for Hinky's Fine Books. Max and Ambria took up positions on either side of me.

"Where do we go now, Conrad?" Ambria's eyes were big like a lost kitten's. "We don't have anything except the clothes on our backs."

All our belongings had been in the house. We'd lost the carpet and two school broomsticks in the destruction and the following chase. I hoped the university didn't know we'd borrowed them. A shock of dismay twisted my stomach as I thought of my most valuable possession. I patted my pocket and, much to my relief, felt the square lump of the phone. With it, we had money and could replace our meager belongings.

I gave our dilemma some thought and arrived at a quick conclusion. "There are a lot of abandoned houses in the area. We could probably find another place to stay."

"I suppose we won't be trapping the Goodleighs." Ambria brushed a tear from her eye. "We've lost the chance."

"We could still take them on," Max said. "We just need to plan it out."

Two separate thoughts found a connection and an idea blossomed. Fairy mushrooms in the fairy cakes had lightened us and allowed us to fly away on one broom. We had to figure out a way to get the other orphans quickly away from the orphanage. How or why those thoughts connected, I didn't really know, but I was pleased with the result.

I had the perfect plan.

Chapter 22

"We can take everyone right from under their noses," I said.

Ambria and Max turned to me and questioned me at the same time. "How?"

I cupped my hands as if holding something. "We need whole fairy mushrooms. The other children eat them, and then we use three brooms to fly them away."

Max's face brightened. "Brilliant! An entire mushroom would last for at least an hour."

"They could hold hands and form a human chain," Ambria said. A wicked look flashed across her face. "Then we go back and burn the place to the ground."

"I like the sound of that." Max smirked. "I still have some fireball scrolls we could use."

I imagined a fireball striking Marcus and Felicity. Picturing them flailing, screaming, and running in circles as they burned alive brought a smile to my face. I saw the smiles on my friends' faces and immediately sobered. *Killing is not good. It shouldn't make me happy.* Unfortunately, it might be the only way to stop the Goodleighs forever. This rationalization made me feel good about the decision. I didn't want to feel good about killing of any kind.

I don't want to be like my parents.

"There's just one problem." Max folded his arms and pursed his lips. "We have to steal the mushrooms without the Lady of the Pond or any dryads catching us."

"Obviously," Ambria said as if she knew all about the challenges. "We'll need to scout the location, but to do that, we'll need brooms."

"Will we get in trouble for losing our brooms?" I asked.

"We're supposed to check them out properly," Max said. "Lucky for us, I can bypass the security."

Ambria tilted her head slightly. "You broke into the shed?"

He shook his head. "No."

She slapped his arm lightly. "Don't be mysterious, Max. Tell us this instant."

"It doesn't matter how I got in," he said in an exasperated tone. "The point is, we can go back and get more brooms without anyone knowing." He looked up at the cliff. "The problem is, we have to go back to the sky lifts."

"I think we should get the brooms first, then hunt for a house," Ambria said. "We might be able to do it all in time for dinner with the old man."

The topic of Galfandor's dinner invitation caused me to realize I had no idea where he lived. I turned to Max. "Where is Galfandor's house?"

"He lives in Moore Manor." He quickly seemed to realize this wasn't enough of an explanation. "Just behind the university is Greek Row where all the fraternity and sorority houses used to be. The first house on the right is where Ezzek Moore, the founder of the university, once lived."

Ambria held up a hand. "Wait, Ezzek Moore founded Arcane University?"

"Yeah. He founded the Arcane Council, came up with rules to protect normal people, and helped pull together the Overworld Conclave." Max smacked his lips. "He's a real legend."

"What happened to him?" Ambria asked.

"Everyone thought he died hundreds of years ago, but found out he was still alive under the name Jeremiah Conroy." He let that sink in for a moment. "Turns out Ezzek Moore was alive back in ancient times under the name Moses. He fought in the First Seraphim War and helped Justin Slade in the Second Seraphim War." Max's lips twisted into a wistful look. "Then Daelissa killed him for good."

Ambria gave me a meaningful look. "Now we know why the Goodleighs thought so much of your potential."

Max squinted. "Huh? What does Ezzek Moore have to do with it?"

"My mother was his descendant," I said.

179

"Ah." Max snapped his fingers. "Yeah, I didn't think even think about it, but her last name was Moore." He chuckled. "I'll bet old Ezzek had a bunch of kids over the centuries."

A heavy sadness formed a tense knot in my chest as I thought about my dead ancestor. He'd been a great man. It made me wonder how my mother could've been so evil. With great effort, I turned my attention back to more immediate issues. "Since Galfandor lives near the university, maybe we should hunt for a house first and then get brooms on our way to his house."

Ambria pinched her lips. "Oh, I suppose, but looking for a house on foot might take a lot longer."

Max pointed to an empty horse carriage being drawn by a tiny goat. "We can take public transportation."

"That poor little goat is going to pull all of us?" she asked in a dismayed voice.

Max laughed. "No, that's just an illusion." He waved a hand and the carriage stopped. "What sort of animal do you want?" he asked Ambria.

"It can be anything?" she asked.

He nodded. "Anything."

"Well, in that case, I'd like a unicorn."

I snorted. "A unicorn?"

"Purple," she added.

Max waved at the carriage. "Well, tell it what you want."

Ambria clasped both hands behind her back and faced the carriage. "I'd like a purple unicorn, please."

An illusionary purple unicorn pulled our carriage back toward the street where Levi's house had stood. We disembarked one street over and peered at the remains. People in black uniforms crawled over the rubble. I hoped we hadn't left anything incriminating.

The row houses on this street looked a lot like the ones on Levi's street.

"How are we going to find out if anyone is living here?" Max asked.

Ambria tapped her chin. "I have an idea. Just follow my lead." Before we could say anything, she knocked loudly on the door of the first house, a tall gray-stoned building with black shutters and large windows.

A moment later, a man in green robes answered. His eyes looked over our soiled clothes and grimy faces. "What do you want?"

"We're selling vacuum cleaners," Ambria said. "Would you be interested?"

"A what?" the man scratched his head. "Are those something new from Science Academy, or are they magical?"

"It sucks dirt off your floor," she said.

"Oh, I don't need that. I've got hedgehogs."

I gave Max a confused look, but he didn't seem to notice.

"Do you think your neighbors would be interested?" Ambria asked. "We're raising money to help orphans."

The man visibly relaxed as if that explained why we filthy ragamuffins stood on his doorstep. "Aw, well that's very sweet, young lady." He motioned down the road. "Don't bother stopping at one fifteen, one twenty-two, or one thirty-seven. I know for sure nobody's lived in those houses for years. I haven't seen the Hendersons for a while either. Terrence mentioned trying to find a job in the nom workplace." He shuddered. "Awful thing to do, but if you can't make ends meet, you do what you have to do."

Ambria put a hand to her mouth. "Oh, how awful. Which house is that?"

He pointed down the block. "The brownstone over on the corner."

"Thank you so much for your help, sir," Ambria said in a sweet voice. "The orphans will be ever so grateful."

He mussed her hair and smiled. "Of course." He nodded at Max and me. "It's heartwarming to see kids trying to do good in this troubled world."

We waved goodbye and walked down the street a little way.

"Heartwarming *indeed*," Max said. "You'd think he'd at least give us a little money for the cause."

Ambria clucked her tongue. "Max, are you actually upset he didn't donate to a fake charity?"

Max straightened. "You know what? I am. The nerve of some people." He shook his head and burrowed a fist into his palm.

"But I just made it up on the spot, you silly boy." She looked at him and rolled her eyes.

"It's the principle of the matter," Max explained. "If it really makes him so happy, he needs to do more than talk. He should donate money and especially candy."

"Candy?" Ambria giggled. "The important thing is, his advice actually will help orphans." A sly smile creased her lips.

I nodded. "Very clever."

"And a bit devilish," Max said in a lighthearted tone. "But I like it."

Ambria crossed her arms and smirked. "Sometimes I surprise even myself."

We pretended to knock on the doors of a few houses just in case the helpful man was watching us, and made our way to the Hendersons' brownstone, skipping the other houses in the middle. I liked that the house was on the street corner. It meant we could keep an eye on the neighborhood more easily.

As with Levi's place, this house and the ones around it bore all manner of statues. A thick stone frame around the front door and windows supported fiercely poised mythological creatures. Griffins stood guard over the front door, front legs raised as if striking an enemy. Smaller versions of the same statues perched at the top corners of the window frames.

I led the group around the street corner in case the man we'd spoken with was keeping an eye on us and walked into the backyard of the house. I peered through the backdoor window and saw only a dim, empty kitchen. I rapped on the door and waited. No answer. I tested the door but it was locked.

"Can we change the door into a frog with one of the scrolls?" Ambria asked.

Max shook his head. "They only work on animals, not dead stuff."

"Hmm." She twisted the doorknob again. "What if we break the window?"

I looked at the houses behind this one to see if anyone might be looking out. Lights shone from the windows of a row house a couple of doors down. "Better not. Someone might notice."

"Wish we had a rot potion right about now," Max said.

"Oh, yes, and demolish this house like the last one." Ambria sniffed. "You really need to think things through, Max."

He stuck out his tongue. "The reason the last house fell apart was because the entire rot potion vaporized it. Just a little bit would be enough to take down the door without destroying the house."

"Then we wouldn't have a backdoor, and wouldn't that look odd to the neighbors?" She raised an eyebrow. Max didn't rise to the challenge.

I noticed a window someone had left cracked open on the second floor. "If only we had a broom."

Max sighed. "Told you we should've gone for the brooms first."

Ambria ran a hand along the thick concrete window frame on the first floor and pointed to the griffins perched on wide ledges at each corner. "Maybe one of us could climb and pull ourselves up to the window ledge."

Max puffed out his chest. "I can do it." He grabbed the lower ledge and balanced a knee on it. He stood and stretched toward the upper window ledge, but his fingers missed by several inches. He looked back at us. "Give me a boost."

Ambria and I pushed on his backside, huffing and puffing to get him up.

Ambria gave up. "You're heavier than you look." Her eyes wandered to me. "Conrad is thin as a stick. Let's help him instead."

Max climbed down and sighed. "Fine."

Scaling the frame didn't look as easy as shimmying up the trees back at the orphanage, but I was willing to give it a try. "All right."

Max knelt, braced his back against the house, and cupped a hand. "Let's try this the proper way." He gave Ambria a pointed look.

I stepped onto his hand. He lifted and I wobbled off balance. I felt Ambria grip my other foot and push. My fingers grasped the top frame. Max shoved hard and I nearly hit my head on the ledge supporting the griffin. I windmilled and somehow wrapped a hand around the statue's head. The others let go and I dangled by one arm.

"Help him," Ambria said.

I looked down and saw Max brace my feet with both hands. "Here goes." He pushed.

I swung up my other arm and grabbed the head. Straining, I managed to pitch my leg over the griffin's back. With the extra leverage, I slowly slung myself up and onto the stone creature. Panting, I rested atop it for a moment until I caught my breath. From here, the ledge was just wide enough to stand on. Bracing my hands against the house, I shuffled my feet up the griffin's back until my feet rested atop its head. From there I was just able to reach the lower ledge of the open window.

"You can do it, Conrad," Ambria said. "Just be careful."

"Yeah, I don't want to have to clean up the mess if you fall," Max added helpfully.

I looked down. The fall wouldn't kill me, but it would probably hurt a lot. I hoped I had the strength to pull myself up to the open window. I took a deep breath and reached my right hand up to the ledge. Once I had a firm grip, I moved my left hand to join it. My fingers slid into the groove where the base of the window fit. An idea sprang to mind. Instead of pulling myself up, I swung one foot at a time and braced them against the rough brick while holding tight with my fingers. Slowly and carefully, I walked up the wall until I could see inside the house.

The opening was just large enough to slip my arm through. I bounced on my feet and flung a hand through the crack. My hand snagged the wooden frame inside.

"Go, Conrad!" Ambria shouted.

"Hush," Max chided. "You'll have every neighbor looking through their windows if you keep shouting like that."

"You can do it," she said in a loud whisper.

I pressed up against the bottom of the window with my forearm. It resisted at first, then slid up a few inches, just enough to admit my torso. I bounced again and used the momentum to reach my other arm inside and grasp the frame. Arms burning with fatigue, legs aching, I couldn't hold on much longer.

Bouncing once more, I kicked a leg up and onto the ledge. My foot bounced off the bottom of the window and my ankle bone cracked hard against the stone ledge. My other foot slipped off the side of the house. My chin banged so hard on the brick my teeth clacked together. Stars flashed in my vision and wooziness threatened to drag me into darkness.

Chapter 23

I heard gasps from below.

The blackness gathering at the edges of my vision faded. I still clung to the ledge. Somehow, my foot had caught on the outer frame or I might have fallen. Straining with all my might, I used this leverage to pull my body up and onto the frame. Panting and sweating, I slid beneath the window and into the house. My back thudded on the wood floor. Arms limp as noodles, it was all I could do to touch a hand to my aching chin. Bright blood glistened on my fingers when I pulled them away.

After taking a moment to catch my breath and test my jaw for any fractures, I pushed up to my feet and stumbled down a staircase. The hallway at the bottom led to the kitchen and the backdoor.

When I opened it, Ambria rushed inside and gave me a hug. "That was so brave, Conrad."

Max patted me on the back. "Brilliant. Do you feel okay?"

I nodded wearily. "Spectacular."

"You're bleeding." Ambria grabbed a dirty towel from the kitchen floor and pressed it to my chin. "It doesn't look too bad—more like a scrape."

Taking the towel from her hand, I managed a smile. "Thanks. I'll hold it for now."

Ambria poked around in the cupboards and drawers. "Looks like they took everything." She opened a door and inspected the pantry. A single burlap sack sat inside. She opened it. "Unless we want to live on oatmeal, we'll need to buy groceries."

Max picked up a scroll from the table and read it. "It's a notice of eviction for not making payments." He dropped it and opened the other papers lying there. "I'd say this house is empty."

I tested a switch on the wall. The chandeliers flickered into flame. "How come they still have gas?"

"Gas?" Max scratched his head. "Oh, most of the utilities are aether powered." He paused at my confused expression. "Magical energy."

"They don't shut it off if you don't pay for it?" I asked.

"Nah, they're powered by ley lines—magical conduits of aether in the ground. They're free to use."

"How convenient." Ambria walked into the hallway and opened a door beneath the stairs. A small cot and some books were inside. She picked up one and read the cover. "*Arcane History*." She dropped it on the cot. "Conrad and I should probably read that at some point."

Another one bore the title, *Elementary Magic*, and the next, *Elementary Potions*. "Are these the classes you take at the university?" I asked.

"Yep." Max nodded. "First year stuff."

An imposing steel door down the hall to the left caught my attention. The antique brass knob didn't budge when I tested it and it didn't seem to have a keyhole. "This must be locked from the inside."

"Probably opened with a spell or arcphone," Max said.

We spent a while exploring the house. The downstairs rooms were bare of furniture, but one upstairs bedroom contained two wire frame beds with mattresses. The bathroom in the middle bedroom was fully stocked with a dizzying variety of shampoos, soaps, and bottled liquids I hesitated to touch. Neatly folded towels sat on a shelf next to the clawfoot tub.

Max pulled the cork from one, sniffed, and immediately broke into a sneezing fit. "Some kind of perfume," he said after regaining control.

Ambria waved it under her nose. "Smells lovely."

Max wrinkled his forehead. "You need your nostrils checked."

I looked at my dirty hands and soiled clothes. "Well, at least we can clean up before going to dinner."

"I don't have a thing to wear." Ambria said.

"You could always wash your clothes in the tub," Max suggested.

I wandered back into the hallway and opened the door to the bedroom at the end of the hall. My eyes widened when I saw the inside. Two racks of clothes stood in opposite corners with chests of drawers situated to the sides. I opened one and discovered male socks and underwear.

Ambria gasped and clapped her hands. "How lovely!" She went to a rack of feminine clothes and looked through the dresses. "Goodness, but these are skimpy outfits." She held a black one against her body. It came down past her knees and was obviously meant for someone a bit larger than her. "Why would they leave all these clothes?"

Max pointed a thumb over his shoulder. "And what's with all that stuff in the bathroom?"

"Could someone else be living here?" I asked.

"Maybe they left the clothes they didn't want," Max said. "They probably took what they could and left the rest."

"Well, perhaps we could make use of them," Ambria said, holding a dress with a checkered pattern. "These are a bit large, but they'll do in a pinch."

The male clothes were also several sizes larger than me, but given my slim build, that wasn't unusual. I checked out a pair of jeans and shrugged. "Guess we can make do with this for now."

An hour later, Ambria and I were ready to go, though we looked a bit ridiculous in our baggy outfits. A checkered dress sagged on her petite frame and a pair of short stockings she'd found wouldn't stay up no matter how many times she tugged on them.

A brown shirt fit me like a burlap sack. The jeans I wore were so long on me I had to roll them up nearly a foot. To keep them secure on my waist, I'd poked an extra hole in a belt just so it would fit tightly.

The only attire that fit us were our shoes since we hadn't found any footwear that came close to fitting our small feet. Ambria stated that even if the stiletto heels she'd found fit her, she wouldn't be caught dead in them.

Max was still fiddling with the locked iron door when we came downstairs. "You look dashing." His sarcastic tone made it clear he thought otherwise.

"Don't make fun," Ambria chided. "We'll find clothes that fit tomorrow."

He chuckled. "You look like a pair of dwarves that stole grown people's clothes."

Ambria held up her dainty fist. "Don't make me use this on you."

Max threw up his hands. "I surrender!"

We left the house by the back door and found an empty public carriage rolling past on the street. Max whistled and it stopped for us to board. Ambria chose a pink unicorn this time to take us across town to Max's uncle Malcom's house.

"Maybe you should wait outside," he said, looking toward the house.

"I don't want to see your grumpy old uncle anyway," Ambria said.

He went inside while we waited in the carriage.

"I hope this new house works out," Ambria said. She tugged on a loose stocking and frowned. "We definitely need to shop for clothes and food tomorrow."

"Okay." Taking care of ourselves seemed like a huge responsibility even though we now had a place to live. In all likelihood, our housing situation was temporary. Someone else might eventually buy the house, forcing us out again. Unless I found a way to make more money, our funds would eventually run out.

"You look tense, Conrad." Ambria put her hand over mine. "Are you okay?"

"I'm worried about the future."

"Do we have enough money to last a while?"

I shrugged. "Maybe. It depends on how expensive groceries are. Then we'll need clothes too."

She squeezed my hand. "We'll find jobs."

I snorted. "We're too young. Nobody will hire us."

"Don't be depressed." She leaned over to meet my downcast eyes. "We've come too far to give up now."

I knew she was right, but the doldrums didn't want to let me go. On top of day-to-day survival, we also had to do something about the Goodleighs. Once they figured out that Brickle was dead, they wouldn't stop until they found us. They'd search Queens Gate from one end to the other.

Max emerged from his uncle's house, his blond hair slicked back so tight against his pale skin, it made him look nearly bald. He wore a burgundy suit with a black bow tie, and shiny black shoes.

Ambria made a face. "Where do you think we're going, Max? A school dance?"

"Mighty dapper," I said, though I didn't mean it. He looked a bit ridiculous. Then again, Ambria and I looked slipshod with our oversized clothes and worn shoes.

Max's frown turned upside down at my comment. "Thanks, Conrad. I want to impress the headmaster. He's the man with the final say over who gets admitted to the university."

"Doesn't a dean usually do that?" Ambria asked.

He climbed into the carriage and waggled his hand in a so-so manner. "The headmaster at the university could also be called the dean. Some of them prefer dean, while some prefer to be called headmaster."

I directed the carriage to take us to the university shuttle. The illusionary pink unicorn took off at a trot.

Ambria remained interested in the topic at hand. "Wasn't Galfandor headed to a dean council meeting?"

"Yeah, probably with Dean Tesla of Science Academy, and Grand Dean Frankenstone—she's the woman in charge of all Overworld education."

"Her name sounds familiar," Ambria mused.

"Yeah, some nom wrote a novel based on her great-great-grandfather's early tests with reanimating corpses." Max pshawed. "It caused a big stir in the Overworld community."

"Did you learn that in Overworld history?" Ambria asked.

He nodded. "Anyway, I want you two to be on your best behavior with Galfandor." He directed his gaze to Ambria. "If you play your cards right, you might be able to get a free ride to the university."

"Oh really?" Her eyes brightened.

"If he likes you, he could award you a scholarship so long as you don't flop the entrance exam."

"That would be great," I said. Once Galfandor discovered I hadn't been the one to make the potion, he'd quickly realize I wasn't very impressive at all. Hopefully, it didn't ruin the chance for my friends to benefit.

The carriage halted at the shuttle zone just as the pirate ship floated in to dock. We headed to the end of the short waiting line as a crowd disembarked. Once the ship was empty, a parrot appeared on the ship railing, whistled a couple of times, and then said, "All aboard, you landlubbers!"

Ambria clasped her hands together and giggled. "How cute."

Once onboard, we took stairs to the upper deck. Though it wasn't large, it had a mast complete with sails, a large wooden steering wheel, and even an illusionary rack of swords. As the ship lifted off for the cliff, I walked to the waist-high railing and peered over the side. I was able to poke out my head by a foot or two before an invisible barrier halted me.

Max climbed up a ladder on the mast to the crow's nest. "Ahoy, mateys!"

I laughed and climbed up after him.

Ambria rolled her eyes. "So immature."

"Oh, don't be such a grownup," Max called down.

She crossed her arms and tried to resist, but finally relented and scampered up to join us. "The view *is* a bit better here."

We reached the cliff top a few minutes later and headed down the path to the university. Max stopped at the broom shed and waved his wand at the door. It clicked open. He went inside and returned with three more brooms.

"I suppose we're thieves now." Though Ambria's tone was disapproving, she still climbed aboard the broom.

Max winced. "We're borrowing them."

"Once the scene clears at Levi's house, maybe we could sort through the rubble and find our old brooms," I said.

"They're probably splintered to pieces." Max climbed on his broom and led us past the dorms to a road that wound up a hill fringed with trees.

Blackened ruins greeted us on the left side of the road. Further down, other scattered ruins gave evidence of once large houses that had been burned or razed by forces unknown.

Ambria sucked in a breath. "What happened here?"

"Used to be fraternity and sorority houses up here." Max halted his broom and pointed to more ruins on the right side of the road past a thick grove of trees. "The Overlord's forces marched through here when he launched a sneak attack on the university. When he took over, he abolished the Greek system, saying it was for elitists."

"Why haven't they rebuilt?" Ambria asked.

"When Galfandor took over, he said that he agreed with abolishing the old system."

I found myself in total agreement. "I've seen films with fraternities and sororities."

"When you were living with fosters?" Ambria asked.

I nodded. "The people in them liked nothing better than beating up and making fun of kids who weren't members."

"My father hated the decision—he was an Alpha Omega himself." Max chuckled. "My father despises Galfandor."

"Well, at least I won't have to worry about joining a sorority," Ambria said. "I think dividing people into silly clubs just makes them dislike each other for no good reason."

"Oh." Max cleared his throat. "Well, even though the old system is gone, they came up with a new one, but I think it's a lot better."

"What sort of system?"

"They're kind of like noble houses named after great Arcanes, but everyone has to be a member."

Ambria sighed. "I may not have been as exposed to the real world as Conrad, but I've read more books than I can name. Dividing people like this never ends well."

Max apparently had nothing more to add to the conversation and abruptly changed the subject. "Well, look, there's Moore Manor!" He flew down a gravel road to our right. We wound through a wooded area littered with felled, rotting trees and huge diagrams burned into the very earth itself. The large manor ahead, however, looked completely undamaged. A white marble statue of a man stood in the center of a patch of green grass and flowers.

Ambria pointed at the burn marks. "What in the world happened here?"

Max's eyes brightened. "Justin Slade and Ezzek Moore fought an epic battle here against Daelissa. There were these huge demons attacking the house"—he held his arms wide—"then Justin Slade summoned an Abyssal demon." He punched the air. "The Abyssal killed the other two demons and wiped out the battle mages."

"Goodness." Ambria shivered. "I can't believe they'd use such awful creatures."

"Well, demons can be pretty useful if you know what you're doing." Max led us over to the statue. "Unfortunately, the story doesn't have a happy ending. The original house was destroyed, and Daelissa killed Ezzek Moore on that exact spot." He pointed to the perfect circle of flowers and green grass at the foot of the statue.

"Didn't that happen years ago?" I asked. "Why are there still diagrams burned into the ground?"

"Well, when you summon demons that powerful, they leave marks that can last for decades."

Ambria grunted. "I suppose we'll learn that in demonology class."

Max grinned. "Yep."

I felt a shock of surprise that they actually taught such an evil subject. Max led us to the front door. The manor stood two stories tall with a steeply pitched roof ringed by large, stone gargoyles resembling winged demons with bald heads and long, pointy ears. I didn't understand why people around here had such fondness for ugly statues. *It must be an Overworld thing.*

The front door opened before Max could use the knocker. Galfandor smiled at us and motioned us inside. "Welcome to Moore Manor. Let's not dither. Dinner is waiting." Galfandor walked briskly for someone who looked so old and led us to a dining room with a round, wooden table large enough to seat six people.

A roast surrounded by vegetables steamed in the center of the table. Galfandor took a knife and began slicing it. "Don't be shy. Hold out your plates and I'll serve you."

Once we each had our plates full with generous portions, he took a slice for himself and sat down.

As we ate, I noticed the headmaster stealing curious glances at me. I wanted to ask him why, but since everyone was preoccupied with eating, it seemed impolite to break the silence. When we finished, a wooden man dressed in butler livery walked in with a tray bearing a pot and teacups.

I stared with wonder at the odd butler. He reminded me of the strange puppet guards at the entrance to Queens Gate. "How—" I stopped myself before asking a question sure to mark me as a nom.

Galfandor didn't miss my reaction. "You've never seen a golem before, Conrad?"

I tried to recover. "Not like that one."

He nodded, bright blue eyes fixed on me. "Servant golems are quite handy in a house this large." He looked around the table. "Tea, everyone?"

Ambria nodded briskly. "Absolutely."

The golem had no visible joints—it seemed to be made from a single piece of wood—yet it bent over and set the table as if it were made of rubber. Once it poured us each a cup, it left, vanishing through a double-hinged door into what I presumed was the kitchen.

Galfandor took a sip of tea and regarded me seriously. "Young man, I couldn't help but notice something rather troubling about you."

I nearly choked on my tea. I swallowed loudly. "W-what would that be?"

He set down his teacup "You're cursed."

Chapter 24

"Cursed?" Ambria's voice rose an octave.

Max scooted his chair away from me. "What kind of curse?"

"Yes, well, I haven't worked that out yet." Galfandor stood. "Let's go to my study. I'd like to get a better look."

I felt woozy from his abrupt diagnosis and had trouble standing. *Cursed? What does that mean?* I wondered if it was something the frogre had done to me. I managed to get up and followed the headmaster as he vanished through a door.

Ambria gripped my arm as we followed. "I'm sure he's wrong, Conrad. You look fine." She glanced behind us. "Right, Max?"

"I hope so," he replied. "Curses are usually pretty bad, though."

"Brilliant analysis," she replied in a tart voice and turned back to me. "Nothing to worry about."

It was all I could do to put one foot in front of the other. My mind felt numb. *Something horrible is wrong with me!* We walked across a hallway and into a room lined with bookshelves. A sturdy wooden desk covered in parchments and scrolls occupied the center. Galfandor opened a drawer in the desk and fished around for a moment before retrieving a pair of spectacles with pink lenses.

"Ah, my rose colored lenses should do the trick." He glanced at me and flinched back. "Goodness. I thought I felt a malevolent aura around you, but this is quite a sight."

"May I look?" Ambria asked in an uncharacteristically timid tone. Her hand on my arm trembled.

"Of course." The headmaster handed her the spectacles.

She backed up a step and hesitantly looked through the lenses. Her face went white and she nearly dropped the spectacles. "Oh, goodness."

Max took the glasses from her shaking hand and held them to his eyes. He jumped back. "It looks like he has black ghosts writhing around his body." He braced a hand on the desk. "What is it?"

Galfandor took back the eyewear. "I've never seen anything like it." He reached under his robe and produced a wand. "Let me see now." He waved the wand and flicked it toward me. A cloud of pale white light sparkled toward me.

I nearly jumped out of the way, but found the presence of mind to stay in place. As the light surrounded me, it revealed ghostly black shadows dancing in my vision.

"Look, Conrad." Galfandor pointed toward a large mirror on the wall. "Don't be afraid."

Clenching my fists to contain the fear, I turned toward the mirror. A harsh gasp escaped my throat. Two wraithlike creatures encircled me. One darted through my body and jutted from the other side while the second slithered around me like a snake. It coiled and struck at the light. Sparks flew.

Ambria shrieked. Max cried out and I heard something thump on the floor.

The other shape clawed at the light, causing it to dim with every attack. A terrible ache formed in my temples and my skin felt as if it was on fire. As the light faded, one of the shadows stood and cast its ethereal hands forward. In a brilliant flash, the light was gone.

The heat on my skin relented, replaced by cold sweat. As the afterimages of the horrifying vision faded, I realized with a shock that I recognized one of the shadows. It looked exactly like the one I'd seen in my dream. Whatever they were, they wanted something from me.

Ambria gripped Galfandor's arm. "What was that thing? Will it kill Conrad?"

The old man seemed nonplussed. He shrugged. "I'm not sure. One thing is certain, however. If I try to remove this curse, it would most likely kill Conrad."

Max picked himself up off the floor. "I don't understand how he's survived this long."

Galfandor dropped into a worn leather chair and regarded me, fingers steepled beneath his chin. "I think the laserphant in the room is *why* someone would bestow such a curse on a child."

"Could it have been the frogre?" I asked.

He shook his head. "No, this is the work of a frightfully skilled Arcane."

Ambria's lips flat-lined into a grim expression. Though she said nothing, I knew what she was thinking.

Her brother, Levi, cursed me when he was trying to kill me.

Galfandor took a sip of tea, set it down, and unloaded a very direct question. "Conrad, what is your last name?"

My throat tightened. Telling the headmaster my real last name would be a mistake. At the same time, he seemed to be the only person who could possibly help me. If anything, he'd been the kindest adult I'd met and seemed trustworthy. *What if this is a ruse?*

"Baker," Ambria said.

At the very same moment, Max blurted, "Huxtable."

Galfandor's gaze never wavered from me. "Be honest, Conrad. You have nothing to fear from me."

While I appreciated my friends' attempts to protect me, I felt being truthful was for the best. "Edison."

For the first time, the old man's eyes flashed with either surprise or uncertainty. "You are the son of Victus Edison and Delectra Moore." His voice sounded tight.

I nodded.

The room went deathly silent for what seemed a very long time. Galfandor finally looked at Ambria. "What is your last name, young lady?"

She took a step back, eyes widening. "Why does it matter?"

He did not answer, but his unrelenting gaze refused to let her remain silent.

Her lips trembled and finally she spoke. "It's Rax."

The old man nodded and his eyes seemed to focus on something a thousand miles away.

"Maybe we should leave," Max said. "You probably don't want people from evil families in your house."

The headmaster rose from his chair. "A name is a name, nothing more, young Tiberius. It is up to an individual to choose his actions." He looked at me. "Conrad Edison, you have it in you to become a great Arcane should you choose the right path."

I nodded, uncertain how to respond.

He turned. "Ambria Rax, you could be a great leader one day if you avoid the temptation of power for power's sake. This was something your father was too weak to resist."

"I'm not that fond of power," she said.

Galfandor turned to the last member of our trio. "Maxwell Tiberius, your father craves power but is too petty and cowardly to take the risks necessary. Thus, he has always remained in the shadow of your late grandfather. If you are not afraid to take risks, you may someday bring honor back to your house."

Max's face turned a bit red. He gave Galfandor a grudging nod. "If you say so, sir."

"Galfandor, I think I should clarify something," I said. "Ambria and I never knew our parents. We were sent to an orphanage years ago. Only recently, I discovered terrible secrets about the place."

"I would be intrigued to hear your history," Galfandor said. "Perhaps once I know more, I can divine who would lay such a curse on you and why." He walked toward the door. "Let's go to the parlor where we may all sit."

We followed him down the hallway and entered a door. Leather divans surrounded a table in the cozy little room. We each took a seat. Galfandor said nothing, but gave me an expectant look. I took a deep breath and told him our story. Aside from a few thoughtful grunts, he listened quietly, without comment. I was extremely hesitant to expose the fullness of our crimes—the deaths of Levi Rax and Brickle—but couldn't think of a good way to leave them out.

He winced when I told him of the shovel to the back of Levi's head, though the part where a demon devoured Brickle didn't seem to faze him in the least. I ended the narrative at the episode with the frogre and didn't tell him of acquiring our new home though that crime was minor compared to murder.

Max looked down when I finished the story while Ambria squirmed in her seat, eyebrows pinched with worry. I felt as though we'd submitted ourselves to judgment. Even worse, I wondered if I'd ruined Max and Ambria's chances for admittance to Arcane University.

Galfandor pulled a rope. A bell chimed.

I expected a troop of Templars to enter, seize us, and throw us in jail. Instead, the butler golem appeared with a fresh pot of tea. "Would anyone like a refill?"

I held out a cup in a trembling hand. Though tea had been a luxury most of my foster parents afforded me, the Goodleighs had been far stingier. If I somehow remained out of prison, I decided tea would become a daily staple.

"Please don't call the Templars," Max said in a whining voice. "I promise destroying the house and killing Brickle were accidents."

"I take full responsibility," Ambria said. "I'm the one who cast the demon scroll."

Galfandor took a sip of tea. "Ah, perfect as always." He smacked his lips together. "Nothing like a spot of tea while listening to a tale of adventure."

"That adventure has been our lives for the past few days," I said.

"You're a very brave boy," the headmaster said. "You risked life and freedom to rescue Miss Rax from an uncertain fate."

"What's our punishment?" Max asked.

Galfandor raised his eyebrows. "Why, anyone with a grain of sense can see your actions were in self-defense. There was nothing malicious about destroying the house or killing those men." He raised a finger. "That is not to say killing is justified if you can find another way. Conrad must have hit poor Levi just right to kill him, and your lack of experience with advanced caster scrolls led to the untimely demise of Brickle Brixworth."

"Does this mean you'll help us rescue the other orphans?" Ambria asked. "We can't let the Goodleighs continue selling them into service."

Galfandor clicked his tongue. "Unfortunately, since the breakdown of Overworld society, such illegal practices have become all too common. Without a strong Overworld Conclave, the factions have drifted apart and the dividing line between the supers and normals has grown dangerously thin."

"There are more people like the Goodleighs?" I asked.

"Why, there are entire organizations devoted to such ghastly enterprise. There is even an underground gladiator circuit where enslaved supers must fight each other, sometimes to the death." His upper lip peeled into a grimace. "I would not be surprised if Ambria was scheduled for sale to such a master."

Ambria squeaked. "What awful, horrid people!" Fists clenched, she jolted to her feet. "I won't stand for this, Conrad. I will not allow the Goodleighs to sell a single orphan more."

I turned back to the headmaster. "Will you help us, Galfandor?"

"I'm afraid I cannot overtly help you, Conrad. There are political complications that would stand in the way." He tapped a finger to his chin. "I can provide you with more spell scrolls—"

I felt my mouth drop open. "You can't help us?" My voice rose in pitch. "What kind of person could just stand by and do nothing?"

The headmaster didn't look angry at my outburst. Instead, he seemed curious about my reaction. "Conrad, there are things you are much too young to understand. Perhaps one day you'll see the truth of it. I will supply you with what I can, but directly helping you is out of the question."

"What about the Templars?" Max asked.

"They are not under my control," he said. "Ask them for help if you wish, but I think you'll find they're much too preoccupied with Queens Gate to do anything in the normal world. I'm afraid the fate of the Overworld was sealed the same day the Alabaster Arches closed behind Justin Slade and his army. What should have been a golden age has instead turned into a dark dystopia."

Ambria's bright red cheeks paled at his words. "You're saying there's too much crime to control?"

He nodded. "I'm afraid it will take centuries for the supernatural society to recover."

"If you won't help us with the Goodleighs, can you at least tell us about Conrad's curse?" Max said.

"I'm afraid the answer is clear," Ambria said. "My brother must have done it when he tried to kill him."

Galfandor shook his head. "No, this curse is far more insidious than an ordinary death curse. In fact, if it is what I think it is, someone has managed something far worse—a living curse."

Max scrunched his lips. "If it helps you live, wouldn't that be a charm?"

"I do not mean it helps Conrad live, I mean the curse itself is alive." He took a sip of tea and continued. "Conrad's many foster parents suffered from mysterious deaths and ailments usually right around his birthday. I believe this curse is the cause. It would also explain why the Goodleighs were so eager to foist you on unsuspecting couples for much of the year, knowing that you would return to them around the same time."

"The Goodleighs put this curse on me?" I asked.

He shook his head. "While I do not know this couple, I can say with certainty they likely don't have the skill required. I also know I do not have the skill to remove this curse."

"What can I do?" My voice sounded thin with despair.

"That would seem obvious," he said.

"Obvious?" Max, Ambria, and I said at the same time.

"Your dream," Galfandor explained. "The creature in your dream was the curse talking to you."

"It told me to go to the doctor," I said.

"And not just any ordinary doctor," he replied. "I believe Rufus Cumberbatch was a close associate of Victus and Delectra Moore, though many refuse to believe this opinion. If anyone was capable of placing this curse on you, it was him."

Chapter 25

Ambria and I stared at each other for several seconds as we processed the troubling fact that Dr. Cumberbatch might have done this to me. The question still remained, why?

Galfandor seemed to read my mind. "If there are answers to be found, young Conrad, you must seek them out with Cumberbatch." He clasped his hands across his lap. "Unfortunately, I know the man well and suspect he won't easily cooperate. He has always been something of a cowardly liar. Though he often spoke out against the Overlord, I believe it was all for show so he could gain useful information for his true master. Otherwise, he wouldn't have survived."

My thoughts bounced back and forth between the Goodleighs and the doctor. Which should I tackle first? I knew removing the curse should take priority, so I decided we should plan our next moves accordingly.

"Do you have access to fairy mushrooms?" Max asked Galfandor.

"For your daring rescue plan?" the old man replied with a chuckle. "I must say, using the mushrooms with brooms to spirit away the other children is quite inventive." He leaned forward. "Though I cannot help you directly, I promise I will help you find good homes for anyone you rescue."

I stood and approached Galfandor, held out my hand. "It's a deal, sir."

He stood and gave my hand a firm shake. "A deal." He reached back and gave the bell rope two quick tugs. Moments later, two golems bearing brooms and a large burlap sack appeared. Galfandor smiled. "Here are your supplies. May they grant you success."

I looked inside the sack and found small satchels. One brimmed with mushrooms. Another held potions, and yet another contained scrolls. *How could he possibly have known what we would need?* Rather than badger him with questions, I decided to accept this help.

"Thank you, sir."

Galfandor placed a hand on my shoulder. "I wish you the best of luck." He paused. "Didn't you say you downloaded information from the Goodleigh's arctablet?"

"Yes, I have it on the phone right here."

"Perhaps I should have a copy. I might be able to find out where these children came from."

"Absolutely." I took out the phone.

He patted his robes, muttering to himself. "Where did I put that infernal thing?" His hand stopped just over his chest. "Ah, there it is." He took out a phone and held it up to mine.

"Phone, send all information from the Goodleigh's tablet to Galfandor's phone," I told it.

"Transfer in progress," the phone said.

Max ran a hand along one of the brooms and chortled. "Whoa, is this a genuine Firefly Special?"

"Built by Screven himself." Galfandor pursed his lips and looked at Max. "Don't be tempted to race them."

"Wouldn't think of it," Max vowed, even as his eyes flashed with desire.

After the data transfer finished, we gathered our supplies and left Galfandor's house as dusk settled across the sky. I wanted to fly my new broom, but Max cautioned me against it. "You can't just hop on a Firefly and zip around, Conrad." He stopped speaking. "Then again, you might be able to just like you did these old brooms, but I wouldn't chance it right now." He slung the new broom over his back with the included leather strap and got on the old broom. He'd tied the burlap sack with supplies to the back of my broom. The added weight made it hover with a slight upward tilt.

Ambria and I climbed on our brooms and followed Max as he headed toward the cliff.

"What's so different about these new brooms?" Ambria asked.

"They're built for speed." Max flashed a wide grin. "These beginner brooms automatically keep you upright and don't go very fast. A Firefly is a boomstick, a supercharged broomstick. You'll have to practice with them or you'll just look silly dangling upside down."

"Lovely," Ambria complained. "Sounds like another delay before we can rescue the orphans."

"Well, these brooms will get us to the orphanage and back a lot faster."

I cleared my throat as we crested the cliff and began our descent into Queens Gate. "Actually, I think we should go to Cumberbatch first and get this curse removed."

Max nodded. "That's a good idea."

"I think that's very selfish, Conrad." Ambria huffed. "For all we know, the Goodleighs will sell another poor soul into slavery in the time it takes us to convince the doctor to help you."

"What if this curse interferes with our rescue operation?" I said. "We have no idea how it'll affect me or others close to me, especially since it apparently killed or injured my other foster parents."

"I think we have until your next birthday before that happens again." Ambria narrowed her eyes. "Don't get me wrong, Conrad. I'm very concerned about your delicate condition, but we can't waste any more time before rescuing the orphans."

I wanted to disagree, but couldn't argue with her logic. "Okay. Rescuing the orphans comes first."

Her frown turned to a smile. "It's much easier to just agree with me, isn't it?"

Max groaned and rolled his eyes.

When we glided into the valley, Max waved goodbye and headed for his uncle's house. "Meet you at Chicken Little at seven for breakfast?" he said.

"See you then," I replied.

Ambria and I reached our new home on Baker Street a few minutes later and entered through the backdoor. I untied the supply sack and set the satchels on the table so we could sort through them, and set our new brooms in the corner of the dining room.

When Ambria opened a bag slightly larger than the others, her eyes lit up. "How nice of him." She withdrew two sets of bed linens and was about to close the bag when she realized there was another lump in it. "Goodness, these little sacks hold a lot."

We were both surprised when she tugged a down comforter from the bag.

I felt another lump in the bottom. "It's still not empty."

"Is it a magic sack?"

I shrugged. "How else could so much fit in there?" I pulled out another comforter followed by two feather pillows. Once I removed the last pillow, the sack flattened.

"Well, this certainly solves our linens issue for now." Ambria ran a hand along the sheets. "They're so soft."

"Let's go fit the beds," I suggested.

"Excellent idea." She sighed. "It's early, but I'm ready to collapse."

We left the kitchen and were about to head up the stairs when the metal door in the hallway clicked and swung open. A young woman stepped out, a yawn stretching her mouth wide. She sniffed and abruptly stopped. Her head flicked our way. She blurred toward us at inhuman speed.

My back hit the wall hard enough to drive the wind from my lungs. I heard Ambria grunt at the same time. Red irises blazing, the woman bared her teeth. Needle-sharp fangs extended from beneath plump pink lips.

We had just met our first vampire.

"Desmond, we've got visitors," the woman shouted.

Another figure blurred into view and stopped right behind the woman. Desmond stood much taller than me. Bulging muscles stretched tight his T-shirt, and his face looked as if an artist had carved it. The woman looked his feminine equal in attractiveness. Unfortunately, they also looked quite deadly with their fangs and glowing red eyes.

Desmond looked at us and laughed. "Children?" He leaned toward Ambria. "What are you doing here, little girl?"

"We should ask you the same thing," Ambria shot back. "This is our house."

"No it isn't," the woman hissed. "This place was abandoned when we moved in."

"Now, Sonia, let's show some manners toward our guests." Desmond pulled back her arm and released us.

Ambria and I took deep breaths. I wanted to run for my life, but Ambria regained her composure and stared defiantly at the two vampires. "How many more of you are there?"

"We're the only two," Desmond said.

Sonia snarled and moved toward Ambria. "Don't come into my house acting like you own the place, you little brat."

Desmond put an arm in front of her. "Behave, Sonia."

The woman stepped back but glowered at Ambria.

I decided to intervene before my friend made Desmond angry as well. "I'm Conrad, and this is my friend, Ambria."

"Nice to meet you," Desmond said. Sonia quietly glowered.

"We're orphans," I explained. "We were chased out of our old home by a frogre. We thought we'd found another place to live. If you already have a claim, we'll move on."

Sonia's face softened. "At least this one is nice." She flashed her fangs. "Can I have him first?"

I gulped and forced myself not to back away. "We'd really prefer it if you didn't drink our blood."

Desmond smirked. "I'm afraid Sonia is just trying to scare you. We don't feed on children."

The woman gave him a disgusted sideways look. "You didn't have to tell them."

"Well, that's very nice of you," Ambria said. "Feeding on children would be cruel."

Sonia's eyes flashed. "Are you wearing my dress, little girl?"

Desmond looked me up and down and burst into laughter. "I don't think my clothes fit you very well."

Sonia erupted again. "How dare you come into our house and steal my clothes!"

"I didn't realize they were yours." For the first time during this situation, Ambria actually seemed scared.

Stealing another girl's clothes must be very dangerous. "We'll put back your clothes and leave," I said. "Please, we didn't mean any harm."

"Of course you will," Sonia said. "I want you gone now!"

Desmond held up a hand. "Come now, sister. Remember when we were the ones looking for a place to live? Remember when we were forced into a life we didn't want?"

Sonia took a deep breath and looked away. "Yes."

"They're orphans, for goodness sake. We can't just turn them out on the streets."

"You seem rather nice for a vampire." Ambria directed the comment at Desmond. "Then again, you're the first vampires we've met."

"We are not vampires by choice," Desmond said. "In fact, we were once just normal people going about our lives."

"Spare them the sob story." Sonia crossed her arms. "My brother took me dancing for my seventeenth birthday. This man at the club gave us what I thought was alcohol, but was really some bizarre blood potion that turned us into blood-sucking leeches. The next thing we knew, we weren't in London anymore, but all the way across the world in Australia fighting our way into a huge castle with an army."

"You don't remember traveling?" I asked.

"The old vampires could control our minds," Desmond said. "We couldn't resist them."

"They call it compulsion," Sonia said. "Apparently, the vampire controlling us was killed during the battle and freed us. We tried to run, but Templars caught us and put us in prison for nearly four months. Later they told us since we'd been forced to fight, we were free to go so long as we took an orientation course and swore not to break Overworld rules."

"Wow," I said. "You've been through a lot."

"Sounds like you've had an interesting time too," Desmond said. "I haven't seen a frogre in years."

"It appears we have some stories to trade," Ambria said with a sigh. "I was so looking forward to bed."

"Can we at least stay here for the night?" I asked the vampires. "We have nowhere else to go."

Desmond nodded. "Be my guest."

Sonia huffed. "Fine, but only because the boy was polite about it." She gave Ambria a pointed look. "Now, kindly remove my dress and hang it."

Ambria curtsied. "At once, madam." She went upstairs.

"Well your day might be ending, but ours is just beginning," Desmond said. He cast a wistful look toward the metal door. "We need to eat, and then have to party the night away." He didn't look enthused about it.

"Oh yes, drink blood, party all night." Sonia frowned. "When I was normal, that was all I wanted to do—well, except for drinking blood. As a vampire, you *must* be social or you'll make someone mad at you." She walked away and stormed upstairs. "I'm going to get ready."

When she was gone, Desmond let out a soft chuckle. "Life is so strange."

"I completely agree," I said.

His eyes softened with sympathy. "Despite what my sister says, I want you two to stay here as long as you'd like. We know what it's like to be homeless. We're still very young by vampire years, and we never had a chance to earn money. With the Overworld economy in shambles, we're barely making it."

"That would be great," I said. "We can help with groceries if you'd like."

Desmond laughed. "That's one thing in our favor. We can eat regular food, but we don't have to." He patted me on the shoulder. "Let's talk more tomorrow evening. We'll discuss an arrangement." With that, he went upstairs.

A sense of profound relief melted the anxiety knotting in my chest. It seemed with every solution we found, another problem surfaced. Living with vampires didn't seem like the ideal solution, but maybe it would work.

Chapter 26

When the vampires left for their night out on the town, Ambria took the linens provided by Galfandor and made the two wire-frame beds in the room at the opposite end of the hallway from the bedroom the vampires used as a walk-in closet.

"I really don't like the idea of sleeping in the same room as a boy," Ambria said. "Maybe we can move a bed into the middle room for me tomorrow."

"I can move my mattress to the other room if you'd like."

She smiled and batted her eyelashes. "Oh, would you?"

"Sure. Can you help?"

"Of course."

We each took an end of the mattress and hauled it into the center bedroom. Ambria helped me put the sheets back on.

"Now I don't have to listen to you snore," I said.

She giggled. "It's nice to hear you making jokes, Conrad. You're always so serious."

I hadn't really thought about it. "Maybe I'm just not a funny person."

"You are what you want to be." She kissed my cheek. "Good night."

It had been a busy, hectic day. I closed my eyes and dozed off quickly.

"Conrad." A faint, whispering voice called my name again and again.

My eyes flicked open. Everything in the bedroom was stark white except for a shadowy visitor and me.

The cat-like wraith strolled forward, eyes glowing bright green. "Release the curse, Conrad."

Black smoke roiled from my nose and mouth. I tried to scream, but the smoke choked my windpipe. I flailed and tried to get up, but an invisible force pinned me to the bed. The smoke morphed into the shape of a large spider with eight large eyes burning red as embers. "Go to the doctor," the spider hissed.

"What does the curse do?" I asked.

The cat purred. "It changes everything."

"*Everything*," the spider hissed.

The nightmares stalked and skittered toward me. I cried out. "Leave me alone! Go away!"

"Only you can make us leave," they said in unison. "Go to the doctor."

They leapt into my mouth, their smoky forms burning into my throat. I couldn't breathe or move. Terror spiked my heart. Everything went black and cold.

When I woke up, it was still dark outside, but the phone clock told me it was six in the morning. My sweat-soaked shirt and shorts clung to my skin. When I sat up, I realized my sheets were every bit as wet as me. I quickly bundled the linens and stowed them in a corner until I could figure out how to clean them. Laughter echoed from downstairs. I threw on the old worn pants and shirt from the orphanage and went down the stairs.

Sonia and Desmond were there with a man and woman who looked about their age. I realized with a shock that blood trickled down the necks of the visitors. The sight stopped me cold. I suddenly wanted nothing more than to creep back upstairs.

Desmond's head flicked around in an instant. His red eyes locked onto me and he frowned. Sonia giggled. Mouth wide, long fangs protruding beneath her lips, she moved as if to bite the other man's neck. Desmond gripped her shoulder and shook his head. "It's time to get ready for bed."

Sonia's lip curled into a sneer. Her nostrils flared and she looked back at me. Anger burned in her eyes. "I told you it was a bad idea."

"A bad idea?" the other woman asked in a very slurred voice. "We're a great idea."

"Been fun, nice having you over," Desmond said as he ushered them to the door. "Time for bed."

"Goodnight!" the man called drunkenly as Desmond shut the door behind him.

Sonia blurred up the stairs too fast for me to see. She stopped, nose less than an inch from mine, eyes burning. "Maybe I *should* feed on you."

"That's enough, Sonia." Desmond's voice was cold and firm. "Go to bed."

Her mouth sprang wide and she hissed at me. I flinched back and struck my head on the wall. Sonia burst into cruel laughter. "That's what you get, little boy." She sauntered down the stairs, making it look easy despite the tall, spiked heels she wore.

After she'd gone through the steel door, Desmond emerged from the kitchen, his lips clean of blood. "She can be difficult at times, plus she's had too much to drink."

"Too much blood or alcohol?"

He grinned. "Both." His eyes wandered up and down me. "Those clothes aren't fit for rats. Do you have anything else?"

I shook my head. "We lost them to the frogre. Is there any way to clean them here?"

He nodded. "There's a wash downstairs. Won't take but a few minutes."

"To wash and dry?"

"Yep." Desmond put a hand to the expensive-looking black shirt he wore. "A magic wash is something no vampire with a sense of style can live without. I supposed that includes most of my kind."

I felt my face grow hot as I asked the next question. "I had a nightmare and got my sheets sweaty. Can you wash them too?"

Some of the levity in his eyes faded. He put a hand on my shoulder. "I'd be happy to."

"Thanks." I went upstairs and fetched my sheets. When I came down, Desmond handed me a stack of folded clothes. "You can wear these if you want. They should fit you better than mine."

"Where did you get them?" I asked.

His eyes saddened. "They belonged to our little brother. He died in the war."

Pain clenched my chest. "I'm very sorry to hear that, Desmond."

"Yeah." His voice sounded tight and dry. "You kind of look like him." He cleared his throat. "You can keep these clothes. Maybe they'll tide you over 'til you buy new ones."

I went into the downstairs bathroom and changed, then gave Desmond my old clothes to wash. "Can I get them to you in the evening?" he asked. "I'm really tired."

"Sure."

He went down the basement stairs, closing the steel door behind him. I stood there for a moment lost in thought about his little brother. I wondered how he'd ended up in the war and how he'd died. It seemed much clearer to me why Desmond had been so nice. *He sees a little of his brother in me.* Sonia, apparently, did not.

Ambria came downstairs half an hour later, showered, and wearing her old gray dress from the orphanage. She stopped when she saw me. "Where did you get those?"

I told her about Desmond's brother.

Her eyes reddened. "How awful it must be to lose someone like that."

"Losing someone is probably always awful," I replied.

We met Max for breakfast, and managed to eat a meal without incident, though he was shocked to hear about the vampires in our house.

"Friendly vampires?" His lip curled up. "Never heard of such a thing."

"Well, one of them, anyway," Ambria said. "So, what's next for the day?"

"Broom practice." Max grinned. "This is gonna be fun."

We took our new brooms to a pasture on the outskirts of town.

Max explained the advanced controls. "The accelerator notch acts the same, but to keep upright, you have to adjust the pressure on the stirrups."

The moment I sat on the seat, I felt right at home and easily kept the broom from toppling over. Ambria, however, flipped upside down and fell on the grass the instant she boarded hers.

"I'd really like to know why you're such a natural," Max said to me. He helped Ambria back onto her broom, holding the handle to keep it from spinning, and spoke in a slow condescending voice. "Use the stirrups to balance."

"I understand that, you nincompoop!" Ambria popped him on the head. Max let go of the handle. Ambria promptly found herself lying on the ground again. "You did that on purpose."

"Of course I did." Max's face reddened. "You hit me on the head."

I took the broom for a lap around the pasture, flying higher and higher. I pulled back on the handle and looped upside down. A shout of joy burst from me. The flying carpet and old broomstick had nothing on this wonderful boomstick. As I zipped around, performing more and more elaborate tricks, my troubles seemed to melt away.

A while later, I saw Max flying nearby and waving his arms at me. "Conrad, will you come here?"

I drifted over and was pleased to see Ambria drift in a complete circle. "She's learning?"

"Yeah." He gave me a strange look. "I hate to say this, but it's impossible to fly one of these things the first time you try. You've obviously been on one before."

I shook my head. "Before coming here, I didn't even know flying brooms existed."

"Even the best racers had to start somewhere, Conrad." He threw up his hands. "Boomsticks require skill and grace. You're neither skilled nor graceful, at least when you're on the ground."

I probably should have been insulted, but he was right. "I know. I can't explain it, but I feel so confident on a broom, it's like I could do anything."

"Hmm." He put a hand to his chin. "We'll have to put that to the test. In the meantime"—he jabbed a finger at his student—"maybe you could teach her a thing or two."

"Oh, I don't think I could teach."

"Why not?"

I hesitated, unsure how to explain. "I can't explain how I'm able to fly so well. It's like I just know what I'm doing."

Max's gave me an incredulous wide-eyed look. "Well, Mr. Expert, if you figure it out, I sure could use a hand. Ambria is awful at this and she keeps yelling at me."

"I heard that!" Ambria shouted up at us. She raised a fist and shook it at him. "Mark my words, Maxwell Tiberius, I'll be better than you in no time."

He cupped a hand to his mouth and shouted back. "Yeah, we'll see about that!"

We spent the entire morning working with Ambria. I tried to explain how to perform maneuvers, but found it impossible to put into words. When Max described the mechanics, it made perfect sense. I discovered that, despite my innate ability, I still benefitted from Max's instructions.

"It's always been my dream to be a broom racer," he explained as we ate lunch. "I want to be one of the greats, like Kyle Korvani or Uta Melder."

As he spoke of racing, a fervor ignited inside of me. "What about Lulu Strazinski?"

His mouth stopped moving mid-sentence. "How do you know about her?"

I tried to answer, but couldn't think of a good reason why. "Maybe I overheard it somewhere."

Max shook his head. "She was one of the top racers back before the Overlord ruined everything."

"Can we stop with the racing talk and go clothes shopping, please?" Ambria gave Max a long look. "I'm sick of wearing these raggedy old clothes."

"I guess." Max didn't sound the least bit excited.

We spent much of the afternoon following Ambria as she went from shop to shop searching for the perfect dresses. I also made her try on black jeans, shirts, and hoodies since we'd need dark clothes for our assault on the orphanage. When we returned to the house, we each had a variety of new clothes, and bags of groceries.

"I want to meet the vampires," Max said. "They're usually too busy trying to suck your blood to be very nice."

"Only Desmond is nice." Ambria sniffed. "Sonia is insufferable."

Desmond emerged from the basement a little after sundown. He handed me my cleaned linens and clothes and greeted Max politely. "It's nice to meet you."

"What's it like being a vampire and drinking blood?" Max asked.

Ambria rolled her eyes. "Don't bother him with your foolish questions."

Desmond chuckled. "I guess it's like being normal and drinking hot tea, except it's red and salty."

213

"Oh." Max didn't seem to find the response very exciting, but didn't pester him further.

I made some eggs and toast for dinner, and then we went upstairs to my bedroom with our tea so we could make plans.

"I've given a lot of thought to Operation Orphans," Max said.

Ambria snorted. "Did you really give the rescue a name?"

"Every successful operation needs a name," he replied. He took my phone and projected an image of the orphanage and the farmland around it then drew arrows from the sheep pasture toward the rear of the house. "We'll fly in from this direction while everyone is eating, sneak in the back door, and throw one of the stun potions Galfandor gave us at the adults while they're pigging out."

"Wait a moment," Ambria said. "You want to attack the adults?"

"We need to put them out of commission so we can get the orphans," he said. "Trying to go in after everyone is in bed won't work because the house defenses will be active."

"Defenses?" I asked.

"Yeah, the hounds, and probably magic wards." He drew a circle around the house. "After you two escaped, I'm sure they upgraded their perimeter." He pointed at the dining hall. "Everyone will be in there at the same time. With the adults knocked out, the orphans can eat the mushrooms and escape all at once instead of us going door-to-door and waking them up."

Ambria looked as if she really wanted to disagree, but finally nodded. "I hate to say it, Max, but your idea is pretty good."

I held up a couple of the small stun potions. "How long do these last?"

"If they're anything like the ones my brothers have used on me, they should last at least ten minutes."

"Ten minutes is a short amount of time to give mushrooms to the orphans," I said.

"Not really. You told me there were only sixteen orphans left after you two left."

"Unless they added more," Ambria replied.

Max shrugged. "Feeding mushrooms to all of them won't take long, especially with three of us there to do it."

Ambria poked her chin with a finger. "How long do the mushrooms last?"

"It depends on the size of the person." He looked up as if calculating. "We should have at least an hour of free sailing."

Ambria looked at a towel where she'd placed the mushrooms. "We have enough mushrooms for two doses per person, and then a couple extra."

I posed another question. "How long is the flight from Queens Gate to the orphanage on these brooms?"

"At top speed, just under two hours unless the wind is in our face." Max looked at the brooms, a dreamy look in his eyes. "It's going to be a fun ride."

We went over the plan a few more times, looking for any holes, but couldn't find any. I wished I had an adult to consult, but as Galfandor had made it quite clear he wouldn't directly help, I decided not to bother asking him.

We spent the rest of the week training Ambria to fly and keeping an eye open for the Goodleighs in case they returned to investigate Levi's house. We didn't see them, but they could have easily come and gone while we were out practicing with the brooms.

The nightmare creatures in my dreams became more demanding with every passing night. I woke up in the mornings with headaches that took hours to fade. I didn't tell the others, fearful I'd worry them about my ability to perform. I was more than ready to start Operation Orphans. Finishing it put me closer to talking to Dr. Cumberbatch and removing this awful curse.

As we ate lunch that Saturday, I announced my readiness. "I think it's time for Operation Orphans."

Chapter 27

Max gave Ambria an uneasy look, but nodded. "I think she's ready enough. It's not like we'll need to do anything crazy."

We gathered our supplies, dividing the magic scrolls and various potions among us and storing them in the pouches of utility belts we'd purchased. Galfandor had included a large bottle of rot potion, clearly indicating what fate he thought the orphanage should suffer once we rescued everyone. *I should stun the adults and bring the house down on them.* I shivered with delight.

I stopped what I was doing and looked at my trembling hands. *What's wrong with me? Why do I want to kill people?*

"Are you okay?" Ambria asked.

I looked into her wide, concerned eyes. "I'm fine. Just the jitters."

"Me too," Max declared. "I'm excited and ready to leap into action, but my stomach feels like it's full of squirmy worms."

Ambria tucked a last potion into her utility belt. "I'm not scared one little bit." She shuddered and quickly stiffened her spine. "Well, maybe just a little."

I tightened a utility belt around my waist, using the very last notch. "It's okay to be scared. You'd have to be mental to think this is going to be easy."

"At least we don't have a lycan to worry about," Max said.

"What if the Goodleighs are magicians too?" Ambria said.

Max groaned. "*Arcanes.*"

She pshawed. "Oh, whatever."

"Learn the proper words or you'll make people angry at you."

"I'm hardly worried about the Goodleighs being upset with me, silly." Ambria giggled. "If all goes well, they'll be furious with us."

I took a pair of goggles from the table and placed them on my head. The potions sloshed in their bottles as I walked to my broom, causing the belt to tug against my waist, but it stayed in place. I picked up the broom and turned to the others who were still debating Overworld terms and calmly announced, "I'm ready."

Max grabbed his broom and held it over his head. "Let's free some orphans!"

"To the rescue!" Ambria shouted.

I left a note for Desmond, telling him where we were going just in case we failed and never returned. At least they wouldn't wonder what had happened to us, though Sonia would probably be happy with us gone.

We went outside, mounted our brooms, and took off for the exit to Queens Gate. Once we were topside in rainy London, we had to search for a concealed area from where we could take flight. People scurried about, heads down beneath their umbrellas, though a few cast curious glances at the kids carrying odd brooms and wearing suspicious belts. I hoped they assumed we were janitors, though we probably looked too young to play the part.

A blind alley offered an excellent launching pad. After a quick look around to make sure there were no witnesses, we mounted our brooms and tugged the goggles over our eyes. Our brooms shot us upward into the blinding rain. Droplets stung my cheeks and chilled my fingers to the bone. Thunder rumbled and a shout of glee erupted from my throat. I felt free as a bird, leaving all life's worries shackled to the ground below.

When I burst above the clouds, the elation dissipated. More troubles lay ahead. I would eventually have to return to earth and face them. I wiped moisture from the goggles and took out the phone. After I selected "broom" as the mode of travel, the device indicated the straightest route back to the orphanage.

Max grinned and slashed his hand in a forward chop. "Onward to victory."

I nodded. "Onward."

The clouds thinned as we flew over the countryside, offering views of towns and rolling pastureland. We reached the outskirts of the farm within an hour and a half. Using a cloudbank as cover, we surveyed the orphanage below. I spotted boys working around the barns, trimming hedges, and maintaining the lawn. Though I couldn't see faces clearly from this vantage, I spotted a tall, thin figure who appeared to be Marcus Goodleigh himself overseeing the work. He apparently hadn't hired a replacement for Brickle.

Perhaps werewolves are hard to come by.

We still had another hour before dinner was served, so we flew away from the orphanage grounds to a neighboring pasture and set down near some rocks we used as seats. Ambria reached into Max's rucksack and unpacked corned beef sandwiches, sausages, and tea that was, sadly, cold. We ate in silence. The others cast furtive glances at our surroundings. The rattling bell of a sheep in the distance brought Max leaping to his feet. He blushed and sat back down.

"I'm on edge too," Ambria admitted. "My nerves feel tight as a drum."

He gave a grim-faced nod. "We just need to act quickly and decisively. Stun the adults, feed the orphans mushrooms, and Bob's your uncle."

"Let's hope it's that simple," I said.

After we finished our meal, the minutes ticked by slowly. We practiced our opening rescue routine: dashing, uncorking our potions, and pretending to throw them. Max would throw first. If he stunned all the adults, Ambria and I would quickly gather the orphans and lead them into the sheep pasture, feeding them mushrooms along the way. If he failed, Ambria would throw her potion. If disaster struck, I would use my stun potion.

I rubbed my thumb against the cork on the bottle of rot. I no longer felt the insane urge to bring down the manor on the adults, but I would destroy the house no matter what.

Finally, it was time.

We mounted our brooms and flew just high enough to clear the pasture walls. Sheep scattered beneath, bells ringing. I hoped the noise wouldn't alert anyone inside since there was still another hour or so of daylight left. Stopping just outside the stone wall around the pasture, I peered over it and made sure no one was outside. Aside from pigs, the barnyard looked clear.

Max went to the upstairs window I'd used to escape and looked through. He held up a thumb, went around the corner to look into the window to the study, and returned to our hiding spot behind the wall. "Nobody upstairs or in the study. They must all be in the dining hall."

We were just about to head for the backdoor when a snuffling noise drew our attention. Brickle's four hounds padded around the opposite corner of the house, nostrils up in the air.

Max's breath hissed between clenched teeth. "What now?"

"Stun potion," Ambria said.

Max shook his head. "That'll alert everyone inside." He groaned. "I thought the dogs wouldn't be out yet."

"I'd hoped the Goodleighs wouldn't release them until after dinner." My mind raced through alternatives. "I'll lure them away from the house and into the pasture. We can use a stun potion on them out here."

Ambria nodded. "That should keep them from alerting the house."

"I just hope the stun doesn't wear off before we're done." Max looked around. "We're bringing the orphans out here while we wait for the mushrooms to kick in, remember?"

His comment gave me a better idea. "How much corned beef do we have left?"

Ambria withdrew a plastic baggy. "Plenty. Don't tell me you're hungry again."

Max looked at the food. "Are you going to drug it and feed it to the dogs?"

A grin stretched my lips. "Something like that." I told them what to do and took a handful of beef with me. Flying just above the trees, I dropped a clump of beef on the dirt road behind the house. The hounds abruptly shifted their attention toward the noise and raced to investigate. The first one gobbled the meat and sniffed the ground for more.

I dropped another meatball and another, leading the pack to the open pasture gate. The hounds raced through and found four meatballs waiting for them. I watched to make sure each dog ate one and then dropped more meatballs to lead the hounds further into the pasture. Once they'd passed the grove of trees in the center, I dropped lower so the hounds could see me.

Growls rumbled deep in their throats. As one, the pack raced toward me, teeth flashing. One of them leapt at me. I swept my broom to the side. Instead of falling back to the ground, the dog tumbled through the air like an astronaut in space. A chorus of whines and yelps told me the other hounds had achieved liftoff. I ducked beneath a flailing canine somersaulting several feet off the ground.

"Fairy mushrooms sure are handy," Ambria said as she and Max emerged from the tree grove.

Max laughed at a hound flying over the heads of startled sheep. "I'm glad we had those extra mushrooms."

"Me too." I motioned the others to follow me. "We don't have time to waste."

They quickly sobered.

Max nodded. "Let's go."

We flew behind the house and left the brooms hovering a few feet outside the backdoor. I eased open the door and peered into the hallway. Dirty boots lined the floor next to the mud bench. I listened and heard the clinking of silverware emanating from the direction of the dining hall. We crept down the hall toward the open double doors, keeping our backs to the wall so we stayed out of sight. My throat felt too tight to draw a breath and my heart rammed against my chest as if it wanted to burst free.

I felt a hand grip my forearm. I looked back into Ambria's large, worried eyes and managed what I hoped was a reassuring smile. Peeking around the doorframe, I saw the Goodleighs, Oadby, and the other three staff members eating a large roast and drinking red wine. Oadby stood to cut himself another generous portion of beef.

The fear and anxiety melted into a low simmering anger. *Their good life is about to come to an end.* The thought made me happy.

I looked back and motioned to Max. He gulped, nodded, and uncorked his stun potion. He took a faltering step and stopped, seemingly frozen in place, right in plain view of anyone who looked through the open doors. I frantically waved him on, but fear had taken control.

Ambria grabbed the bottle from him, dashed into the open door and threw the potion. "Get stunned, you evil rotters!"

The people at the table barely had time to register what was happening when the potion landed in the middle of the table. It detonated with a brilliant flash and resounding clap of thunder. People flipped over backward in their chairs. Oadby let out a loud cry and stumbled backward, dragging the tablecloth and with it, several plates of food on top of him. The Goodleighs went limp face-first onto their plates.

Pandemonium erupted.

Children ran screaming, many cowering beneath tables, while others seemed too shocked to move.

I ran into the room and jumped on a table, waving my hands and shouting. "Calm down, everyone, we're here to free you!"

I saw William and Stephan holding spoons in their hands as if they might use them to fight. Their eyes went huge at the sight of me prancing around on the table.

"Killer Conrad?" Stephan shouted. "He kidnapped Ambria and murdered her."

"He's come to kill us all!" William screamed.

The children's cries intensified. Someone threw their oatmeal at me. I ducked as a spoon whizzed past my head.

I held up a hand. "We're here to save you, not kill you."

Ambria leapt atop the table. "Quiet!" she screeched at the top of her lungs.

Everyone froze in place.

"Wait, how is she still alive?" William said. "The Goodleighs said you'd killed and eaten her."

"He saved me you little fools." Ambria pointed toward the exit. "Now, let us save you before the adults wake up and chop us to bits."

"Save us?" Stephan snorted. "We have a home and food. What are you saving us from?"

Ambria kicked a bowl toward him. "Because, stupid, the Goodleighs were going to sell me on the black market."

William chortled. "You're mental."

Ambria picked up a spoon and threw it at him. "Believe what you want. If you want to come live in a place where magic works, follow us."

"Magic?" asked a little girl named Beth. "Like unicorns and fairies?"

"Beautiful magic," Ambria said.

The younger boys and girls gravitated toward her.

"She's lying," Stephan said. "There's no such thing as magic."

William put a hand out to stop them from coming to us. "Don't listen to her."

Some of the adults groaned and began to stir.

Ambria whipped out a scroll and unrolled it. "I don't have time for this." She chanted the words and cast a hand at William. In a flash of green light, he turned into a frog.

Stephan yelped and tripped backwards over his own shoes in his haste to get away.

Little Mary squealed and clapped her hands. "A frog prince!"

Catherine, a girl a little younger than Ambria, grimaced. "Just don't make me kiss him."

Another girl her age stepped forward. "We believe you, Ambria. Lead the way."

Ambria smiled. "Thanks, Alice."

William croaked once more and flashed back into a very frightened looking boy. He scrambled to his feet and stared with horror at Ambria. "You're a witch."

"An Arcane, you idiot." She pointed at the door. "Are you coming or not?"

He didn't hesitate to answer. "Yes, I'm coming. Just don't turn me into a frog again."

Ambria opened a pouch and began distributing mushrooms. "Eat these once you get outside."

Stephan emerged from beneath a table and took one, though he regarded it suspiciously. "Will these turn us all into frogs?"

"No, they'll make you light as fairies," she replied.

"Pixie dust!" little Mary shouted with glee.

I looked beneath the tables to make sure nobody else was hiding and found the little boy the Goodleighs had kidnapped the day Ambria and I had left. I gave him a reassuring smile. "Hi, I'm Conrad. What's your name?"

"I'm Toddy." Tears glistened in his eyes. "I'm scared."

I reached a hand for him. "We're here to protect you."

He backed away.

"Hurry," Ambria said. "The adults are waking up."

"Please come, Toddy. If you don't, you'll be left all alone here."

His eyes went wide as saucers. "Don't leave me alone!" Toddy scrambled from beneath the table.

Ambria took his hand and led him and the others to the exit. "We'll never leave you alone."

I took another look around and then turned to follow.

"Conrad," a weak voice hissed. Marcus tried to push himself up from the table, but his arms collapsed beneath him. "You little traitor."

"You're the traitors," I replied in a cold harsh voice. "Selling children into slavery for profit."

He began to chant the strange song I'd heard during our drives in the car. My legs went weak and it was all I could do to remain standing. A sudden realization struck me. This was no song, but a sleeping spell. Try as I might, I couldn't resist the haunting lullaby. Black dots formed at the edges of my vision. My knees hit the floor. Felicity rose behind her husband and pulled a gleaming butcher knife from the bloody roast on the table.

Her lips peeled back in a snarl. "More trouble than you're worth, brat."

I tried to grab the potion at my belt, but my arms were limp. My body swayed, and toppled to the side. Watching helplessly as Felicity staggered closer with the knife, I hoped Ambria and Max could escape without me.

I heard a loud shout. A stone struck Marcus right in the nose. He yelled and fell off his chair. Another stone hit Felicity in the forehead. She screamed, dropped the knife. The light pushed back the darkness in my vision and the world snapped into focus.

"Get up, you lazy git." Max's grinning face appeared. "Look, Conrad, I'm awful sorry about freezing up back there. I was so scared—"

"Save the apologies for later." I held up a hand. "Now help me up."

He tugged me to my feet and looked back at the adults. "Should we stun them again?"

I fingered the rot potion and thought about it. Stunning them again would ensure their deaths. I didn't want so many souls on my conscience. "No. Let's go."

We ran down the hallway. I uncorked the rot potion and threw it into the central corridor. Black smoke poured from the bottle. Within seconds, every wooden object it touched disintegrated. The ceiling

223

began to buckle, and I knew it was time to leave. Max and I raced outside and spotted Ambria leading the orphans down the dirt road to the pasture. We grabbed the three brooms and followed.

The central part of the manor imploded in a cloud of dust. I saw Oadby and other adults coughing and running from the back kitchen entrance. Of the Goodleighs, I saw no sign. If they died in the collapse, I would shed no tears for them.

Chapter 28

By the time we reached the field, several of the smaller children were already floating and giggling with delight. Thankfully, Ambria had instructed everyone to join hands so no one floated off.

"I'm feeling really weird," William said. "My stomach is all wibbly wobbly."

Stephan unleashed a loud belch. "I might toss up my gruel."

"Don't be a ninny," Ambria said. She looked at Max and me. "Are you ready?"

Max didn't meet her gaze, but nodded. "We're ready."

"What are those brooms for?" William asked.

I dropped mine and let it hover. "This is how we're getting out of here."

"Ambria is a good witch," little Mary declared as she floated several feet off the ground with Alice and Catherine holding hers and Beth's hands.

I grabbed a strand of diamond fiber and fastened it to the back of Ambria's broomstick and then threaded it around the waists of five girls. I repeated the procedure with Max's broom, attaching William, Toddy, and the smaller boys together.

"Why aren't you tying me with William?" Stephan asked.

"Because you two are the heaviest," I said. "Even with the fairy mushrooms, we'll need to balance the load."

He cried out as his feet left the ground. "I don't like this at all. I'm afraid of heights."

Ren, Johnny, and the other boys squealed with glee as they flipped through the air. I grabbed the broom to keep them from dragging it away. "Well, by the time this flight is over, you shouldn't be scared anymore."

"I think they're light enough to go," Max said.

Ambria mounted her broom. "Up, up, and away." She eased forward, letting the slack in the rope tighten and then angled up, trailing giggling girls behind her, except for Alice, who squeezed her eyes shut and curled into a ball as they gained altitude.

"That's smart," Max said. "I was about to take off at full speed."

I didn't want to admit it, but had been about to do just the same. "Easy does it," I told him. "Don't want to give anyone whiplash."

We followed Ambria's example and ascended at a gentle angle. Stephan gibbered with fear and clenched the diamond fiber rope so tight his knuckles went white. Soon, we were flying fast, though nowhere near top speed. We hadn't brought goggles for the other children and didn't want them to be too uncomfortable.

I heard a pop and a whiz. Max cried out and grabbed his shoulder. He pulled away his hand to reveal blood. Another pop startled me. I turned and saw Marcus's black car flying not far behind us. Felicity hung out the passenger window with a long rifle. She took aim and fired.

Stephan screamed and grabbed his leg. "I've been shot! I've been shot!"

The sedan closed quickly. I saw Marcus reach a handgun out the window. Shots popped, but they must have all missed, because nobody screamed.

"Evasive action!" Max yelled.

Ambria and I looked at him with confusion.

He shouted again. "It means, split up!"

More shots rang out.

I shook my head. "We can't split up. Someone needs to get rid of the Goodleighs."

"We can't just fly willy-nilly with children in tow," Ambria said.

I angled down, then flew sideways beneath Ambria and the others while Stephan continued to cry in pain and the other children burst into screams and tears. "I'm going to attach my group to yours," I told Ambria. "Then I'll take care of the Goodleighs."

Her forehead wrinkled into a worried look. "Be careful, Conrad."

I unfastened the diamond fiber from my broom and attached it to the rope trailing behind Alice, the last girl, in Ambria's train. "Will do."

226

Using my mysterious, innate flying skill, I looped the broom upside down to reverse direction and rolled upright. Bullets sang past me. I hugged the broom and flew in circles, making myself a hard target. I felt no fear, only grim determination. It was time to finish the Goodleighs once and for all.

Felicity cocked the rifle bolt and fired. Pulled the bolt to eject a shell, and fired again. I dodged back and forth, up and down. As I drew to within a few yards, she sneered and took out a shorter gun with a long clip. She pulled back a small lever, squeezed the trigger. A hail of bullets exploded from the muzzle.

I yelped and did a wide barrel loop followed by a steep dive. Sharp pain bit into my leg. I clenched my teeth and ignored it the best I could. The black car swerved through a small cloud to follow me as I whizzed past. I looked back and saw Felicity jam another clip into the automatic gun. The car caught up to me quickly. The rat-a-tat of bullets warned me to dodge. I jerked left then hit the brakes hard. The sedan flew overhead. I increased speed and flew just beneath it.

"Where is he?" I heard Marcus shout.

I grabbed a metal flange beneath the car and held on. The car veered around as they searched for me. Felicity's upside-down face appeared from my right. The gun barrel appeared a split second later. I turned off the broom and released the pipe. Bullets exploded as I tumbled toward earth. I felt a rush of wind as one narrowly missed my head. Felicity burned through the ammo within seconds and the gun went silent. I flicked on the broom and angled up toward the driver door as Felicity withdrew inside the car to reload.

Marcus saw me in the rear view mirror and angled his handgun out the window. He fired, but missed every shot without me even moving. I put on full speed, reached into my pouch, and flicked a cork from a potion. Felicity jammed a clip into the gun and pulled herself into a sitting position halfway out of the window just as I drew even with Marcus.

"I hope you burn," I said in a cold voice and threw the stun potion in the window.

I veered away an instant before the interior of the car detonated in a brilliant white flash. Felicity shrieked and Marcus screamed. The car careened out of control, rolling, spinning, and diving. It plunged into the woods with a loud boom and screech of metal. I almost flew away, but stopped and turned toward the area.

I need to be sure.

A trail of broken saplings led me to the final resting place where the sedan had struck a large oak. The front section was crushed and the windscreen shattered. Marcus's broken body draped across the steering wheel. Felicity lay on the hood, eyes wide and unseeing. Blood pooled around her head. I shuddered and looked away. They were dead.

I cut power to the broom and fell to my knees, vomiting. Shadowy voices whispered in my head.

Good boy, said a masculine voice in my head. *Leave no enemy alive.*

"No, I'm not a good boy," I said. "I'm evil. I kill people."

You make us proud.

"I make me sick!"

A feminine voice, like that of the cat shadow, spoke. *Gather the blood for a ritual. We will destroy their entire lineage!*

The voices grew louder and more demanding. I couldn't silence them no matter how hard I tried. An ache grew in my head, the pain pounding against my temples.

"No!" I cried. "Leave me alone!"

In an instant, there was silence.

"Hello, Conrad," said a familiar voice.

I opened my eyes and saw Dr. Cumberbatch standing on a flying carpet not far away. "What—how—"

"I set wards around the farm and pastures in the hopes you might someday return. The moment you appeared, they alerted me." He smiled. "It was very brave of you to confront the Goodleighs, Conrad. Now it's time for you to be brave once more."

"Brave?" I rose to my feet. "What's wrong with me? Why am I cursed?"

He took out a wand. "You'll find out in due time." He flicked the wand. Dark mist swallowed the light.

Consciousness fled.

Cora's feeble hands touch mine. She sucks in a harsh breath. In a matter of days, the cancer has taken everything from her, but she still manages to smile at me.

"I'm sorry, there's nothing more we can do," the doctor says to her.

She nods.

"I notified the orphanage," he says.

A tear wells in her eye.

I can't hold back any longer and burst into sobs. "Please don't go, Mummy." I want to hug her, but I know it will only hurt her fragile body.

I hear a familiar voice behind me. "It's time to go, Conrad."

I look back and see Mr. Goodleigh, his face flat and emotionless.

"She's still alive." I say.

The doctor gives Mr. Goodleigh a disbelieving look. "Sir, you need to wait in the hallway."

Mr. Goodleigh's eyes harden and I know I'll be punished when I return to the orphanage. I don't care.

I kiss my true mother on the cheek. "I love you, Mummy."

"Be good, son." Her breath rattles in her throat. "I will always love you."

Her chest deflates, and the light fades from her eyes.

I have lost everything.

Finally! The cat shadow stretched as if waking from a nap. *We are here.*

The other shadow hovered overhead like a dark cloud. *The curse will be ended.*

I jolted awake but couldn't move. I lay flat on something hard and wooden, my limbs, chest, and head secured by what felt like leather straps. I could turn my head, but try as I might, couldn't slip beneath the bond. The table rotated upright. Cold stone kissed my bare feet. The phone in my pants pocket pressed against my leg, but I couldn't reach it.

Dr. Cumberbatch stood in front of me, eyes bright. "Ah, Conrad, you're finally awake. Time to begin." He slid the strap from my head. "That should make you more comfortable."

"What are you doing to me?"

"Preparing to remove the spell I placed on you so long ago." He sighed with satisfaction. "I'd planned to release you on this birthday, but the Goodleighs refused to leave you with me."

I used my new freedom to crane my head. We were in the doctor's wine cellar. Two large oak barrels sat to either side of me. "Did they know about the curse?"

"Of course not." He chuckled. "I, of course, knew about the deleterious side effects of demon magic, so after putting you under this enchantment, I knew the best thing to do was get you far away from me."

"You put me in the orphanage?" A terrible anger burned inside me. This man was responsible for Cora's death. He was responsible for more deaths than I could count.

"I'd worked with the Goodleighs for quite some time in their little enterprise." He shrugged. "It seemed a very good place to keep tabs on you."

I realized I was asking the wrong question. "Why did you put me under this enchantment in the first place?"

His eyes brightened. "I summoned a minor demon to possess you. It was the only way to preserve souls."

Horror twisted my stomach. "I'm possessed? Were those demons I saw in my dreams?"

He clapped his hands together once. "This is the exciting part, Conrad. Brace yourself."

"I'm already braced, thank you very much." Nausea crept up my throat as I thought of the evil parasite feeding off my body and soul.

"Get ready for a late birthday surprise, young man." He stepped to the barrel on my right, undid a clasp on the side, and swung it open like a coffin. A man's body lay inside, a shimmering nimbus surrounding his body. Cumberbatch moved to the second barrel and opened it as well. A woman, hands across her chest, rested inside. The doctor splayed his hands like a magician who'd just opened a cabinet to reveal the conclusion of a trick. "Ta-da!"

My eyes went wide as I recognized the corpses. "My parents!"

"Yes, yes, yes!" He puffed out his chest. "I'm surprised you recognize them." Cumberbatch leaned in close. "In a moment, you'll get to meet them."

"Meet them? But they're dead!"

"They've never been *dead*, my boy, just temporarily out of body." He bent down and examined a demon-summoning diagram at my feet. "When they were cornered and facing defeat, I knew there was only one way to save them." He stood and brushed off his hands. "If everyone thought they were dead, nobody would look for them. With my specialty in demonology, I knew of a way to make that happen."

Somehow, I suddenly knew the answer. "You summoned the demon to siphon their souls, using my body as a vessel so the demon wouldn't consume them." I knew right then that the shadowy cat and snake I'd seen in my dreams had been the twisted souls of my parents.

Cumberbatch seemed disappointed at my revelation, but his face brightened. "Ah, the knowledge of the souls living within you must have leeched into your subconscious." He tapped his chin. "It must have finally countered the dampening effect of the enchantment on your intelligence."

"Is that why I was so stupid?" I asked.

"Indeed."

My lips peeled back. "What kind of a doctor are you?"

"A very skilled one." He tested my bonds. "I was once but a healer until I discovered a wealth of other magics to complement those skills."

"Like demon magic."

He pursed his lips. "Precisely."

I strained against my bonds. "You're as evil and twisted as my parents."

"No, you're wrong there, lad. Evil is a term used by those who don't understand greatness, by those who lack the intelligence to grasp the power afforded them." The doctor's eyes narrowed. "Your parents were—are—great visionaries. With the Overworld on the brink of collapse, and Ivy Slade gone, there will be nothing to stop them this time."

I wanted the curse removed, but didn't want my parents back. It was an odd admission for an orphan, I realized, but my family had murdered their way into power. I calmed down and tried to reason with the man. "Don't bring them back, sir. Why don't you let the demon have them and take power for yourself? You're obviously brilliant."

Cumberbatch chuckled. "I'm a genius, boy. My playground is hypothesis and theory, not policy-making or governing the brainless masses. I prefer to work with people who support my quest for knowledge—visionaries like your parents." He picked up a thick rod from the table behind him and flicked it. It sprung into a long staff with a large green gem at the top. "Speaking of which, it's time to begin."

He began to chant strange unfamiliar words.

"No!" I wriggled and pressed futilely against the straps. "Stop!"

He ignored me and continued. I felt something writhing inside me, reacting to the spell. My vision blackened for a brief moment and my head lolled forward. When I jerked back to full consciousness, I suddenly understood the foreign language. It wasn't just any language, but the demon tongue.

"Sovodorak, I call you forth. Show your form. Release the souls." He repeated the chant over and over again. I felt something tear loose from me, like tape peeling from my skin. A dark presence stepped forward and slammed into an invisible barrier. It turned toward me, snarling.

It was like looking in a mirror of shadows, for the face was my own.

I shouted and pressed my head against the table, desperately wishing I could get away from this thing before it tore me apart.

The demon's face and body sucked inside out and suddenly its back was to me once again, a wispy umbilical cord stretching from it and into my stomach. "You broke your word, Arcane," it hissed. "You swore to give me a body to use all those years ago. Instead, I've been a prisoner inside a heap of flesh."

Cumberbatch held up a hand. "Apologies, Sovodorak. The spell did not work quite as envisioned, but it worked well enough."

"Well enough?" the demon spat. "Look at me." He spread his arms. "My form is now that of the boy's. This possession has irreparably harmed me."

"I'm certain you'll eventually return to your normal form," Cumberbatch assured him. "For now, I need you to return the souls to their vessels."

"Not until you restore me."

"Don't make me force you to do this, Sovodorak." Cumberbatch sneered. "You know I can make it very unpleasant."

"You already have, *magician*."

The doctor stiffened and scowled. "How dare you!" His fists clenched. "Very well. You leave me no alternative." He pounded the butt of his staff on the ground and began to chant again.

Sovodorak slammed against his invisible prison. "Release me or I will send your soul to the Abyss!"

Terror froze me. I prayed the demon wouldn't turn his rage on me.

The demon stiffened. His arms splayed as if invisible strings pulled at him. He howled in agony. Cumberbatch slammed his staff again. I felt as if a giant worm was crawling up my gullet. I wanted to scream, but only produced a ghastly choking noise. Oily smoke poured from my mouth. It clouded my vision, obscuring everything. The smoke morphed into the faces of my parents. Ghostly shrieks tore from their mouths. Their souls drifted apart and funneled into their bodies. Their ghastly cries faded.

Cumberbatch roared in a commanding voice. "Return to Haedaemos, Sovodorak. Return to your realm!"

The ground beneath the summoning diagram bubbled thick and black. The demon roared. "I will return, Cumberbatch. When I do, I will devour your soul!" The tar writhed like snakes around the demon and sucked him into the ground.

I suddenly felt alone.

A great weight lifted from my body—from my very soul. If I hadn't been bound, I might have flown away. The world sharpened into focus and every color became richer and deeper. Sounds became crisper, and a mélange of odors suffused my nose. I felt a hollow space deep within me, and then a craving. Unseen energy suffused the air around me. I drew it in like taking a deep breath and felt the hunger dissipate. I was no longer living beneath the smothering blanket of a demon and my parents' souls.

I was free!

Groans emanated from either side of me. I flicked my head this way and that and saw movement in the barrels. My parents sat up. Slowly, they looked at each other and smiled.

The Overlord and his wife were once again alive.

Chapter 29

This moment would have brought tremendous happiness to most people. Seeing my parents risen from the dead was, for me, frightening beyond belief.

Victus crawled slowly from the large cask like an old man rising from bed. He walked around me without a word and helped Delectra out of her barrel coffin. They exchanged a passionate kiss.

My father raised his fist as if to pump it in the air, halted, and grabbed his back. "I am stiff and sore, Cumberbatch. I have lain dormant far too long."

"I too feel wretched," Delectra said. "But it is good to be among the living once again."

The doctor rubbed his hands together. "I've prepared potions that should fix you two right up." He retrieved bottles of sparkling blue liquid from his table and handed one to each.

They gulped them down. Victus stretched and twisted his back. "Ah, much better." He spread his arms as if soaking in the air. I felt the invisible energy around me move, as if drawn toward him. He frowned. "I still don't feel quite right."

"In time, in time," Cumberbatch said. "You've only just risen from the dead."

Delectra walked in front of me, looking me up and down. "I find it hard to believe this puny thing is our child."

Her condescension infuriated me. "I suppose you're not as superior as you believed."

Cumberbatch cleared his throat. "Ah, well, the spell took a toll on him physically and mentally. I assure you there is nothing wrong with your offspring. He should rebound with the demon magic lifted from his soul." He picked up a pair of rose-tinted spectacles like the ones Galfandor had used and looked me over. "Hmm, this is odd."

"What is?" Delectra snatched the spectacles from his nose and held them in front of her eyes. "What is that odd glow around him?"

"It would appear some fragments of your souls have stuck to him." He prodded me with a finger. "Perhaps I could compose a spell to free them."

Victus pursed his lips. "How long will that take?"

"Perhaps a month or two." Cumberbatch lifted my chin and shrugged. "Maybe longer."

"There must be a quicker method," Delectra said. "If we freed his soul, would that release the fragments?"

The doctor nodded. "Most certainly, but—"

"Then do it," Victus commanded. "We don't have time to waste if we're to seize the government."

I couldn't believe what I was hearing. "I'm your son, you evil buggers!"

They ignored my outburst.

Cumberbatch nodded at Victus's assertion. "Yes, the time is ripe for a coup as I'm sure you overheard while still trapped within Conrad." He backed up a step. "Consider this. Your son has an excellent pedigree and is of age. He could be turned into a powerful Arcane."

My parents seemed to ponder his suggestion.

I pressed against my bonds. "What sort of parents would kill their son for power? Is there no limit to your wickedness?"

Delectra pressed a cool hand to my forehead and pressed me back against the platform. "As our son, you should want what is best for the family." She released my head and then slapped the daylights out of me. "Now shut your mouth and do as you're told."

"We can always have another child." Victus folded his arms and gave me a dispassionate look. "You served your purpose as others have before you." He gave me an almost human-looking smile. "Conrad, you have the distinction of living longer than your other siblings. You should count that as a blessing."

The revelation slammed me in the guts. "I have siblings?"

"I'm afraid demons require sacrifices to teach their magic," Cumberbatch said. "Your parents have always been willing to donate."

The scream of horror that erupted from me sounded animalistic even to my ears. I thrashed in desperation, screaming until my throat went raw. When my energy ran out, I sagged against the leather straps, tears dripping from my eyes and onto the cold floor. "Monsters," I croaked. "I hope a demon eats your souls."

"Be glad that is not your fate, boy." Victus put his forearm against my throat and pressed hard. "You will die quickly, your soul released to the aether."

I looked him in the eyes and peeled back my lips. "Then finish me, you bleeding rotter."

The sound of a metal blade being drawn rang out. Delectra appeared, a curved, scythe-like knife with a gleaming razor edge in her hand. "I see you've kept my favorite knife, Cumberbatch."

He bowed. "Of course, Mistress. I knew you would want it back."

"This blade has tasted the blood of many enemies," Delectra said, tracing the cold metal tip against my forehead. I felt something warm trickling down and over my nose. "Now it will slaughter you like a beast."

I felt an odd, detached calm. I was about to be killed by my own parents, but at least I'd done some good in my short life. Perhaps someone else would eventually defeat Victus and Delectra. Perhaps Ivy would return. *Nothing lasts forever.* They would one day get their due.

I'll be with you soon, Cora—Mum.

I took a deep breath and stared Delectra straight in the eyes. "I'm ready, *Mother*."

She smiled. "Brave lad. You do us proud by not cowering and begging for your life." Delectra swung back her arm.

I saw a flash of movement near the entrance to the basement. A bottle clattered on the floor, rolled behind the three adults, and exploded. My head slammed back against the platform. My parents and Cumberbatch flew forward, slamming face-first into the floor. Delectra's scythe clattered to the floor.

The bodies of the adults must have shielded me from the brunt of the stun potion, because my vision was only slightly blurry. Ambria

236

zipped up to me on a broom and chanted loudly. She abruptly grew to the size of a giant and the world around her swelled to immense proportions. I looked up as her huge hand scooped me up.

"Ribbit!" I said. "Ribbit, ribbit!" I felt an intense craving for flies.

Seconds later, the world shrank back to normal.

"Sorry about the frog spell," Ambria said. "It was the fastest way to get you out of those straps." She patted the back of the broom. "Now, get on, Conrad!"

I hopped on the bare handle behind her seat and grabbed her waist. She took off for the exit. Max waited there on his broom. He grinned like a madman. "I did it, Conrad! I stunned the adults!"

"Good job." My voice emerged as a weak croak.

"You look awful," Ambria said. "I watched that woman cut you. I tried to convince Max we should kill the lot of them, but I don't think we have it in us to do it."

"I do," I said. If I'd had the presence of mind after the blast, I would have slit their throats. Now it was too late to go back and finish the job. *I am my parents' son.*

Max held out my broom as we flew away from the doctor's mansion. "This was in the forest next to the Goodleighs' car."

"We combed the entire mansion," Ambria said. "I didn't think we'd ever find you."

I wiped blood from my face. "How did you know where I was?"

"Max and I set down in the woods to hide with the orphans when you went to fight the Goodleighs." She looked at him. "Then he decided to go help you."

"I saw the Goodleighs' car crash in the forest," he said. "Then I saw a flying carpet go in after you. A few minutes later, that man came out with you unconscious on the carpet. I followed him to his estate and then went back for Ambria. That's why it took so long to rescue you."

"Are you well enough to fly your own broom?" Ambria asked.

I nodded. "Well enough."

Max handed me the broom. I activated and mounted it while we hovered in the air. Then we took off to where Ambria had left the other children. The mushrooms had long since worn off by the time we reached them.

"What happened to you, Conrad?" William asked. "You've got blood all over your face."

Stephan grimaced. "Did someone try to sacrifice you to the devil himself?"

"You might say that," I replied.

"Thank you for saving us from the Goodleighs, Conrad," Alice said. She kissed me on the cheek. "You're our hero."

"Conrad the hero!" little Mary chirped at the top of her tiny lungs.

"Hero!" Beth chimed in.

Before I knew it, all the younger kids were hugging me. Stephan and William gave me begrudging nods.

I looked at Ambria. She seemed to be glaring at Alice for some reason. "How are we going to ferry everyone to Queens Gate?"

Max quirked his lips. "We might have to go get some flying carpets."

"Flying carpets?" Stephan blurted.

I laughed. "After seeing flying brooms you're surprised?"

He looked down. "Well, it's just weird."

"Of course it is." I looked at Max. "Well, let's get some flying carpets."

Max and I sped back to Queens Gate. He borrowed an extra-large flying carpet from his parents' house and we took it back to Ambria and the others. By the time we got back to town, it was nearly three in the morning. The vampires were still out, so we piled everyone into Ambria's room and let them share the sheets from our beds.

I didn't even bother with bathing and collapsed on my bare mattress. When I woke up, it was nearly noon. I heard talking in Ambria's room and went inside. The other children were eating toast and eggs. Ambria walked into the room with a tray laden with more toast and a heaping plate of sausages.

Stephan and William jumped from their spots on the floor and tried to grab more food, but stopped cold when Ambria glared at them. "Don't you dare take anything until I say you can."

The two boys backed away.

"You're bossy," William said.

Ambria set down the tray and set her arms akimbo. "When you're in my house, you do what I say." She looked over at me and smiled. "Good morning, sleepyhead."

I managed a smile. "I'm going to get cleaned up."

She walked over and whispered in my ear. "I set a plate aside for you. It's downstairs in the kitchen."

"Thanks." I took a shower, went downstairs, and dug into the food Ambria had prepared. The flavor of the eggs exploded on my taste buds. I tasted a sausage and groaned with pleasure. The colors in the kitchen seemed so vibrant, as if I'd been seeing things in muted detail all this time. I clenched a fist and felt stronger. In the air around me, I sensed that strange energy I'd first detected at Cumberbatch's after he'd lifted the curse.

Maybe this is what it's like to really be alive.

I savored every bite of the food, and relished hot Earl Grey tea. I'd been numbed for so long, that everything before this day seemed like a shadow reality. My enthusiasm dimmed when I thought about the challenges ahead.

Max showed up when I was nearly finished eating. "How's the hero feeling this morning?"

I jabbed a fork in my sausage. "I'm not a hero. You and Ambria rescued me. You're the heroes."

"Maybe we all are." He shrugged. "Can I have a sausage? I'm starving."

I grinned and gave him one.

Ambria came downstairs a moment later and raised an eyebrow at Max. "Really, now, haven't you already had breakfast?"

"At my parents'," he admitted with a sheepish grin. He jabbed a thumb to his chest. "But a growing boy needs a lot of food."

"Apparently, you need *all* of it." She released a little sigh and sat down. "It's still early, but I'm exhausted. Cooking for so many mouths is hard work."

"We need to figure out what to do with the children." I put down my fork. "I think we should ask Galfandor. He might know how to help."

Ambria nodded. "I think that's the best idea I've heard all morning. We're just children ourselves, and I know Sonia will lose her mind if she discovers the new additions to the household."

I stood and put my dishes next to the sink. "Let's go."

"Now?" Max asked, his mouth full of toast. "I haven't finished eating."

Ambria put her hands on her hips. "Now, Max."

I went upstairs and put William and Alice in charge while we left. "Under no circumstances is anyone to wander around the house or go outside," I said.

"Why not?" Stephan complained. "It's boring up here."

I flattened my expression. "Because vampires live in the basement, and they'll be very unhappy if you wake them."

That comment drew gasps from everyone except for Mary who demanded she get to see the vampires right away.

"Uh, we'll wait right here," William said.

"We'll be back soon." I left and grabbed my broom on the way out. Max, Ambria, and I flew to Moore Manor and knocked on the door.

Galfandor answered a moment later. "Conrad, Ambria, and Max, what a pleasant surprise." He didn't look surprised. "Please, come in." He led us to the dining room where a steaming pot of tea waited. The three of us exchanged confused looks.

"Were you expecting us?" I asked.

"In a manner of speaking, yes."

Max gave him an uneasy look. "You can see the future?"

"Well, he is a magician," Ambria said.

Max winced and hissed, "Arcane, you dummy."

Galfandor chuckled. "I've had the golems set this table for the past several days in anticipation of your return." He smiled. "I thought it would make me look clairvoyant."

"If that's the case, why would you tell us?" I asked.

"I'd rather hoped you wouldn't ask about it." He poured us each a cup of tea. "Now, tell me all about your mission of mercy."

Ambria narrowed her eyes. "I think you really can see the future, but you don't want us to know that, so you're pretending you can't."

Galfandor simply smiled and took a sip of tea.

I enjoyed a mouthful of the Earl Grey as well and then told him the story of rescuing the orphans, but left out what had happened afterward.

"We need someplace for the orphans to live," Ambria concluded.

"Thankfully, I was able to make use of the information Conrad took from the Goodleigh's tablet." Galfandor withdrew an arcphone from his inside pocket and fiddled with it for several seconds before finally finding what he wanted. "All but two of the children have living parents."

Ambria gasped. "Really? That's wonderful."

Galfandor nodded. "It appears the Goodleighs preferred to kidnap children and later tell them they were orphans."

"What about the two without living relatives?" I asked.

He peered at the list. "Ah, well that would be you and Ambria." He gave us an apologetic look. "In any case, you may bring the children here and I will notify their parents. I imagine there will be some very happy reunions."

"Brilliant!" Max declared.

"Every child is also from an Arcane family." Galfandor turned off his phone. "Some of the older ones are even eligible to take the entrance exam to Arcane University."

"We'll bring them here right away," Max said.

Galfandor leaned back in his chair. "There is another matter to discuss."

I tensed. "What would that be?"

"I took the liberty of finding homes for you and Ambria as well."

She and I glanced at each other.

"We're fine where we are," Ambria said.

I didn't quite share her enthusiasm about our current home, but also didn't want to go live with strangers. "We have a house."

"Yes, well, I think it best if you live with adults for the time being." Galfandor regarded us seriously. "Queens Gate is not as safe as it once was."

Max furrowed his brow. "Hang on, now. Didn't you just let us go on a dangerous mission without any adult supervision at all?"

Ambria bolted from her seat. "Exactly. We are perfectly capable of taking care of ourselves, thank you very much."

The old Arcane held up his hands in surrender. "Very well. But if you're interested, I've found relatives for you to live with. They are, unfortunately, noms and as such, don't live in Queens Gate."

"We'll keep it in mind," Ambria said.

The more I thought about Galfandor's proposal, the better it seemed to me, and not simply because we lived in a house with vampires. It was time to tell the old man the rest of the story.

Chapter 30

"There's more to our little adventure," I said.

Galfandor raised an eyebrow. "I'm listening."

"Cumberbatch showed up after the Goodleighs crashed. He knocked me out and took me to his estate where he removed the curse."

"I thought your aura felt different today," Galfandor said. "What made Cumberbatch decide to help you?"

Max snorted. "He didn't exactly help him."

I held up a hand to quiet my friend. "The curse used demon magic."

"No surprise." Galfandor shrugged. "When Cumberbatch first came to Arcane University, he wanted nothing more than to be the best healer. He thought conventional techniques were too limiting and added specializations in demonology and necromancy."

"He summoned a demon to possess me in order to preserve two souls." I let that sink in.

Judging from the troubled look growing in Galfandor's eyes, he probably knew what I'd say next. "Go on, Conrad."

"My parents are alive again."

"Apparently, Conrad still has some of their soul fragments stuck to him," Ambria said. "They were going to kill him."

"I don't think they're a hundred percent," Max added.

"Are you certain your parents are alive again and that Cumberbatch wasn't simply using necromancy on corpses?" Galfandor said. "It can be very hard for most people to discern the difference."

"They were up and talking like normal people, not zombies, if that's what you mean," I said.

"Yes, but did they do magic?" he asked. "People revived by a skilled necromancer will still act like their old selves, provided the bodies were well preserved."

I thought hard but didn't remember my parents doing any sort of magic. "No."

The old Arcane seemed to relax. "Then it's likely he simply revived their corpses. Demon magic doesn't preserve souls. Demons devour souls to perform magic."

"It looked like it worked to me," I said. "How else did I know things that only my parents knew?"

"It's possible, if he tried this insane theory of his, the demon took your parents' souls, and because he possessed you, some of their memories transferred during all those years." He pursed his lips and nodded. "Yes, the curse makes much more sense now."

"So the Overlord and Delectra aren't back for round two?" Max asked, sounding somewhat disappointed.

Galfandor shook his head. "Cumberbatch attempted an impossible feat and failed. I am certain of it."

I didn't know what to say. Despite the extra knowledge drifting around in my head, I knew little about magic. If my parents weren't truly alive, but simply reanimated corpses, then my worries about them were unfounded. I decided to trust Galfandor's word on this.

"We'll bring the orphans—children—to you," I said. It was odd knowing that everything I'd known for most of my childhood had been a lie.

We returned to the house and announced the good news to everyone.

Alice flung herself into my arms. "Oh, Conrad, it's a miracle!" She squeezed me so tight I could hardly breathe. "You've saved us all."

"Saved us all," Ambria said in a mocking voice. "I suppose Max and I simply slept through the ordeal."

Stephan held out his arms. "I'd be happy to hug you, Ambria."

She dropped open her mouth slightly. "I'd rather hug a toad."

"That can be arranged," Max said with a grin.

Alice kissed both my cheeks. "You're very brave, Conrad. I hope to see you again."

Ambria groaned. "Let's load them on the flying carpet."

As she herded the children outside, Max came up to me. "I used to think girls were gross, but I kind of wish Alice would kiss my cheeks too."

I raised my eyebrows. "I could always ask her."

He waved his hands. "No, no, no. That would just be embarrassing." His expression grew serious. "By the way, I figured out how you can fly brooms so well."

I raised an eyebrow. "Tell me."

"Your mother used to be a professional racer." He grinned. "When she was young, she was the champion. Then she met your dad and stopped racing."

"I guess with her soul inside of me, I must have soaked up the skill." I just hoped it would stick with me. And that I soaked up nothing nastier. The thought gave me a shiver.

When we arrived at Galfandor's later that day, several parents had already arrived. Galfandor matched them up with the proper children while Max, Ambria, and I stood by and watched with great satisfaction.

Galfandor also spoke to Stephan, William, and Alice about taking the entrance exam for Arcane University.

"I can be a magician?" Stephan looked astonished. "That's always been my dream since I was little."

"Pulling rabbits out of hats is boring," William said.

Galfandor smiled. "I believe you'll discover there's a bit more to it than that, young man."

Alice squeezed my hand. "Are you going to school too, Conrad?"

I shrugged. "I guess. I don't know if I can do magic, though."

"You might surprise yourself," Galfandor said.

"I'll be there," Max said.

"What will I need to study?" I asked.

"I can tell you *all* about it," Max said. "I have the scroll with the requirements."

Over the next few hours, all the other parents arrived and collected their children. Little Mary's mother and father were the last to arrive. Before she left, she gave us each a hug and a kiss.

"I'm going to be a fairy princess when I grow up," she declared. "I'll always share my pixie dust with you."

244

"I don't understand how this is possible," her mother said to Galfandor, "but you have our eternal gratitude."

"Thank these brave children," he said, waving an arm to us. "They are the ones who rescued them."

The mother hugged each of us. "If you ever need anything, just ask me."

"We thank you from the bottom of our hearts," the father said as he shook our hands.

Most of the other parents had said something similar. It felt good to know that, despite the sins of our parents, Max, Ambria, and I had done something wonderful.

Galfandor's golem butler brought us a basket with a hot meal packed inside for us to take home.

"I hope to see you soon," the old man said. "If you need anything, don't hesitate to ask."

"Can we keep the brooms you gave us?" Max asked.

Galfandor chuckled. "Yes. I believe you've earned them."

As we flew over the cliff and back toward Queen's Gate, I closed my eyes and imagined Cora smiling at me, green eyes bright with love.

She would be proud of me.

I hoped that was true.

A great sense of purpose swelled in me. I had broken the chains of the past and now had a future to look forward to. I had two great friends and a place to live. With the burden of the living curse gone, I felt more alive than I'd ever been.

Now it was time to take this new life and live it to the fullest.

###

I hope you enjoyed reading this book. Reviews are very important in helping other readers decide what to read next. Would you please take a few seconds to rate this book?

For the latest on new releases, free ebooks, and more, join John Corwin's Newsletter at www.johncorwin.net!

Meet the Author

John Corwin is the bestselling author of the Overworld Chronicles. He enjoys long walks on the beach and is a firm believer in puppies and kittens.

After years of getting into trouble thanks to his overactive imagination, John abandoned his male modeling career to write books.

He resides in Atlanta.

Connect with John Corwin online:
Facebook: http://www.facebook.com/johnhcorwinauthor
Website: http://www.johncorwin.net
Twitter: http://twitter.com/#!/John_Corwin